This book belongs to

THE HISTORY OF THE SMALL WORLD:

SAVING THE SMALL WORLD

Thunderforge Pubs

U.S.A.

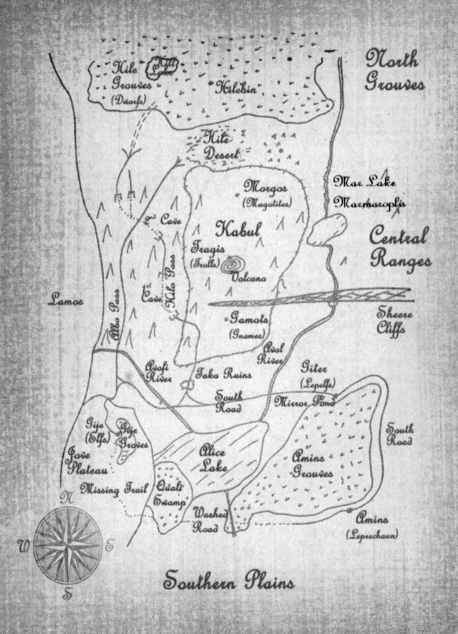

THE HISTORY OF THE SMALL WORLD:

SAVING THE SMALL WORLD

By
Dr. Gerhard Plenert

Illustrations and Art
Johathan Noronha Pushnam

Thunderforge Pubs
Publishers Since 2012
An imprint of DonnaInk Publications, L.L.C.
601 McReynolds Street, Carthage, NC 28327

Thunderforge Pubs

Library of Congress Cataloging-in-Publications Data.
Name: Plenert, Dr. Gerhard, author.
Title: "Saving the Small World" / Dr. Gerhard Plenert

Description: Thunderforge Pubs an imprint of DonnaInk Publications, L.L.C. presents: *"Saving the Small World" the third book in the fantasy fiction series titled, "The History of the Small World."*
This series follows the lives of a group of leprechauns whose world has been disrupted and they go on a challenging and eventful quest to restore harmony.

Identifiers: ISBN – 13 – 978-1-947704-58-9 (alk. paper).
Subjects: BISAC: FIC009100 FICTION / Fantasy - Action & Adventure; FIC009040 Collections & Anthologies; FIC009120 Dragons & Mythical Creatures; FIC010000 Fairy Tales, Folk Tales, Legends & Mythology; FIC002000 Action & Adventure.
Classification: LCC - PS3600-3626; LCC - PN6120.15-6120.95.

340 p. cm.
Printed in the United States of America

Book design by: Ms. Donna L. Quesinberry.
Book illustrations by: Johathan Noronha Pushnam.

For more information contact:
DonnaInk Publications, L.L.C.
www.donnaink.com

601 McReynolds St.   1390 Chain Bridge Road, #10029
Carthage, NC 28327   McLean, VA 22101

REVIEWS

This book is a must if you are a fan of the "Fantasy" genre!!

As an author, Mr. Plenert has a captivating style. If you are into fantasy (i.e.: The Hobbit, etc.) you will thoroughly enjoy "The Siege of a Small World". The characters are easy to associate with and the storyline is a hook right off the bat! Kudos Mr. Plenert! Eagerly awaiting the sequel!!

PMB

Take the time to read this book, you will thoroughly enjoy this great story.

Mr. Kenneth Smith

The Siege of the Small World is imaginative. Dwarves, elves, and many more populate the Small World. (The big world, of course being filled with humans). I enjoyed learning about the world and its inhabitants . . .

Liliyana

The History of the Small World is a well-crafted "clean" series from start to finish. Many of fantasy, mythology, and science fiction novels are risqué ~ it is refreshing to entertain oneself in reading a series where profanity and/or graphic situations are not necessary, expressly for juvenile and/or Christian readers.

Beyond this, the world Professor Plenert has created features masterful imaginative high watermark epic fantasy with film appeal. Filled with unforgettable characters who are engaging and colorful; you share this novelist's vision as your mind moves from sight, to sound while becoming a part characters' journeys.

Gerhard has written many business titles and has effectively transitioned from technical business writing to the world of fantasy fiction and he continues to refine this process. Books one and two (i.e.: The Siege of the Small World and The Uniting of the Small World) deliver an imaginary world filled with elves, giants, gnomes, leprechauns, and other creatures who come to life in an entertaining and pleasurable guise. The illustrations are exceptional and deliver an enhanced sense of participation.

Ms. Donna L. Quesinberry
Founder and President
DonnaInk Publications, L.L.C.

OTHER BOOKS
BY DR. GERNARD PLENERT

THE HISTORY OF THE SMALL WORLD SERIES

- *The Siege of the Small World* - Dr. Gerhard Plenert
- *The Uniting of the Small World* - Dr. Gerhard Plenert
- *Saving the Small World* – Dr. Gerhard Plenert

OTHER FICTION TITLES

- *Dawn of the New Templars* - Gerhard Plenert
- *Activating the New Templars* - Gerhard Plenert
- *The Dragon Pit* - Gerhard Plenert
- *Montana Rising* – Gerhard Plenert
- *Montana Scourge* – Gerhard Plenert

BUSINESS TITLES

- *Discover Excellence: An Overview of the Shingo Model and Its Principles* - Edited by Gerhard Plenert
- *Driving Strategy to Execution Using Lean Six Sigma: A Framework for Creating High Performance Organizations* - Gerhard Plenert | Tom Cluley

- *Finite Capacity Scheduling: Optimizing A Constrained Supply Chain* - Bill Kirchmier | Gerhard Plenert | Gregory Quinn

- *International Management and Production* - Gerhard Johannes Plenert, Ph.D.

- *International Operations Management* - Gerhard Plenert

- *Lean Management Principles for Information Technology* - Gerhard J. Plenert

- *Making Innovation Happen - Concept Management Through Integration* - Gerhard Plenert | Shozo Hibino

- *Module 17 Operations Management* - Gerhard Plenert

- *Reinventing Lean: Introducing Lean Management into The Supply Chain* - Gerhard Plenert

- *Strategic Continuous Process Improvement: Which Quality Tools to Use, and When to Use Them* - Gerhard Plenert

- *Strategic Continuous Process Improvement: Which Quality Tools to Use, and When to Use Them* - Gerhard Plenert, Ph.D., CPIM

- *Strategic Excellence in the Architecture, Engineering, and Construction Industries* - Gerhard Plenert | Joshua Plenert

- *Supply Chain Optimization through Segmentation and Analytics* - Gerhard Plenert

- *The eManager: Value Chain Management in an eCommerce World* - Gerhard Plenert

- *The Plant Operations Handbook: A Tactical Guide to Everyday Management* - Gerhard J. Plenert

- *Toyota's Global Marketing Strategy: Innovation through Breakthrough Thinking and Kaizen* - Shozo Hibino | Kolchiro Noguchi | Gerhard Plenert

- *World Class Manager* - Gerhard Plenert, Ph.D.

DEDICATION
TO THOSE THAT MATTER

This Book is dedicated to the leader of the
Small World of my life,
Renee Sangray Plenert

My parents George and Ida Plenert
(Who gave me the chance to live in the greatest country.)

And my 8 Kids
(Who mean the world to me.)
And the yet to be Numbered Grandkids
(A process which is beyond my control.)

Who Work Hard Trying to Save Me From Myself

Within My Own "Small World"

TABLE OF CONTENTS

EPIGRAPH

That thy way may be known upon earth,
thy saving health among all nations.
Psalms 67:2

A great civilization is not conquered from without
until it has destroyed itself within.
Durant

That which is governed by law is also preserved
by law and perfected and sanctified by the same.
Doctrine and Covenants 88:34

FOREWORD

By Ar. Perumal N

This is an enlightening series of interesting events which holds the reader captive. The vivid details engage the reader with glimpses of Small World which includes dwarfs, lepelves, elves, gnomes and leprechauns. The story is a reflection of the challenges of a world where light and truth triumphs narrowly but only when sought by the few good.

It enthralls the imaginative mind, bringing it into a world of fantasy. The journey focuses on enclaves of leprechauns and leads us to culminating heights of tragedy, thrills, deception, snares and dangers throughout a journey which addicts the reader and leaves them thirsting for more.

I thoroughly enjoyed reading this book and recommend it for people of all ages and interests. This adventure would make a wonderful movie.

Ar Perumal Nagapushnam, Architect
Post Grad Dip Architecture
Selangor, Malaysia

PREFACE

HOW IT ALL BEGAN

The Southern Plains became dependent on trade with the North Groves. Each had their own areas of expertise and each had come to rely on the other for their survival. But for some unknown reason this vital trade came to an abrupt halt. The Dwarfs no longer came to the south to trade. Most Southerners believed the Dwarfs of the north couldn't be trusted. What was their game? Were they trying to starve out the south? Were they trying to increase the price for their goods? Where were they? What game were they playing?

In the first book in *The History of Small World* series, titled *The Siege of the Small World* we journeyed with the leprechauns as they organized an expedition to the north in order to find out why trade had stopped.

The second book in the series, titled *The Uniting of the Small World* begins with their arrival at the North Groves and continues with their trials and challenges, eventually uniting the peoples of northern and southern Small World in a unified effort against the threats of the evil Kabul.

This third book, *Saving the Small World*, brings the unified efforts of the various species of Small World together in their efforts to save themselves from the planned destruction coming from the Kabul.

ACKNOWLEDGEMENT

WITH GRATITUDE

This book has been many years in the making and there are numerous individuals that need to be recognized. Of primary importance would be my conscience that validated the flow and identified any holes in the plot, Renee Plenert. And secondarily my publisher, Ms. D. L. Quesinberry, Chief Execution Officer (CEO), President & Founder of DonnaInk Publications, L.L.C. of Carthage, North Carolina with satellite addresses in Virginia and Maryland.

I want to give special thanks to my illustrators and artists. The cover design and all the illustrations throughout the book were done by an artist out of Selangor, Malaysia, Johathan Noronha Pushnam. As you can see, he is an incredible artist. Thank you for your help.

My many years of reading fantasy novels on airplanes as I traveled for work taught me a lot and I need to share my appreciation to the many fantasy authors that came before me. Their ideas, approach, and style have been an inspiration to me and I offer my sincere thanks.

THE HISTORY OF THE SMALL WORLD:

THE UNITING OF THE SMALL WORLD

Introduction

How It All Began

Many years ago, far too many for anyone to remember, the smaller inhabitants of the outer world became overpowered by their larger brothers. The "bigger ones" (men and giants) wanted more land forcing the "smaller ones" (dwarfs, elves, leprechauns, and lepelves) into increasingly tinier corners of the world. Before long they didn't have enough land to farm and they were forced to be dependent on the bigger ones. As the legends tell us, the smaller ones were pushed out of the flat lands and into the mountains. Searching the mountains for a new home, a few of the dwarfs were more courageous and entered into tunnels that they had been afraid to enter. Tradition had them believing that the tunnels housed evil spirits. But the courage of the dwarfs allowed them to discover a new world, a world "underneath." Luckily they found that these tunnels were too small for the bigger ones to enter. The tunnels provided a sanctuary from the fears of the outside world. And the tunnels easily fit the size of the smaller ones but were too low for the "bigger ones".

As the dwarfs delved deeper and deeper into the tunnels, they found a new world. Eventually the tunnels opened into an enormous cavern, much bigger than anyone could see across. This new world had mountains, rivers, lakes, and forests. It even had a bright glowing orb somewhere near the ceiling, which simulated the sun. The orb's brightness would cycle, glowing brighter during the day, and going completely dark at night. This world had trees, and grass, and insects. In fact it looked much the same as the world they had come from on the surface. The dwarfs called their new world Small World.

The adventuresome dwarfs worked their way back to the surface to retrieve their dwarf cousins and bring all of them to this new world. Initially there was fear at entering the tunnels, but after some time it was decided that the dwarfs would all migrate to this new world. They proceeded with the migration determined to leave everything they had ever known behind. They also hoped to leave other creatures that they feared, bigger or smaller, behind. But it didn't work out that way. The other smaller ones, the elves, leprechauns, and lepelves had noticed the dwarf migration, and how they never returned, and they followed suit. Before long the entire smaller population had resettled in this new world. The departure was successfully concealed, and the bigger ones were left with the mystery of never knowing what had happened to any of the smaller ones.

The geography of Small World developed into three major sections, the North Groves, the Central Ranges, and the Southern Plains. The tunnels through which the dwarfs had initially entered Small World were near the south. In their attempt to separate themselves from the other smaller ones, the dwarfs migrated as far away from the entrance to Small World as possible. The dwarfs ended up in the North Groves.

Population growth and migrations built up farms and cities, much the same as in the bigger world, except now everything was built to fit the smaller inhabitants. Three cities were developed in the Southern Plains. The first of these was Gije on the Jove Plateau, which became the land of the elves. A second was Amins on the southern edge of the Amins Grove, which became the land of the leprechauns. The third city was Giter on the northern edge of the Amins Grove, which became the land of the lepelves. The lepelves evolved from a blend of the elves from Gije and the leprechauns from Amins. Being half-breeds and therefore outcastes from each of these communities, they created their own home.

The North Groves became home to the dwarfs and had two cities, the commercial city of Hilebon and the capital city of Hilebin. The North Groves and the Southern Plains relied heavily on trade between themselves. They traded fruits, clothing, baskets, and furniture using the Albo Pass over the Central Ranges. Trade was primarily conducted by the dwarfs, since their southern counterparts were less adventuresome and preferred to avoid traveling.

The Albo Pass was the safest route of travel for the dwarfs between the North and the South. An alternate route was the Kilo Pass, but this route involved passage through the dangerous and feared Kabul which was in the middle of the Central Ranges. The only other remaining route was along the Avol River which required a treacherous three hundred leprechaun length ascent at the Sheere Cliffs.

The Albo Pass traveled along the west edge of the Central Ranges and posed no serious dangers. It was the highest of the trails and therefore had the most treacherous weather. This trail also ran along the Lamos, a cliff that was believed to drop off to the center of the world. Many of the Small World inhabitants, particularly dwarfs, allowed curiosity to get the better of them and had tried to scale down into the Lamos to see what they could find, but none had ever returned.

To the east of the Albo Pass was the Kabul ruled by Lord Krakus. Lord Krakus was an old leprechaun wizard of the south who one day, during evil experiments, was engulfed with flames causing burns all over his body. By using his wizardry and pieces of dead animals, he was able to reconstruct a grotesque body for himself. The residents of Small World feared the Lord causing him to flee the populated areas in total rejection. This rejection caused the Lord to develop a hatred for all the inhabitants of Small World. In isolation, he established his own land in the wasteland area of the Central Ranges known as the Kabul.

In the Kabul, Lord Krakus vowed to take revenge on the other regions of the Small World. He developed three major cities. The city situated furthest north was Morgos, the home of the Magotites. Magotites were maggot-eaten dead animals brought back to life by the Kabul Lord so that he could use them for his evil designs.

The central city in the Kabul was Tragis, on the edge of the Kabul volcano. This volcano contained many tunnels, including the laboratory of Lord Krakus wherein his evil experiments continued. Tragis was also the home of the trolls, the tallest and strongest, but also the ugliest of the Small World creatures. Tragis contained the Kabul Lord's castle where Lord Krakus and his army of trolls controlled all the activity of the Kabul.

The third major city of the Kabul was Gamotz, the home of the gnomes. Gnomes were irresponsible and illogical creatures with bodies of deformed Small World beings. They were the mutated result of a holocaust that occurred in the Upperworld, soon after the "smaller ones" came to Small World. The gnomes were rejected by the inhabitants of Upperworld and found their way to Small World where they found sanctuary in the Kabul. This was where they established their new home.

The Kabul was a region avoided and feared by both the North Groves and the Southern Plains. The reign and fear of Lord Krakus caused contact between the Kabul and the other areas of Small World to stop. Both sides wanted to avoid the contact and conflict. But the North Groves and the Southern Plains knew little of the evil designs of the Kabul Lord.

In the first book in *The History of The Small World* series, titled *The Siege of the Small World* we learned that trade was disrupted between the northern dwarfs and the southern leprechauns, lep-elves, and elves. In an attempt to learn why this trade had been disrupted, the leprechauns organized an expedition to the north. The first book recounts the adventures of these Small World creatures as they struggled through a never-ending series of trials, eventually arriving at the North Groves. The second book in the series, *The Uniting of the Small World*, begins with their arrival in the north and continues with their trials and challenges in the hope that the northern and southern relationship can be reestablished, but discovering that the real culprit is to be found in the Kabul. This third book, *The Saving of the Small World*, goes through the attacks by the Kabul on the remaining species of Small World in the hope of conquering all of Small World. The adventure continues.

PROLOGUE

A STRUGGLE BEGINS

The Southern Plains became dependent on trade with the North Groves. Each had their own areas of expertise, and each had come to rely on the other for their survival. But for some unknown reason this vital trade came to an abrupt halt. The Dwarfs no longer came to the south to trade. Most Southerners believed the Dwarfs of the north couldn't be trusted. What was their game? Were they trying to starve out the south? Were they trying to increase the price for their goods? Where were they? What game were they playing?

In the first book in the History of Small World series, titled "The Siege of the Small World" we journeyed with the leprechauns as they organized an expedition to the north in order to find out why trade had stopped. The second book in the series, titled "The Uniting of the Small World" begins with their arrival at the North Groves and continues with their trials and challenges, eventually uniting the peoples of northern and southern Small World in a unified effort against the threats of the evil Kabul. This third book, "The Saving of the Small World", brings the unified efforts of the various species of Small World together in their efforts to save themselves from the planned destruction coming from the Kabul.

THE HISTORY OF THE SMALL WORLD:

SAVING THE SMALL WORLD

CHAPTER ONE

THE TRAITOR

The sun had now set and it was slowly becoming dark over Gije, the elfin kingdom in Small World. Gijivure, the elf, wanted desperately to know more about the plans of Lord Krakus, the evil wizard of the Kabul. Was he going to attack any of the southern cities? What were his plans and when will he be carrying them out?

The elf decided to go out into the fields around Gije and risk the possibility of encountering any werewolves. He didn't want anyone to notice him. The late evening, when it was dark and everyone was settled into their homes, would be the best time for secrecy. He especially didn't want to encounter the dwarf, Egininety-one, who had been left behind in Gije as a representative of the dwarfs to the elves.

The elf was getting ready to leave, slipping on his overcoat when there was a knock on the door of his small apartment. He lived alone in this apartment, so he knew the visitor was someone who needed to talk to him.

He answered the door and was surprised to find his brother standing there. Gijivure asked,

      "What's going on?
          Why are you coming here,
          So late in the evening?
    There must be something wrong."
The brother answered,
          "I had a fight with our mother,
              and she kicked me out.
      I need a place to stay the night.

Can I stay here and pout?"
Gijivure responded,
 "Sure you can,
  I have to get something.
  I'll be right back,
 Stay here till then."
To which the brother said,
 "What do you have to get?
  Should I come with you?
 I can help,
  Be with you too."
But Gijivure insisted,
 "No. Just get to bed.
  I'll be back soon enough.
  It won't take long,
 I'll join you in bed."
After Gijivure left the brother stayed up for a few more minutes waiting for his brother's return but soon he decided he was too tired and proceeded to go to bed. He soon fell asleep.

In the meantime, Gijivure snuck through the exterior gates of the city, and went out into the fields. He went around the back side of a hay bale, blocking any views from the city. He sat down and started his humm, hoping that the Prince would hear him. He crossed his legs, folded his arms, closed his eyes, bowed his head, and began to hum. "Hummmmm ummmmm ummmmm," went Gijivure's chant for several minutes.

It took a long time before the Kabul Prince Kakakrul arrived in his eagle form. He landed in front of the elf and transformed himself into the prince. Angrily he barked, "What do you want at this late hour? I had to come all the way from the Kabul. This is a real nuisance."

Gijivure was taken aback by the prince's attack, but recovered quickly and said,
 "I want to know,
  What's going on.
  When are you attacking?
  Who are you attacking?
 What is the plan?
 Am I in danger?"
The prince responded, "We've already attacked and destroyed Giter. We've wiped out the lepelves. We're preparing for another

attack, this time our target will be Amins. It should be completely destroyed in a couple of days. Then comes Gije."

Gijivure was visibly afraid,

"Do I need to get away from here?

Where should I go in order to be safe?"

"Don't go away yet," responded the prince. "I may need some information from you about the attack strategy. Let's talk each day over the next few days so I can ask any questions that may come up."

Gijivure was worried about himself when he asked,

"You're sure I'm going to be safe!

I need to be safe"

"Of course. I need you for information so I'm going to make sure you're safe. I'll keep you posted on our progress and plans in the Kabul."

Suddenly the prince jumped into the air and transformed into an eagle in the middle of his jump. Gijivure was surprised by this action, but it wasn't long before he discovered the reason for the prince's strange behavior. Three werewolves were snarling at the elf as they stood in a menacing stance. One charged and jumped up, unsuccessfully striking at the eagle. Unfortunately for the elf, he landed on Gijivure and scratched him on the arm. Then the eagle flew into action, taking a dive at the werewolf and viciously pecking a hole in its head. The eagle's attack frightened the werewolves and the three ran off, whimpering in fear.

Gijivure knew that the scratch meant that he was now infected by werewolf venom. He needed to get treatment as soon as possible or he would suffer the fate of the other werewolves and become like them, which he considered a fate worse than death.

The prince flew off towards the Kabul. The conversation between the prince and the elf was over. Gijivure slowly worked his way back toward the city. He didn't want to rush because that would drive the venom into his blood stream. He snuck through the gate and back into the city. He decided to go directly to the doctor, hoping that he would still be in his office. Unfortunately for the elf, the doctor's office was closed.

He headed back home. Off in the distance he saw a couple of dwarfs and an elf making their way out of the city causing him to say,

"I thought only one of the dwarfs,
stayed in Gije.

All the other dwarfs,
Left for Amins.
I could have sworn that,
I saw two of them there."
He didn't realize that it was Egininety-one, Egiforty-four, and Gido that were exiting the city and heading back to Amins.

He returned to his home, entering the house quietly hoping not to wake his brother. He turned on a light and made his way toward his bead. He was shocked to find his brother dead, apparently stabbed to death, lying in his bed. He stared at the brother for several minutes and then the reality of the situation struck him and he said to himself,

"That could have been me!
Who would do something like that?
Why would they do it?
I'm lucky I wasn't here."

Murders were unheard of in the elvan kingdom. Now he knew that he would have to go to the doctor's house and wake him to find out what he should do. He arrived at the doctor's house and explained,

"I have two big problems.
The first is that I have been bitten,
The second, my brother is dead.
He is lying in my bed murdered.
A werewolf bit me.
Those are my problems."

The doctor perked up in surprise,
"What are you saying?
Your brother has been murdered?
That's horrible.
I'll come and see what has happened,
Wait while I get a coat,
I'll come with you."

Then Gijivure protested,
"But what about my bite?
The werewolf bit me."

The doctor was surprised by Gijivure's selfishness and said,
"Just come to my office,
Tomorrow is good,
I'll start the treatment.
You'll be bedridden,

For several days,
The drugs will knock you out.
Plan on not doing anything else.
Where were you anyway,
That you would be bitten?"
Gijivure responded,
"I was out in the fields,
I didn't realize,
How late it was,
I shouldn't have been in the fields."
To which the doctor said,
"That wasn't very smart,
At night in the fields,
Big mistake."
The doctor's response, caused Gijivure to wince, recoiling at the insult.

A couple minutes later the two were headed to Gijivure's home. After arriving the doctor carefully studied the injuries of the dead elf. After he finished, he stated,
"I'll have someone come,
Pick up the body,
In the morning.
I want to spend,
A little more time studying the body,
Seeing if there are clues."
Gijivure questioned,
"Can't you take him now,
Where am I going to sleep?"
The doctor made his way to the door, again bothered by Gijivure's rude response.
"Try the floor,
It's good enough for you,"
responded the doctor as he exited the residence.

Gijivure was extremely frustrated. He wanted the doctor to stop everything else that he was doing and start immediately with his treatment against the werewolf venom, but the doctor seemed to push everything off until the next day. The elf took the doctor's suggestion, laid out a blanket on the floor, and went to sleep. His day was finished and his meeting with the prince had gained him nothing.

Giant council meetings were more like mini riots and shouting sessions. There was no agenda and anyone could say anything. But what they said the most was, "Why did we get attacked by a bunch of trolls?" and "Where did they come from?" and "We lost far too many lives defending our home from these invading trolls."

After about thirty minutes the outbursts started to die down and the leader of the giants, who was referred to as the "Giant-giant" was able to get everyone's attention. "Apparently, from what I've learned, the Kabul Prince Kakakrul led the invading party. He had discovered our entrance through the tree trunk, and he led his troll horde into our caves using that route."

Giant-giant continued, "The first thing we need to do is we need to close that access point and create another. After completing that, we need to ask ourselves why the Kabul is terrorizing the giants? What have we done to deserve this unkind treatment? I think we learned part of that answer from the dwarf that was in this cave recently. He said that the Kabul Lord Krakus is reigniting the Life-fight wars and that his plan is to take over the entirety of Small World. That would include us as well. We have always been peaceful and have tried to avoid contact with the other members of Small World, but I don't know if we can stay out of this fight. The Kabul has brought this fight to us, and we may need to respond."

That last comment sent the entire council meeting into mayhem. Everyone was jumping, yelling and sometimes screaming, questioning the last statement of the Giant-giant. The majority of the giants didn't want to get involved in the fight. There were just too many other Small World species and they didn't want to continuously be bothered by them. However, there was a small and very insistent group that kept reminding everyone that in order to keep their privacy they would need to keep the Kabul from attacking them again.

After about one hour of meaningless debate which ended up not changing anyone's mind, Giant-giant again took charge of the meeting. He was starting to stand up when suddenly a mudwump came smashing into him, crashing him to the ground and depositing a muddy slime on his clothes wherever he made contact. Giants had a reverence for these mud creatures. They were the caretakes of the Creator. They seemed to randomly appear out of nowhere. They only showed up when they are delivering a message from the Creator. However, the challenge is that they do not have any way to communicate. They can speak, but they can't hear or understand any communication from the giants. The arrival of this mudwump, and his act of ramming into the Giant-giant, could only mean one thing; the Creator has a message for the giants.

"Come," was all the mudwump said and Giant-giant knew immediately that he was to travel with him to see the Creator.

Giant-giant stood up and announced, "A mudwump has arrived and I must go with him to the Creator. We need to learn what the Creator wants us to do. After I learn the Creator's message I will return to you and share the message with you. Then we can continue our discussion about the Kabul."

With that the council meeting was closed and Giant-giant waved his hand at the mudwump signaling for him to lead the way. The creature moved directly toward a solid wall of dirt and magically a cave opened up large enough for the giant to enter without bending over. After the creature and the giant had passed through the entrance, the cave magically closed so that no one was able to follow behind.

Being sealed in didn't concern Giant-giant. He had survived previous mudwump encounters in the past and he knew how meeting with the Creator could be confusing and disconcerting. But this time he was just excited. He wanted to hear what the Creator had to say. He knew that the Creator was able to see the "big picture" of what was occurring in Small World, much bigger than the giants were able to see secluded in their world of caves. The Creator's insight would be critical in determining how the giants would interact with the rest of their world.

The mudwump led the giant through a myriad of tunnels going deeper and deeper into the mountain. At one point they passed under Mirror Pond. The pond was visible above them and the giant couldn't resist sticking his finger up into the pond. It was the only place in Small World where the top of the lake was actually at the bottom. Sticking his finger into the pond was like sticking it into any body of water, but it was above instead of below him. He stuck both his hands into the water and used it to wash some of the mud off that had been deposited on him earlier by the mudwump.

traveling through the tunnels took about an hour but eventually they arrived at the cavern where the Creator was located. The cave had a very large opening, larger than any they had encountered previously during their travels through the tunnels. The opening to this cave was even wider than the cave they were coming from. The room was almost an exact circle. It made Giant-giant feel as though he had entered into a ball. It seemed as if he was standing at the bottom of an enormous ball.

The mudwump that he had been traveling with immediately bowed down to the floor paying homage to what appeared to be a large, cubic, polished rock that was floating and slowly spinning in the center of this cylindrical cave. This rock wasn't being suspended by anything noticeable.

The cave was enormous, so much so that the giant was at least two giants away from the spinning rock. Its surfaces were smooth with no decorations. The only discernible blemish in the entire structure was the entrance through which he had just come.

The smoothly polished rock glowed in an orange light that filled the entire room. This was the same rock light that lit the caves the giant had walked through previously but the brightness of this new rock was so strong that the entire room shone even brighter than he had ever seen. But it was a strange mysterious light. He could look directly at the light and not have his vision affected. As with the previous visits to the Creator, he was stunned. He wondered if this rock was where the Creator resided.

Giant-giant followed the lead of the mudwump and dropped to his knees, bowing his head, out of respect for the Creator.

"Raise my friends," came what sounded like a calm, gentle, elderly voice. The voice seemed to emanate from all directions of the cave at once, but Giant-giant assumed that it must have come from the rock and then somehow echoed throughout the cave.

"Leave me alone with him," said the soft voice, and the mudwump somehow understood the Creator's voice and rolled out of the cave. The door magically closed behind him. Once the door was closed the giant could find no outline of the door to mar the inner surface of the cave. It was as if the door had never existed.

The giant found it difficult to form words. He had so much he wanted to ask, but found himself too captivated to talk. He waited for the Creator to talk first.

"You need me," spoke the Creator. "The Small World hopes to defeat the Kabul and continue with life as it is, yet all of you know very little about what you risk. Krakus has found power by aligning with the root of all evil. I am proud of the many species in what they are attempting. I am proud of their strength. Unfortunately the power of evil needs more than merely high-spirited and strong willed leprechauns, dwarfs and amazonionites for the Kabul to be defeated. I need the giants to join with the rest of the Small World.

Your role, and the role of all the giants, in the defeat of the Kabul is critical. The rest of the world needs your support to succeed. I need you to join with the various species in Amins and participate in the planning. Otherwise, it will be impossible for them to be successful."

"I will personally go to this meeting," responded Giant-giant. "When is it being held?"

"Right now," responded the Creator. "Go to Amins as soon as you get back to your city. Additionally, I will be giving you messages in your mind that are intended to be helpful and to give you direction. You have not experienced this in the past, but I am giving you this ability using the Protee power. This is a power that I have also given to one of the Leprechauns."

"That's exciting," respond the giant. "Having your direction and support will make a big difference in this fight."

The Creator continued, "I will be able to read your thoughts. If you want to communicate with me, just think as if you're talking to me, much like a prayer. Think your thoughts and I will try to respond. I may not always respond, and that just means that I don't care which way you go, so don't bother me with trivial nonsense. Only ask for my help if it is vital to your mission of saving Small World."

"Thank you," responded the giant. "Your help will be critical to our success."

"Go now and hurry," said the Creator.

A mudwump reentered the Creator's cavern. Giant-giant knew that this was to be his guide back to the giant's city and he started to follow him.

The journey back was uneventful and about one hour later the giant found himself back in the large chamber from which he had departed earlier in the day. After their arrival, the mudwump returned into the dirt wall and the cave quickly closed up behind him as if he had never been there.

Giant-giant found many of the other giants still waiting in the chamber, anxious to hear what had occurred in the conversation with the Creator. Giant-giant stood up in front of the crowd and spoke out, "The Creator has spoken. We are to join in a meeting in Amins with the other species that are trying to prevent the Kabul from taking over Small World. We are to share our strength with them and work on a plan with them. Unfortunately, this will mean that we can no longer be isolated as we have been in the past."

Someone in the crowd yelled out, "The Creator has spoken. We can always return to our normal life after we have stopped the Kabul." However, Giant-giant had a feeling that life would never return to normal again. Their world would be changed forever.

Several giants in the group yelled out, "The Creator has spoken."

Giant-giant called out, "I need Egglac and Hector to join me and the three of us will leave immediately for the meeting that has been directed by the Creator."

A cry went out from the group, "The Creator has spoken."

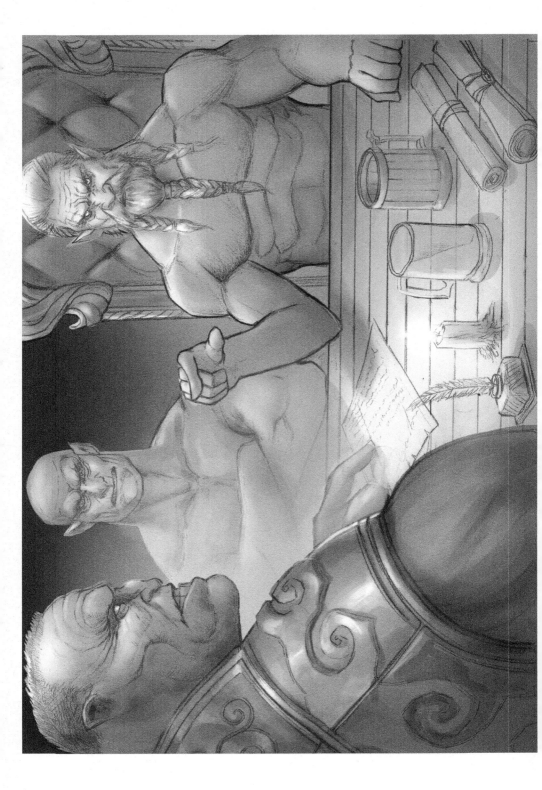

CHAPTER TWO

THE COUNCIL

After several attempts Amaz the elder leprechaun who was the leader of the community was finally successful in quieting the group thereby allowing him to start the meeting. His handsome face showed aged lines of concern. He started the emergency Amins council session with a fury; "We have learned a lot over the last couple weeks. We now know that we're in extreme danger of being attacked any day and possibly even at any minute. Our citizens are scattered and in hiding in the forests around us, afraid that when they return to the city their homes may be destroyed. We are grateful to know about these potential attacks thereby giving us a chance to prepare. We are sorry for those who have died and who have been seriously injured in the pursuit of this knowledge. And we will forever be grateful to them for their sacrifices."

He paused, and then continued, "Having said all that, we now need to make a plan thereby helping assure our survival. We have with us here in the council chambers all the travelers from the north and I would like each of them to introduce themselves so that we know who they are and what their role has been in this grand adventure. Then we'll talk about what we need to do in order to protect all our futures." With that, Amaz looked at the person to his immediate left, who was the wizard, giving him the queue to start the introductions.

The wizard, with his long grey beard, strange spiked hat that leaned to one side, and tall staff that reached a foot over the top of his head, said, "I am the Wizard of Havinis and I was awakened by the crossing of the Northern and Southern Swords. This was accomplished at great risk to the heroes that you sent to the north to meet with the dwarfs. We want to remember and honor the life of Yanon and the numerous injuries and the suffering of all the team members. Many dwarfs lost their lives in the process of acquiring the Northern Sword during the battles that we fought at Hile Lake, and their memory is special to us all. Four dwarfs lost their lives helping us get here and we want to remember the memories of Egififty-one, Egiforty-nine, Egiforty-five, and Egininety-nine. I know you southerners don't necessarily like the dwarfs, but you need to know that they have sacrificed a lot in order for us to be here together. The dislikes you have for each other need to be put aside while we push ahead trying to protect ourselves against the threat that the Kabul now poses. Later I will offer up my thoughts and ideas on how we need to proceed, but for now we will continue our introductions."

The next person in line was the leprechaun Elasti who said, "You all know me. I was on the first expedition where my friends Agot and Broch were killed, and I went on the second expedition to the dwarfs. For those of you who may not have heard, Obydon, our sword carrier, stayed in the north and is now the keeper of both the southern and northern swords. He lost one of his arms in a battle with the gnomes. He is also a hero of this expedition, but he stayed in the north so as not to put the swords at risk. I personally am thrilled to be home and to help Amins survive and I will gladly share what I have learned."

The next person, also a leprechaun, spoke up, "I am Bydola who went on this mission because of my strength. However, during our journeyings I met with the Creator and he gave me Protee powers. Some of you have already experienced the healing capabilities of this power. I will answer questions about that later."

Continuing with the next seated leprechaun since they had all grouped together by species, was Hasko who said, "I went on the expedition north because I was supposed to be such a wonderful scout, and I was the only one who got lost from the group when we were in the Kabul. But I'm back and I'm safe."

Then came Hiztin who introduced himself by saying, "I went because Hasko couldn't go without me. We experienced a large number of trials, but we made it and we're here to help."

The last leprechaun was Jesves, who said, "I went with because I'm the best tracker. But as we worked together as a team, we became totally dependent on each other, whether it was a dwarf, a lepelf named Garbona, who stayed behind in the north, an elf, an amazonionite, and at one point we even had the critical help of a Mermaid. It has been an incredible journey."

Next came the amazonionites, starting with their leader who said, "I am Goglbarj, an amazonionite. I have been raised to hate every one of your races, but I have learned that these prejudices are poorly conceived. I and my two friends are here to help and save all of small world. We realize we have to work together in order to be successful."

The next Amazonionite spoke up, "I am Goglchin."

And then the next, "I am Goglhick."

Then came the only elf in the group,

"I am Gido from Gije,
I am an elf,
I come from the elfin council,
All by myself.
We were the last winner,
From the Lifefight struggle,
My elf traveler Gijivure,
Stayed home from trouble.

Next it was the dwarfs' turn for introductions and their leader went first. "I am Egisix, the leader of the dwarf military. This has been a very difficult journey and I think that only the lepelves have lost more people than us. The battle at Hile Lake was savage for us and we also lost four dwarfs during our travels here to the south, Egififty-one, Egininety-nine, Egiforty-five, and Egiforty-nine. They will not be forgotten."

This last remark triggered a load groan from the other dwarfs, signifying their approval of Egisix's comment.

"We also left one of our dwarf party, Egininety-one, in Gije with Gijivure and the elves in order to build up support there. But he has since been reunited with us here. I need to give you a report on the travels to the Tako Ruins and what happened afterward."

"We'll do that after our introductions," suggested Amaz. "Let's finish the introductions."

The remaining dwarfs introduced themselves, "I am Egiforty."

"I am Egiforty-four."

"I am Egitwelve."

"I am Egininety-one."

"I am Egififty-seven."

That ended the introductions and everyone in the room returned their attention to Amaz. He was about to open discussions when

Gilbon, the lepelf military leader from Giter, burst out with, "How rude. I'm also a visitor. Why didn't you let me introduce myself?"

Amaz responded with, "You're not new to this group but go ahead and give your introduction."

"I'm Gilbon, the lepelf military leader from Giter. I am here to protest the lack of help from any of the other southern Small World cities. Lack of help has now resulted in the destruction of Giter."

After the lepelf's rant Amaz again attempted to start a discussion. Unfortunately, before he could say anything, Balbot, one of the younger and more outspoken members of the leprechaun council, burst in; "I can't believe that the Kabul Lord would do something so stupid. He lost the last Lifefight war. Why would he start another?"

To which the wizard responded, "Didn't you hear? Giter has been destroyed and Amins is next on the list. Your arrogance will prevent us from getting ready."

Algo, the leprechaun elder, spoke up immediately; "It's obvious that we need to get united and move forward in our preparations. Any discussion on why the Kabul is attacking is meaningless at this point. It's too late for that conversation. We need to get ready and that's all there is to it."

This meeting was very important for the council members, much more so than most meetings which were usually entangled with bureaucracy. The city of Amins was convinced that they were the next target for the Kabul. They were surprised that they had not already been attacked. There was a lot of tension in the council. It seemed as if everyone was talking at once. The rumblings of many private conversations echoed through the chambers. The twelve members of the council led by Amaz, the "wise elder", along with all the guests who had experienced the wrath of the Kabul, waited in anticipation for Amaz to continue the meeting.

The council chambers were inside the immense State Hall. It was a beautiful old hall built by the old ones many ages ago. The "old ones" were the first inhabitants of Small World. They were the first to settle the area and the work that they did was still held in high esteem.

The hall had huge windows with colored glass brought in from many parts of Small World. The council members enjoyed speaking in this hall since their high pitched voices could be heard many times over with the echoes that the hall created. The furniture in the chamber was simple. It contained one oversized round table with beautifully crafted chairs made from the wood of the rare Karkat tree, a tree that was unique to Small World.

Outside it was a miserable winter morning. It was pouring rain and the streets were muddy. The people were so hampered by the weather that it had put everyone into bad spirits.

Amaz stood out from the crowd. He was taller and stronger looking than the others. He had the look of a great intellectual. His appearance gained him the respect of everyone he encountered. Today however, his face looked aged with concern.

Amaz stood up and slapped his hand on the table several times in an attempt to bring the council members and visitors back to order after the previous outbursts. It would be a difficult job to control this unruly group. He knew he must work on the major issue of the Kabul or no other business would be possible.

"Let's get a report about the most recent travels to Gije and to the Tako Ruins. Who wants to give us this update?"

Egisix suggested, "I think the Wizard should go first."

The Wizard jumped in and said, "Two expeditions went out, one to the Tako Ruins and another to Gije. I went with Egisix and Elasti to the Tako Ruins where we went to the ruins of the great Tako Library. There we found the scrolls that I critically needed, which taught me how to cast spells. While we were there I cast a flying spell on Egisix so he could travel to the north. That way north and south can stay in communication and work together. I'm going to ask Egisix to give an update of what he learned while he met with the dwarf King Egione."

Egisix picked up the conversation and said, "The wizard's spell turned me into a hawk. I just have to use the magic word that he gave me and I can transform back and forth between a hawk and a dwarf. It's really dangerous being a hawk because the eagles want to attack me. In my hawk form I flew to Hilebin, transformed back into a dwarf, and met with King Egione. I had to tell him all the news about our travels and the destruction of Giter. He was very upset that we had lost one of our Small World cities, and possibly an entire species. I informed him that I would be traveling back and forth between the north and the south carrying messages and updates. I asked him what he thought we should do about the Kabul and he said that we should probably both attack simultaneously, one from the north and one from the south. He thinks we should do this before the Kabul has had a chance to regroup. Then, a little

later, he suggested that maybe we would be better off if we held a defensive war and
just wait until we are attacked. He was concerned that we may cause more damage than necessary if we attack first. In the end I'm not sure which option he preferred. But I know that he is anxious to hear what this meeting will come up with as a plan and if the wizard is in support of the plan that we come up with."

The wizard responded, "Thanks for the update. That was extremely helpful and confusing at the same time."

Egisix jumped in again saying, "There's one more thing that I should mention. I also travelled to visit the Princess of the Northland, Ejijone. She is the spiritual leader of the dwarfs and it is always respectful to keep her informed."

The wizard spoke up again and said, "Thanks for that information. Now let's listen to Gido for an update on the team that went to Gije."

With that Gido spoke up,

"I learned from Egininety-one,

We have a traitor elf.

I went with him and Egiforty-four,

To remove himself.

The traitor elf,

Met with the Kabul Prince,

And gave him information,

That would make you wince.

I had to kill,

The traitor elf,

And do the deed,

All by myself."

He looked at Goglhick, hoping to see her reaction, and was pleasantly surprised to see her look of support. Now Gido finally felt that he had a chance to have a relationship with her. He had something to look forward to.

With that the wizard spoke up, "You can see that these are trying times for everyone. We worried about the dwarfs, and instead we have an elf betraying us. The elves are the species that defeated the Kabul during the Lifefight wars so you can imagine what a surprise it was for us to learn that there was a traitor amongst them."

The conversation returned to Amaz who said, "Now that we have had an update from the most recent adventures let's start a discussion about how best to deal with the Kabul. We have all the species represented here so we should be able to come up with something that works for everyone. We already had a couple plan options suggested by King Egione. Let's start with that. Any thoughts or suggestions?"

There was a hub of conversation around the room. Strong agreement with Egione was obvious. After allowing a few moments of debate, Amaz had to again slap his hand firmly on the table to bring the council back to order. "I see that we're generally in agreement with King Egione's idea of an attack from both the north and the south, but I think we should also hear what the wizard has to say. We need to see how all of this fits into his plans."

The wizard took the lead and asked the question, "I need to share information about the spells that I learned while reading the scrolls that I retrieved from the Tako Ruins. You already heard Egisix talk about the flying spell. There are also other spells that would be useful like the invisibility spell and the night vision spell. Unfortunately, these spells have limits on them. There are a limited number of individuals that can be kept under any spell at one time. So, we can't turn the entire town invisible, as much as you would probably like me to."

Avre, a member of the council, asked, "I'm confused about something that Egisix said. What is this magical word that he was talking about?"

The wizard explained, "It is a word that only the spell holder can know or invoke. Each person that is put under a spell will be given their own secret name and they use it to execute the spell."

Again the council went into a hub of side conversations. Algo, the elder, was calm as he asked the wizard; "How do you see these spells helping us defeat the Kabul?"

The wizard answered, "The flying spell is already helping us keep all the species united. The invisibility spell may help us in a spy effort against the Kabul. We may be able to infiltrate the very chambers of the Kabul Lord and listen to his plans and conversations. And the night vision spell will help us if we end up in a battle at night."

"So where do we begin?" asked Amaz. "What is the first thing we need to do in order to get ready?"

"Train your people to be ready for war. Prepare weapons and make them if needed," explained the wizard. "Additionally, I will put the invisibility spell on two individuals and send them into the Kabul as spies. Hopefully they will be able to learn about the Kabul Lord's plans and be able to come back and report."

Algo asked, "Can't you put the invisibility spell on all of us? Then the Kabul will never find us."

The wizard explained, "There is a limit on how many spells I can do. The limit is based on energy extended. I can do at most five spells, and I already used up one on Egisix. We need to use these spells wisely. They are a great and valuable tool, but we can't just throw it around randomly. We have to use the spells strategically. I think that sending spies up to the Kabul would be useful. What do the rest of you think?"

Algo asked, "Can't we use Egisix to fly into the Kabul and see what's going on?"

Again the wizard responded, "Since the Kabul Prince is an eagle, it's dangerous for Egisix to travel into the Kabul. We can use him at a high altitude to see if there is any movement, but we can't use him to fly low enough into the Kabul to hear or learn anything. That's why I'm suggesting we send a couple spies with the invisibility spell."

Balbot agreed with this saying, "I think the wizard has a plan that might work. With spies we can get early warning of any attacks, and with Egisix, if we need to attack the Kabul, the north and south can do it in a united effort, if it comes to that."

Amaz called for a vote asking, "We need a vote. Do we go with the wizard's plan of getting everyone prepared for war, and sending spies into the Kabul."

The vote was quick and unanimous. Then Amaz asked, "Who are the two that should be sent into the Kabul?"

Algo spoke up saying, "Sadly it should be a couple of individuals who have already experienced the Kabul and know what to expect. I know we've overworked these heroes, but it is these individuals that would be the best choice."

Amaz reviewed the list verbally and said, "That group could include Elasti, Bydola, Hasko, Hiztin, Jesves, and Gido. Of you six, let's start by asking if there are any volunteers?"

Gido jumped up immediately and said,

"I will go,
My people asked for,
Me to be,
Their ambassador."

Avre burst in, "You can't send Bydola. We need his healing power here if there is indeed an attack."

Looking around at the hesitancy of the remaining individuals, Elasti spoke up and said, "Looks like it's me again. Hasko, Hiztin, and Jesves have already experienced some rough times in the Kabul, leaving me as the best option."

Hasko objected, "I don't want to go out there again, but in order to save Elasti, I would do anything. He's been our hero all along during these several journeys."

Amaz spoke up, "Unfortunately I have to agree that Elasti is by far the best option for this spy mission." Then, looking directly at Elasti he said, "I know how rough this is on you. It's hard sending you out a third time. But I think you are by far the best option with the most experience. Will you be the second volunteer?"

"Noooooo," was a cry out from outside the chambers. It was Jizeel. Elasti was soon to be wed to Jizeel, the daughter of Amaz. "I've had to live in fear of losing Elasti and now you're going to put us through this again. I can't stand it any longer."

Amaz spoke up, "I'm sorry Jizeel but we have to look at the survival of not just Amins, but all of Small World. Your future husband Elasti is a hero of the leprechauns, and we now need to utilize his talents once again." Then turning to Elasti again he asked, "Will you go?"

"Of course," he replied. "I must go because of the sacrifice that many of my friends have already suffered. I must go for their sakes so they did not suffer and die in vain. I would feel too much guilt if I backed out of this fight when it is just beginning."

CHAPTER THREE

THE PLAN

Gijivure did his best to try to sleep on the floor. About two hours into his sleep he was awoken. He felt something on his feet. At first it felt like an itching sensation and felt good. But after a few minutes, it started to hurt. Something was attacking the bottoms of his feet. He abruptly woke up enough to be aware of what it was. It was a rat nibbling on the bottom of his feet. Gijivure jumped up, but the pain of the sores on the bottom of his feet made him jump back down to the floor. He could hear the rats scurrying off, but the damage had been done.

Gijivure ripped up a shirt and wrapped his feet. This reduced the stinging pain of the punctures on the bottom of his feet and he was able to stand. It surprised him how much the wrappings were able to reduce the intensity of the pain.

He had a miserable night's rest for several reasons. First off his dead brother was lying in his house. Second the killers might return and kill Gijivure, which kept him from falling into a sound sleep. Third was the rats. Gijivure started the day finding his brother still lying in his bed, dead. Speaking out loud to himself he said,

"I guess to mother I must go,
And tell her about my brother,
But I need treatment,
From the Werewolf,
The Werewolf bite,
The doctor must cure,
But my brother he must get,
I'll tell my mother later.

It has been miserable,
Someone is torturing me,
The prince didn't answer me,
The werewolf bit me,
I'm infected with venom,
My brother has been killed,
I couldn't' sleep in my own bed,
And now the rats."

Just then there was a knock on the door. It was the doctor and a couple of assistants, arriving to pick up the body. The doctor said,
"We are here to further investigate,
The murder of your brother,
And remove the body,
Is there anything you can tell me?
Have you told his mother?
About your brother's death?"

Gijivure's selfish attitude kicked in,
"I want treatment,
For the werewolf bite,
The bite is dangerous,
I need to be cured."

The doctor could see through his attitude and said,
"Come to my office in two hours,
And we will start treatment,
Now help us with your brother."

Gijivure responded,
"I'll come to your office,
In two hours' time,
I need time now,
To do some urgent business."

With that Gijivure left the house limping. He didn't want to help. His feet hurt. And unfortunately, he just didn't care. He was more concerned about saving his own skin. He limped out into the fields but struggled to find an isolated location. He wanted to know what the Kabul had planned before he went into lockdown with the doctor's treatment for the werewolf venom.

After a lengthy struggle, and a lot of painful walking, Gijivure found a place at the edge of the fields that was just inside the woods. It seemed isolated and away from the field workers. He sat down and started his humm, hoping that the prince would hear him.

As before, he crossed his legs, folded his arms, closed his eyes, bowed his head, and began to hum. "Hummmmm ummmmm ummmmm," went Gijivure's chant for several minutes.

It took a long time before the Kabul Prince Kakakrul arrived in his eagle form. He landed in front of the elf and transformed into the prince. Angrily the prince barked, "What do you want? I had to come all the way from the Kabul. This is a real nuisance. I can't keep talking to you five times every day."

Gijivure was frustrated by the repeated attack but recovered quickly and said,

> "I still want to know,
>> What's going on.
>>> When are you attacking?
>>> Who are you attacking?
>> What is the plan?
> Am I in danger?"

The prince responded, "Like I said yesterday, we're preparing for another attack, this time our target will be Amins. Then comes Gije."

Gijivure was visibly afraid,

> "Do I need to get away from here?
> Where should I go in order to be safe?"

"Again, like I said yesterday, don't go away yet," responded the prince. "I may need some information from you about the attack strategy. Let's talk each day over the next few days so I can ask any questions that may come up."

Gijivure was worried about himself when he asked,

> "You're sure I'm going to safe!
> I need to be safe!"

"Of course. I need you for information so I'm going to make sure you're safe," he lied. "Call me again tomorrow so we can talk."

Gijivure responded,

> "That may be a problem,
>> Werewolf venom is in me,
>>> I need to be treated,
>>> Treatment may knock me out,
>> It may take several days,
> I may have trouble communicating."

"Do what you can," responded the prince. He really didn't care. His father's goal was to wipe out the elves, and Gijivure was just one of them. "I have to go now." With that the prince transformed back into an eagle and flew off.

Gijivure was again disappointed in the response. He wanted to get away to somewhere safe and he wanted the prince to tell him where to go and what to do. Instead, he now has to deal with werewolf treatments and he might still be under the influence of the drugs when the actual attack occurs. He might be wiped out along with the rest of the elves. To Gijivure this was unacceptable. He wanted to be protected by the Kabul as a reward for the betrayal of his people. He wanted more from the prince, but he wasn't getting it.

Gijivure hobbled back toward the city, hoping none of the field workers noticed him, but he was disappointed when one of the workers yelled out to him,

"It's good to have you back Gijivure
It must have been rough,
Having to deal with all those dwarfs,
Nice to have you here."

Gijivure just waved but didn't say anything. He didn't want to engage in chitchat. He wanted to go straight to the doctor and get his treatment started. When he arrived at the doctor's office, he went directly to the back room where he knew the doctor would be studying his brother's wounds. When he entered the room, he found the doctor, his assistants, and Gijivure's mother. His mother had lost her composure and was yelling and sobbing. When she saw Gijivure she yelled out,

"What happened?
How did your brother get killed?
Was it you that killed him?
What happened?"

Gijivure wasn't ready for this type of drama. That's why he didn't go to his mother earlier to tell her about the death of her son. He responded,

"Of course I didn't kill him,
He came last night,
I let him sleep in my bed,
Then I left to do some errands,
When I came back,
He was dead in my bed,
It was probably me that they wanted,
It's fortunate that I was away,

But while I was out,
I was bitten by a werewolf,
This bite is the real problem,
I need the doctor to start treatment."
The doctor was astounded by the non-caring attitude and he burst out,
"Can't you see,
Your mother is hurting,
Don't you have any sympathy,"
Gijivure barked back,
"Just do your job,
Don't worry about my attitude,
I only need you to start my treatment,
Hurry up there so we can get started."
The doctor and mother were so surprised by the attitude of selfishness that they couldn't think of anything to say in response. After a few minutes to recover from the shock of Gijivure's uncaring attitude, the doctor directed him to another of the rooms and told him to wait there till he was finished studying the brother's injuries.

It was another hour before an impatient Gijivure was finally given the first dose of the werewolf anti-venom. Ten minutes later, Gijivure was asleep, and he would stay that way for the next few days. Much to the doctor's pleasure, he wouldn't be hearing for Gijivure for a while.

***

The wizard presented his plan for defending against the Kabul, which included a plan of attack. He suggested the following,
1) Train everyone in weaponry.
2) Prepare defenses, like building up walls and digging trenches, and setting up traps and snares.
3) Hide the elderly, youngsters, and anyone else not capable to fight in combat, away from the city.
4) Plan an attack on the Kabul's weakest points which should distract them away from their own attacks on Small World.
5) Send spies into the Kabul.
6) Communicate back and forth with the dwarfs in the north so they can have a coordinated attack.

Amaz challenged the council by asking them to vote on the wizard's plan. Acceptance of the plan was unanimous. The next step would be a discussion of how each step in the plan would be carried out. The wizard led the discussion by suggesting, "I will leave responsibility for the first item to Amaz. We also need to communicate this list of activities to the elves and the dwarfs so that we can have a coordinated effort."

Amaz suggested, "For number one we have brought up the weapons that were locked away under these chambers. They have all been brought out and blacksmiths have been duplicating them in order to make more for everyone. Additionally, for item two we will begin working on that immediately."

Amaz continued, "Egisix will need to travel back to the north and give Egione the plan. We'll send Egininety-one and Egiforty-four back to the elves in Gije, since they know what route to take and because they've been there before. Gido can give them a letter of introduction. Then they can explain our plan to Lord Gimans. As for Amins, we will follow the second item of the plan and organize a workforce and use them to start building defenses, and we will continue our weapons training. The third item on the wizard's list has already been accomplished."

The wizard continued his explanation, "The fourth item on the list, finding the Kabul's weakest point, may need discussion but my thoughts on it are that Morgos is probably the weakest spot since the magotites are highly disorganized and the city has the poorest of the defenses."

"Hold it," challenged Goglbarj the amazonionite. "Don't discredit the amazonionites. They need to be included in this plan. And someone needs to go to them and tell them about the plan, so they can prepare."

"Would you be willing to take on that mission?" asked the wizard. "Goglchin and Goglhick can stay here with us and help us prepare and train."

"Can you give me the power to fly like you gave Egisix?" she asked. "Going over the Sheere Cliffs makes travel between here and there extremely difficult."

"That would be an excellent idea," responded the wizard. "That would be a good use of one of the few remaining spells. When you go to your people, tell them to prepare for a defensive war. We don't want any offensive attacks until all the species are ready so we can all attack at the same time."

Amaz added, "That expands item six in your plan to include both the dwarfs and the amazonionites."

Goglbarj was thrilled to hear that she would be able to receive this power. In the back of her mind, she had her own plan brewing, and this spell would help her develop her plan.

"Correct," added the wizard. "Let's return to item four." Then turning to Egisix he asked, "Can you challenge the dwarfs to attack Morgos and throw the Kabul completely off guard?"

Egisix responded, "I will give them whatever message you want to give them, but I can't guarantee that they'll do it. They tend to prefer defensive rather than offensive battles."

The wizard continued, "Please tell them our plan and encourage them to be a part of it. We need to work together if we are going to be successful." After a pause he said, "I need to get items five and six going. I need Elasti and Gido so I can put the invisibility spell on them, and I need Goglbarj so I can put the flying spell on her. Additionally, Egininety-one and Egiforty-four need to head for the elves in Gije."

"We're off," said Egininety-one. "We'll report back to you when we return."

"Excellent," said the wizard. "Off you go." The two dwarfs departed for the elven kingdom. Then he instructed, "Elasti come here."

The wizard put his hands on Elasti's head and mumbled a series of incomprehensible ritual words. When he was finished he commanded, "Stand up." After Elasti was standing the wizard continued, "I will give you a magic word that you must not forget." Then he whispered, "The word is 'gillgal'." Returning to his normal voice he said, "That word is what you need in order to command a transformation into invisibility. Don't be invisible more than necessary because it will drain your strength. When you do a transformation, you will need to be in a location where no one can see you. You don't want anyone to see your powers. Now, with these powers you will be able to spy out the activities of our enemies. You will need to be extremely careful."

The wizard performed a similar process for Gido and give him his secret name. Then it came time for Goglbarj and a similar process occurred, but her transformation consisted of her changing into an Owl. She was given her secret name and she was warned about eagles, especially the eagle that the prince transformed himself into.

Then it was time for them to depart. However, Elasti had something he had to do before they left. He went to Jizeel, his future bride, and gave her a little box saying, "You probably thought I forgot. I didn't forget. Here are the dwarf earrings that I promised to bring you from the north."

Jizeel gave Elasti a big hug and started to cry. "Please stay safe and hurry back to me."

Elasti answered, "You know I will." With that Elasti and Gido started their departure up the South Road that Elasti had travelled several times before, but not before Goglhick ran up to Gido and shocked everyone by giving him a hug and a kiss. They, and everyone around them, especially the other dwarfs and amazonionites, looked on in shock. This behavior was unheard of in both species. Then, without saying a word, the two separated and Elasti and Gido departed, Gido staring back at Goglhick with a big smile.

After getting over the shock, and without saying a word to Goglhick, Goglbarj transformed herself and flew off toward the north. All of the travelers knew their mission. They all knew the importance of what they were about to do. And they were eager to do something that would help to protect Small World.

The Wizard of Havinis then returned to address the council meeting with a warning, "The danger that exists in Small World is not just that of the Kabul. The real danger lies in the dark alliance with evil which Krakus has made."

Amaz asked, "I'm not sure what that means. What are you telling us?"

The wizard explained, "The Creator is a greater power for good, no matter if you call him the God of the Rainbow that the southerners worship, or God of Light that the amazonionites worship, or God of Thunder that the dwarfs worship, it's all the same. Similarly, there is an enemy God who believes that lies, deception, and murder are the standards that we should live by. This God is called the Destroyer. Krakus has an alliance with the Destroyer. In that alliance, the Destroyer agrees to help Krakus conquer Small World and in return everyone and everything that remains must worship the Destroyer. They must pay allegiance and homage to him. What I am saying is that we have a double enemy, the Kabul and the Destroyer, and we need to conquer both elements if we are to bring peace back to Small World."

"Will the Creator help us battle the Destroyer?" asked Amaz.

"He already has and will continue to do so," responded the wizard. "Bydola's Protee power is just one example. Another example is the power of the spells that I am able to cast. You're not going to see the Creator out on the battlefield wielding a sword, but he is helping and supporting our efforts. We still have to do the work."

"I feel honored to know that he is supporting us," responded Amaz. "Let's end this meeting and get to work building weapons and traps to fend off the enemy, as you suggested. We have a lot of work to do and we have no idea how much time we have left in order to prepare."

"Agreed," said several council members. "Let's get to work."

The meeting was dismissed and everyone went to work doing their assigned duties.

CHAPTER FOUR

THE TRAITOR

After their departure, Elasti and Gido worked their way up the South Road toward Giter, carefully watching to make sure they avoid any encounter with Kabul forces. They had been warned that if they use their invisibility too often it will weaken them physically and possibly cause it to fail, so they were instructed to save the use of it as much as possible until they arrive at the Kabul.

The road was completely devoid of any travelers. It was eerily deserted. As they passed Giter, they were in awe of the devastation. "There's nothing left," exclaimed Elasti.

Gido responded,

"The trolls left nothing,
No one is alive,
This ruin is intended,
For none to survive."

"That's for sure," Elasti agreed.

They walked a short way into the town, just to see if there was anything left of the king's palace, but it was also in ruins, just like all the rest of the city. There was nothing but destruction and bodies strewn everywhere. "They never had a chance," declared Elasti.

Elasti and Gido had been instructed to go up to the Kabul, but they decided to briefly follow the troll tracks into and out of Giter, hoping to find them or their encampment. Gido insisted,

"We are spies,
That's what we know.
Finding trolls in the south,
Is where we should go.

Let's follow tracks,
            Of the Kabul,
And maybe then,
            We'll know what to do!"

They successfully found the tracks coming into the city from the south, and they found the remnants of a troll camp to the north. Trolls make a mighty mess and their camps are easy to discover. Then, to the surprise of the two spies, they saw troll tracks leading north, toward the Sheere Cliffs. The tracks led right up to the cliffs and then, looking over the edge of the cliffs, Elasti and Gido were horrified to see a pile of troll bodies lying at the bottom of the cliffs.

"I can't believe the trolls just came here and committed suicide," exclaimed Elasti. "Does that make sense?"

Gido responded,
            "Suicide does not,
                        Make any sense.
            I don't understand,
                        The troll's defense."

"Is this some kind of Kabul ritual for the winning trolls?" asked Elasti, not really expecting Gido to know.

Gido responded,
            "I've never heard,
                        Of this before.
            This didn't happen,
                        During the Lifefight War."

The two stared at the carnage for a few more minutes, not realizing that the giants might have been involved, and then they returned to their journey. The two continued along the South Road, heading for the Avol River. They crossed the river without incident, still wondering what had happened to the Kabul forces that had so completely devastated Giter. They saw the remnants of a troll camp along the side of the river, but no more trolls. They scouted out the tracks of the trolls but only saw them going in one direction. The tracks led to Giter, but there were no tracks coming back the same way. The two became convinced that the trolls had all committed suicide, but they couldn't understand why.

"At least we know our homes are safe for now," commented Elasti.

Gido responded,
            "I wish we could,

Tell our homes,
The trolls are gone,
At least for now."

"Correct," responded Elasti. "It would be comforting for them to know that. But we have no way to share that information with them." Then, after pausing for a few minutes he suggested, "We were instructed to go to the Kabul using the Kilo Pass, since that is the route we took the last time, but I think it would be better if we followed the tracks of the trolls, since that will probably be the route that the next attack party will be taking. What do you think?"

Gido responded,

"I agree with your logic,
I think you're right,
The route the trolls took,
Will give us better sight."

Having revised their travel route, the two started working their way backwards along the troll's path. After a short walk along the South Road, the troll tracks started heading northward. It was easy following their tracks, because they made a destructive mess, in spite of the thick forest undergrowth that existed everywhere. The trolls trampled everything in their path as they stumbled along.

The two had to camp out a couple times, because of the length of their journey. Each time they would camp out in the forest, hiding their location in case anyone from the Kabul would pass by in the area. They avoided making a fire or doing anything that would indicate their presence.

On the fourth day of their travels, Gido and Elasti arrived at the mist wall that surrounded the Kabul. It was the same mist wall that Elasti had encountered when he and his companions had travelled north earlier when they went along the Kilo Pass toward the North Groves.

The misty wall was new to Gido, and he expressed his hesitancy,

"I cannot go,
Through this wall of mist,
I do not know,
If I will still exist!"

"I've been through it before and it is scary because it messes up your mind," responded Elasti, which offered very little comfort to Gido.

Suddenly, to the surprise of both spies, about one hundred paces to their left, a gnome came walking through the mist wall. Elasti and Gido were in a panic, and the Gido remembered their invisibility powers and said the magic name. Gido instantly disappeared, but Elasti wasn't as quick and the gnome saw him before Elasti was able to say his magic name.

The gnome was stunned. He knew he had just seen a leprechaun, but now the leprechaun was gone. Seconds later a second gnome came through the mist, then a third and a fourth.

Elasti and Gido were afraid to move for fear that their footsteps would be visible. They stood there in shock as they listened to the first gnome explain what he had seen to his three companions. Fortunately, the companions dismissed his explanation as ridiculous. The gnome who appeared to be their leader declared, "It must have been the mist wall that's giving you hallucinations. There's no way a leprechaun was standing there and then suddenly disappeared. That would be impossible."

"I know what I saw," insisted the first gnome, but then dropped the conversation.

Then the leader declared, "We have a mission. We need to spy out the southern cities and see if they're easy targets. But for now, let's set up camp."

The gnomes quickly built a fire, shot a couple rabbits, and settled in for the evening. In the meantime, Elasti and Gido continued to be frozen in their spots, afraid to move. They desperately wanted to get back to their homes and warn them about the Kabul spies. They wanted to kill the Kabul spies themselves. Maybe after it became dark, they would be able to kill the gnome spies as they slept. But for now, the two southerners were stuck in place.

***

Goglbarj transformed herself into an owl, using the magic name that Bydola had given her, and flew off toward the north. She knew that her instructions from the wizard were to prepare for a defensive war. But she wasn't in a defensive mood. She had never been in a defensive mood in her entire life. Mumbling to herself she said, "This wizard and his compatriots move too slow for me. They plan a defensive war with the Kabul. Why do we just sit around waiting for something to happen. We need to make things happen."

She flew directly to her amazonionite tribe, landing by a tree close to the Gogl tribe, and transforming herself back into her amazon body. She went directly to the Elderess and asked, "Can we talk somewhere in private? I have a lot to tell you about what's going on and what has happened."

"Let's take a walk into the forest and find a private place," responded the Elderess.

After a short stroll into the surrounding forest the Elderess asked, "Tell me everything."

Goglbarj reviewed her travels to Amins including the destruction of Giter and the plans of the Wizard. Then she expressed her frustration, "These guys are moving too slow. We Amazonionites aren't comfortable waiting for trouble to happen to us, especially if we can do something that will stop it from happening. The lepelves are destroyed, and the elves and leprechauns are no match for the forces from the Kabul. The dwarfs are tough. I am extremely impressed by their skills at battle. But they are so badly outnumbered by the Kabul that they don't stand a chance either."

"What are you suggesting?" asked the Elderess.

"I think I should go and talk to the dwarf princess, and the elven queen and see if we can organize a team of female warriors and go on the attack. Maybe you can get the various amazonionite tribes to join together. With a united front, I think we should attack one of the Kabul cities. What do you think?"

"You go ahead and visit the dwarfs and the elves, and I'll talk to the Elderesses of the different tribes," responded the Elderess. "I support your aggressive attitude. It fits with the spirit of the amazonionites. Let's take care of this Kabul threat. If we just disable one of the Kabul cities, it should significantly help the rest of Small World in their efforts." Then she reflected and asked, "Exactly how do you plan to go to the elves and the dwarfs? They're in opposite directions and it will take weeks to get all this put together. Maybe we should just stick with the amazonionites and create our own army."

Goglbarj felt embarrassed but decided to explain, "The wizard gave me the ability to fly. I can travel to each of these locations in just a few hours."

The Elderess looked at her as if she had lost her mind and said, "Now I have trouble believing anything you said. You've gone nuts on us."

Goglbarj now said, "I guess I'll have to prove it to you." She said the magic word and slowly transformed into an owl. The Elderess' amazement was noticeable. Her mouth gapped open and she was speechless. She even took a couple of steps backward in fear that maybe Goglbarj had become obsessed in some way.

Goglbarj flew up into a tree, then flew down again and transformed herself back into her normal form. Once she was again standing in front of the Elderess she said, "Now you can see the power that I have been given and how I am able to travel long distances in a short amount of time."

The Elderess took another step backwards and asked, "Have you been bewitched or possessed? I have never heard of a power like what you are displaying?"

Goglbarj responded, "Nothing like that. The wizard found the Tako Ruins library and in there he found a book of spells that he wants to use in our battle with the Kabul. It included an invisibility spell, which is being used by two individuals to go and spy on the Kabul. Another special power that has been given the leprechauns by the creator is the Protee power which has made it so that they have been able to do a lot of healings, which has saved numerous lives. The wizard also gave a dwarf the ability to convert into a hawk so that the north and south can be in constant communication. There is nothing evil in theses spells. The only evil is the Kabul."

The Elderess, still being cautious but willing to accept what she was being told stated, "Then go ahead and communicate with the dwarfs and elves and find out if we can work together. I'll hold council with the other Elderesses and see what kind of an army of amazonionites we can build up here."

With that direction, Goglbarj returned to her owl form and flew off while the Elderess returned to her encampment. Goglbarj flew north toward the dwarf camp. Strangely she felt more comfortable around dwarfs, who she had travelled with and fought battles with, than around elves who she knew very little about.

She flew over the Mar Lake where the mermaids lived, and then over the Hile Desert. Then she travelled over the North Groves, hopefully heading for Hilebin. She had never been in the North Groves so she wasn't exactly sure where to go, but she was sure she would be able to find it even if she needed to follow a search pattern to do it. It took several hours but eventually she was able to find an area that was highly populated, enough so that it looked like a forest city.

Goglbarj slowly drifted toward the city and then flew away from the town area, looking for a place where she could land and transform into her normal body. She ended up traveling a long distance before she found a deserted area where she could land and do her transformation. Once she had made the necessary change, she started to walk toward the center of the town. It wasn't long before she was stopped by a dwarf who barked out, "Who are you and what are you doing in our forest?"

"I am a visitor from the amazonionites, and I am here to visit your Princess. Can you show me the way?"

"How did you get here? Our guards should have stopped you a long time ago." demanded the dwarf.

"I have special powers," replied the amazonionite, not wanting to give away too much information.

Initially the dwarf was stunned. He heard about amazonionites but he never dreamed he would ever meet one. He had convinced himself that they were legendary and that they weren't real. After recovering from his initial surprise, he said, "Follow me. I'll show you the way."

She started to walk with the dwarf, but he waved her back stressing, "You can't walk next to me. They'll think we are connected in some way. You have to walk behind me!"

Goglbarj was slightly insulted. How dare him say that she had to walk behind him. She felt like shooting an arrow into his butt just out of spite. But she knew that if she did anything aggressive, she would have a whole horde of dwarfs on top of her.

They walked further towards the center of the town. Dozens of dwarfs stopped and stared, not knowing what to make of the strange sight. They rarely had visitors, especially not one that was tall. And never a woman by herself. It was all extremely strange.

The dwarf brought Goglbarj to an elaborately decorated tree, the bottom of which was a door, and he instructed her to knock on the door. He said, "A guard will answer and ask you what you want. He'll decide if you can go in or not!"

Goglbarj did as instructed. She knocked on the strange tree door that was in the center of the tree and suddenly a small hatch, around stomach height for the amazonionite, came flying open. "What do you want?" challenged a voice from inside the tree.

Goglbarj responded, "I am sent from the Amazonionites. I am here to speak with the princess of the northlands. I have urgent business which effects the survival of the Small World as we know it. Let me in so I can speak with her."

"Wait here," responded the voice, as if Goglbarj had any other place to go. Then the little hatch slammed shut.

It took several minutes before the hatch was reopened. Goglbarj was starting to become concerned that the voice had somehow forgotten her. She was about to knock again when suddenly the hatch flew open.

"She doesn't believe in amazonionites. She wants you to go away!" barked the voice and the hatch was once again slammed shut.

Goglbarj was stunned. "Now what?" she asked herself out loud.

CHAPTER FIVE

THE GIANTS

Giant-giant called out, "I need Egglac and Hector to join me and the three of us will leave immediately for the meeting as directed by the Creator."

A cry went out from the group, "The Creator has spoken."

With that the three giants immediately advanced up the stairway to the doorway that went through the tree. This doorway would soon be permanently closed, thereby avoiding future troll attacks through that access point. A new doorway would be created to replace this old door. But they would not be locked out because they would use a second doorway when they returned. This door was hidden in a rock and was seldom used because it was difficult to use. Its lock was challenging to engage.

The three giants walked south toward the South Road. After arriving there they followed the road toward Amins. Going to Giter would require that they travel west, but they knew that the leprechauns were to the south, and they knew from previous conversations when the dwarfs, elves, and leprechauns that had passed by the Sheere Cliffs, that the leprechauns were heavily involved with the wizard in saving Small World.

It didn't take them long to arrive at Giter. Their stride was long, and they travelled at twice to three times the speed of the shorter Small World species. Upon arriving in Giter they were met by stares. The few leprechauns that were left in the city, and which hadn't left the city to hide in the forests, had never seen giants before and they were awestricken. They were too shocked to even give the giants a welcome greeting.

Giant-giant asked one of the leprechauns, "Who is your leader?"

The leprechaun pointed to the council building and said, "Amaz and the wizard are in that building."

The giants went toward the building, but they knew they would never be able to enter the building because of their size. Giant-giant spoke to a couple leprechauns who were standing outside the building and who were staring at the giants and said, "Can you tell your leader to come out here and talk to us?"

Without saying a word, too awestricken to even think about responding, the leprechauns ran off into the council chambers yelling, "The giants have come, and they want to talk to you."

Skeptical that there really were giants outside, but nevertheless following the instructions to go outside, Amaz and the wizard, followed by everyone else that was still in the council chambers, worked their way outside to greet the visitors. Amaz, after composing himself at the surprise of seeing the giants, was the first to speak, "Welcome to Giter."

Giant-giant responded with, "The Creator commanded me to come and work with you. He said that the Destroyer is working with the Kabul Lord in trying to take control of all of Small World and that we giants needed to help. We don't want to help, but after the trolls attacked us in our home, and after the Creator commanded that we join you, we decided that we needed to get involved in this struggle to save Small World."

The wizard was the next to speak, "Thank you for joining our struggle. With your help we have a much better chance of eliminating the Kabul's threats and attacks. As you probably already know, the city of Giter has been completely destroyed and the lepelves have nearly all been eliminated."

"We did not know that Giter was destroyed," responded Giant-giant. "Maybe it was by the same trolls that attacked us."

"Then that explains why the trolls just disappeared," explained Amaz. "We expected them to attack Giter next but they never came. You must have wiped them out."

"We did our best," responded Giant-giant. "They did attack us, but we successfully wiped them out. Do you think there are more trolls?"

"Yes," responded the wizard. "There are a lot more. That was just a small party of trolls. There are probably ten times as many in the Kabul."

"What are your plans," asked the giant. "How can we help?"

"Now that we know we have your help, our plans will be changing," responded the wizard. "Utilizing your help against the trolls, which is the worst threat coming from the Kabul, the rest of the Small World species can concentrate on the gnomes and magotites. I think the smartest strategy is for us to wait for the trolls, gnomes, and magotites to come out of the Kabul, and then catch them by surprise. We can retrace their tracks back to where they came out of the Kabul, and then catch them there. We can wipe them out as they come through the mist wall, before they even know what hit them."

"How do we do that?" asked Giant-giant.

The wizard continued, "Go back to your city and prepare your soldiers. Then go to Giter and follow the troll tracks backwards until you get to the border of the Kabul. Hide out there and make camp and wait for the Kabul warriors to come across. Then kill them as they cross."

"How do we know where the Kabul wall is?" questioned the giant.

"You'll know it because the Kabul is surrounded by a mist wall," responded the wizard. "Crossing through the wall will put you into the Kabul. Stay on this side of the wall and wait there for the Kabul warriors to come through."

"Your instructions have been received and we will follow your plan," instructed Giant-giant as he started to turn and leave.

"Wait," yelled out the wizard. "Please leave someone here who we can communicate with and who can bring messages back and forth between us and you."

Giant-giant turned to Egglac and said, "You stay!"

Egglac made a grumpy face but replied, "Yes."

With that Giant-giant and Hector departed, returning to their city of giants where they rallied the giant community together in order to get ready for war.

***

The two dwarfs, Egininety-one and Egiforty-four head for the elves in Gije in order to update them on the plans and activities of the wizard. They cut through the Amins Groves specifically trying to avoid Giter, just in case there were any trolls still lingering around in the area. They didn't want to take any risks.

They travelled toward the South Road and jumped on it just before the Avol River. They crossed the river using the pull boat that was there. They were familiar with this route since this was the second time in the last couple days that they had travelled to the elven kingdom of Gije. The trip took several days, and they were careful to camp out in the surrounding forests now that there was a real threat of the Kabul forces being somewhere in the area and they needed to be extra careful. It wasn't long before they arrived at the point where the road heads northward to the Tako Ruins and on to the Kabul. A few short hours after that they arrived at the Avoli River crossing. Their journey had thankfully been safe and uneventful up to this point and they hoped it would stay that way for the remainder of the journey.

After another good night's rest, the two travelled on to the Albo Pass junction where the road could be taken to the north or to the south. To the north was the way home for the dwarfs, but to the south was the road to the elves.

"Do you think anyone will notice if we accidently went the wrong direction?" asked Egininety-one.

Egiforty-four responded with, "Don't tempt me! No one would love to turn north more than me. But we have a mission that is critical to everyone's survival, and that has to take priority."

"I know! It's just tempting," responded Egininety-one.

"Don't I know it," answered Egiforty-four as the two of them turned toward the south. "We need to get to Gije before nightfall. It's not smart to camp out on the Jove Plateau with those werewolves running around."

"You're right," responded Egininety-one. "We better get moving."

It was just becoming dark when they passed through the elaborately decorated gates of Gije. The doorkeepers were just beginning to shut the gates for the night.

"Where can we spend the night?" asked Egininety-one of one of the gate keepers.

"There's a tavern,
            With a few rooms,
            Just up the street,"

was the hesitant response he received. It was obvious that the gate keeper didn't like dwarfs.

The two dwarfs made their way to the tavern. Upon entering, the open hall they saw numerous tables set up for guests who were eating and drinking their dinners. The room, which had been noisy with excited conversation when they entered, suddenly became silent and all eyes were on the two. It caused the dwarfs to feel extremely uncomfortable.

The two proceeded to an empty table, sat down, and waited to be served. One of the elves came quickly to their table, more to find out why they were here than anything else. The elfin waiter asked,

"What brings you here?
When did you get here?"

Egiforty-four responded, "We have been sent here by the wizard with a message for the king. We just arrived in town a few minutes ago, just as they were closing the city gates."

"What message do you,
Have for the king?"

asked the nosey waiter.

"We are instructed to only give the message to the king," responded Egininety-one.

"Fine you can,
Keep it to yourself."

barked the waiter as he turned to walk away.

"Can't we order any food?" barked Egininety-one, frustrated by the rudeness of the waiter.

The waiter turned around and replied,

"Okay you can!
What do you want?"

"Some soup and bread," responded Egininety-one.

"And a bed to sleep in," added Egiforty-four.

"Sure, you can,
Have them both."

responded the waiter as he walked off. Slowly the novelty of the two dwarfs wore off and the room returned to its previous noisy state, but the word "dwarf" could be overheard in many of the conversations.

The evening and night were uneventful, and, in the morning, the two dwarfs went down for breakfast. When they arrived in the open hall where food was served, they discovered it to be crowded with guests. There were so many that there was no room to sit and most of the visitors were lined up against the wall. Egininetyone asked the waiter, "What's going on that there are so many visitors?"

The waiter responded,

"They heard there were dwarfs,
Staying here at the inn,
They wanted to see,
What dwarfs looked like,
And they want to know,
If you had anything to do,
With the death of,
Gijivure's brother."

"Wait! So Gijivure's brother is dead and Gijivure is alive?" asked Egininety-one. No sooner had he asked the question when he realized that his question made him a prime suspect. The question made it sound like he expected Gijivure to be dead, which is in reality what he expected to hear, but the news caught him off guard.

The waiter was surprised and responded,
"You know about the murder?
I thought you just arrived!
So you tried to kill Gijivure,
But made a mistake?
How do you know,
About the murder?"

Egiforty-four was quick to jump in and lied, "We heard about the death when we came into the town but we were told it was Gijivure that was killed. That's why Egininety-one was surprised."

The waiter seemed to accept the explanation and commented,
"Gijivure is with the doctor,
He has a werewolf bite.
The doctor must treat him,
Or he may not survive.
He will be unconscious in the doctor's room,
For several days."

The two dwarfs stared at each other in complete understanding. The wrong person had been killed, but now they must finish the job.

After breakfast they returned to their room and started to discuss the mistaken identity of Gijivure. Egiforty-four suggested, "One of us must fake sickness or injury so we can get into that doctor's office and have another chance at eliminating Gijivure."

"I agree," responded Egininety-one. He was about to make a suggestion about how to get into the doctor's office when there was a knock on the door. The dwarf answered the door and asked, "What is it?"

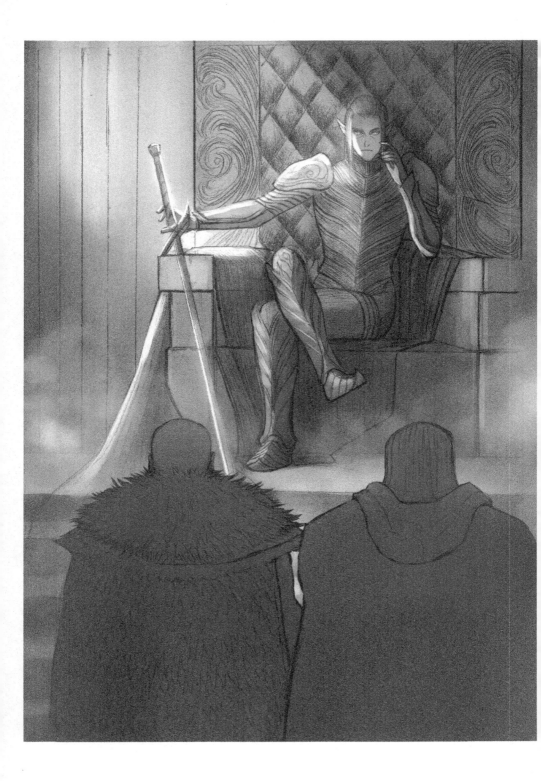

It was the waiter and he said,

> "The king heard you were here,
> He heard that you wanted to talk to him.
> He wants you to come right now,
> And tell him what you know."

"We need someone to show us the way."

The waiter answered,

> "I will take you,
> To where the king is."

The two dwarfs and the waiter left the tavern and briskly walked up toward the palace. The waiter complained,

> "You walk too slow,
> You must move faster,
> The king is waiting,
> To talk to you."

It wasn't long before the two dwarfs and the waiter arrived at the gate of the palace. The dwarfs announced, "We are here to speak to the king at the king's request. Lead us to him."

The elves weren't used to being commanded by a commoner, and they resented the dwarf's attitude, but since the request came from the king, they decided to tolerate the dwarf's rude behavior.

The guard barked,

> "Follow me,
>   You dwarf trash,
> And hurry along,
>   Before I bash."

The dwarfs looked at each other, wondering what the guard meant, but they decided not to push it and hurried along behind the guard.

Once they arrived at the king's reception room where he met his guests the guard instructed them,

> "Do not speak,
>   Until spoken to,
> Or you'll be thrown,
>   Out with a boot."

"More elf rhymes and riddles," grumbled Egininety-one to Egiforty-four, hoping the guard wouldn't hear him. The guard had heard and gave him a dirty look.

It wasn't too long before the king recognized the dwarfs and said,

> "You dwarfs have come,

> To bring me news,
>> Tell me what you know,
>>> Give me some clues."

Egiforty-four proceeded to update the king on the destruction of Giter and the plan of the wizard. He stressed the need to get prepared because the next attack from the Kabul could happen soon. Then the king asked,

>> "Why send two dwarfs,
>>> Why not an elf?
> Is not Gido,
>> Still by himself?"

Egiforty-four explained, "Gido has been given special powers by the wizard. He has the invisibility spell, and he was sent to spy on the Kabul along with Elasti. The two of them are on a special mission to the Kabul. The only other elf that was part of our mission was Gijivure and he is here in Gije under the doctor's care. For now the wizard wants everyone to train up as many able bodied individuals as possible, giving them weapons. He also wants you to prepare you city for the possibility of attack. Later, when he learns more about each of our capabilities, he will organize an attack plan."

The king responded,

>> "I will do as the wizard requests,
>>> It seems only reasonable,
> But tell me more,
>> About this invisible capability."

"It's just a spell that the wizard learned about from the scrolls he found at the Tako Ruins," responded Egiforty-four. "I don't know much more about it."

The king restated,

>> "Tell the wizard,
>>> I will comply,
> With all his wishes,
>> And wait for a plan."

The two dwarfs were dismissed and departed from the king's reception room. As they walked along alone Egiforty-four asked Egininety-one, "What about Gijivure?"

"After we get back to the tavern and to our room, I'll act like I've been poisoned, and you get me to the doctor. Then, when no one is around, I'll finish the job that apparently, we messed up on last time," was Egininety-one's frustrated reply.

"It's a plan," replied Egiforty-four.

They didn't waste any time. As soon as they were in their room Egininety-one immediately started screaming and acting as if he was about to die followed by Egiforty-four running out of the room yelling for help.

The waiter that had previously been friendly and helpful to them helped the two dwarfs out of the tavern and directed them to the doctor. When they arrived at the doctor's office they immediately entered and the doctor asked,

"What is wrong?

Is he injured?

Why is he yelling?"

Egiforty-four explained, "He is having extreme stomach pain and he thinks he was poisoned."

The doctor responded,

"Bring him inside,

Lay him on a bed,

I will give him something."

The response wasn't very satisfactory to Egiforty-four but he was glad that his companion was now inside and maybe he would be able to finish killing Gijivure as they had planned earlier. "Okay," was his response as he half carried and half drug Egininety-one to a bed close to Gijivure.

Gijivure was completely drugged and did not know anything about what was happening next to him. However, the two dwarfs knew immediately that this would be their golden opportunity to eliminate the dreaded spy.

Then the doctor told Egiforty-four,

"You must leave now,

Come back in three or four hours,

For an update."

Egiforty-four didn't want to leave his companion, but he knew it would be the best if he departed. Staying at the doctor's office would just keep him in the way and may have prevented his companion from completing his mission.

Egininety-one was given a pill which he pretended to take but later took out of his mouth. He was afraid that the pill would make him sleepy and he didn't want to fall asleep and miss his opportunity to eliminate Gijivure. It would require several hours of the dwarf pretending to be asleep before an opportunity presented itself. The doctor left the office for some unknown reason, possibly to visit a patient, and Egininety-one jumped into action. He wanted to do something that wouldn't leave a trace, so stabbing, which was his preferred option, was not an option. Instead, he chose suffocation. I took his pillow and put it over the mouth and nose of Gijivure, holding it firm. The elf squirmed in an attempt to breathe, but eventually quit squirming and lay still. The dwarf checked for a pulse and found none. He was convinced that he had accomplished his mission. Then he made his way back to his own bed and returned to a sleeping position. He knew that if he ran off, which was what he would have liked to do, he would raise suspicion that he was the killer. But if he stayed there, then the doctor would have to believe that the dwarf had slept through the entire event.

It was about one hour later when the doctor finally returned. He peeked into the room and found his two patients laying in their beds and he assumed they were asleep and resting peacefully. All seemed well. The doctor went about his business. He had another patient visit his office and soon that patient was dispatched, being taken care of by the doctor. Then the doctor came up to Egininety-one's bed and shook him in an attempt to wake him up.

The dwarf pretended to be groggy, but responded to the doctor by saying, "What's going on?"

The doctor asked,
"How are you feeling?
Are your stomach pains gone?
You should be better by now."

Egininety-one replied, "I'm feeling great. Whatever you gave me seems to have worked."

To this the doctor responded,
"I'm glad to hear it,
If nothing else I can do,
You return to your friend."

The dwarf climbed out of the bed, took one last look at Gijivure who was starting to look pale, and said, "Thank you again. You've been a great help." Then he left the doctor's office and rushed toward the tavern to join up with Egiforty-four. On the way there the two encountered each other on the street. Egiforty-four said, "We need to go back to the king. He has summoned us and has a message that he wants us to bring to the wizard. Were you able to complete your mission?"

"Yes," replied Egininety-one. "It was pretty easy because the doctor left for about an hour and I did what I needed to do during that time. Then I pretended to still be asleep so he wouldn't suspect that I did anything. I think we're free to go with no repercussions."

"Excellent," was all Egiforty-four could think to say as the two hurried off to the king's reception room where they were welcomed in as soon as they arrived.

The king spoke to them immediately as they arrived saying,
"Tell the wizard,
I have heard his request,
And we will be ready,
At his bequest."

Egiforty-four responded, "We will give him your message." Then the two dwarfs bowed and left the reception room. They wasted no time in leaving the elven city, hoping to get away before the doctor realized that Gijivure was dead. They didn't want to have to answer any questions. They rushed to get safely off the Jove Plateau before nightfall.

CHAPTER SIX

THE DWARFS

Egisix flew to the window of his home in Hilebin. He carefully looked around to make sure no one would see him. Flying through the open window he landed on the floor inside the house. After landing he transformed himself from a hawk back into a dwarf.

He immediately exited his house and went directly to Egione, the king of the dwarfs. He waited outside the king's chambers until he was invited in and then bowed in front of the king waiting to be recognized. The wait wasn't very long before the king said, "Stand up Egisix. Before you tell me what's going on you have to tell me how you were able to get here so quickly."

Egisix was hesitant to explain his ability to transform into a hawk. He knew that the dwarfs feared sorceries, and this would be considered a sorcery. He asked the king, "Would it be possible for me to explain this to you in secret without anyone else hearing?"

"Of course," responded Egione. "Everyone please depart." He waited till the room was empty and then he repeated his request, "How did you get here so fast?"

"Please King Egione, don't be surprised by what I am about to show you. This was a gift given to me by the wizard. It is something he learned from the Tako Ruins library and he considered it essential for the north and south to be able to communicate so I volunteered to be transformed in a way that you are about to see." Egisix said the magic word and suddenly transformed himself into a hawk.

Egione jumped out of his throne and ran behind it, peeking out to see the hawk that had once been Egisix. He was visibly shaken.

Egisix could see the king's fear and quickly transformed himself back into a dwarf. Then he said, "That is how I am able to travel back and forth between the north and south so quickly."

The king walked back around the throne and sat down. Then he said, "You are extremely brave to allow the wizard to give you such powers. We must make sure no one else learns about this because it will raise fears." Then he instructed, "Go to the doors and let all my aids back in. Then please explain what message the wizard has for me."

Egisix did as instructed and when the king's entourage was back in the room, the king said to Egisix, "Please proceed."

Egisix explained the travels of the party after they left the North Groves back down to the south. He explained the devastating destruction of Giter, and the preparations that are going on in Amins where the wizard was now located. He explained how the wizard wanted everyone to be trained and ready for an attack. Then he dropped the surprise on Egione. He said, "The wizard thinks the dwarfs should attack Morgos, the home of the Magotites, because they are the closest Kabul city to the north. He feels that it would be easy for us to eliminate that threat and that would quickly reduce the Kabul's ability to organize an attack against any of our cities."

King Egione was quick to respond, "You know that's not the way of the dwarfs. Why didn't you tell him that right away? We only fight defensive wars. That is the way of the dwarfs. We do not attack. We wait until they attack us. Then we proceed to wipe them out."

Egisix responded, "I told him that, but he instructed me to make the request anyway. Now I have made the request, and I will return to the wizard and explain that you refuse to do an offensive attack."

"Good," replied Egione.

One of the advisors to the king spoke up, "How are you going to get that message back to Amins before they organize another attack. You'll probably be too late to do any good."

The king answered the question, "He has his ways. Trust him. He'll get the message to the wizard."

Everyone in the room was visibly surprised by this statement, but no one dared ask the king how this was possible. They knew better. If the king wanted them to know he would have told them.

Egisix was leaving the kings chambers and starting to walk toward his home when he noticed a fuss a little way off to the side. A large crowd had gathered and there seemed to be a lot of confusion. It was too large a group for Egisix to see what all the commotion was about, so he decided to go over and investigate. When he arrived at the gathering, he was surprised to see Goglbarj the amazonionite in the middle of the group. She stood out because she was taller than the rest and was dressed peculiarly compared to a dwarf. The dwarfs were asking questions like, "Who are you?" and "What are you doing in the North Groves?"

Egisix jumped to the rescue. He pushed his way in to Goglbarj and when he was next to her he said, "That's a good question. Why are you here?"

At first Goglbarj ignored him and didn't answer him. She had already answered that question a dozen times and she was sick and tired of repeating herself. Egisix saw her confusion so he blurted out, "I'm Egisix. Don't you remember me from our meeting in Amins?"

"Thank goodness," responded Goglbarj. "I didn't recognize you at first. You dwarfs all look the same."

"Not to us we don't," responded Egisix, slightly offended. "So why are you here?"

"I'm here because I wanted to introduce myself to the Princess of the Northland. I was hoping we could set up communication and possibly work together," explained Goglbarj.

"That's an excellent idea," explained Egisix. "But first I need to introduce you to the king. He will want to meet you."

"Actually, he's already met me during the meeting between the dwarfs and the amazonionites. But if you think it's important, and if you think it will help me meet with the princess, then let's do it."

Egisix commanded everyone to disperse, and they responded, knowing that he was the head of the military and police forces. Then he led Goglbarj to the king's chambers. After entering the chambers, and being recognized by the king, he asked, "You came here to speak to the princess. She has very little power amongst the dwarfs. Why bring your request to her rather than to me?"

Goglbarj responded, "You already have communication with the leadership of the amazonionites. That's the leader-to-leader connection that we need. But I was also interested in a less formal, girl-to-girl relationship between our kingdoms. Wouldn't that be a reasonable relationship?"

The king saw no reason to object, so he stated, "Sure. Go with my blessing. Tell her I sent you and then she'll receive you."

Egisix and Goglbarj exited the king's chambers and he escorted her back to the tree that served as the door to the princess' living quarters. Egisix couldn't resist asking her, "What do you transform into?"

She answered, "An owl."

They arrived and this time it was Egisix who knocked on the door. When the guard answered the door Egisix said, "I have a visitor that, at the request of the king, the princess has been invited to talk with."

The guard looked at Goglbarj and said, "Why didn't you tell me earlier that it was the king that sent you? I will check with the princess, but I am sure she would have gladly let you in."

It only took couple minutes before the guard returned and opened the door. In parting Egisix said to Goglbarj, "I need to get back to the wizard, so I'll leave you to do your own introductions."

"No problem," said Goglbarj. She preferred a private audience with the princess, and this would make it easier.

Egisix returned to his house, preformed his transformation, and headed south.

In the meantime, Goglbarj was escorted to Ejijone, the Princess of the Northland. Upon entering the room, Goglbarj, ignoring any dwarf etiquette, walked directly up to the princess and said, "I am Goglbarj, an amazonionite warrior, and I would like to speak to you in private. Is that possible."

Princess Ejijone was caught completely off guard and it took her a few seconds to recover before she could respond. Then she said, "I thought you were myths. I didn't believe there were really amazonionites. I am thrilled to meet you. Of course, we can have a private conversation." The princess waved the guard, her entourage, and everyone else out of the room. Once they were gone, she instructed, "Let's sit down here together and learn about each other. And maybe you can tell me what this mysterious secret is that you want only me to hear."

Goglbarj proceeded to explain who the amazonionites were, where they lived, and how they lived. Then Ejijone gave a similar overview of the dwarfs. Not surprisingly, in the amazonionites it was only the women who were warriors and leaders, and for the dwarfs it was only the men. Their cultures had driven them in completely different directions.

Then Goglbarj asked the question that had driven her to have this visit, "Here is what I am proposing. The men are moving too slow. They want to wait around until the Kabul is ready, and then, when they attack, the men want to fight a defensive war. We already know that the Kabul is coming after us because they destroyed Giter and almost completely wiped out the lepelves. There are only a few remaining. And the Kabul wants to do the same to all the Small World cities. I want to form our own little army and attack the Kabul. If we only wipe out one city, it reduces the threat and impact significantly."

Ejijone responded, "I know that the dwarfs will only fight a defensive war. That's just the way we are. That's our culture and history. I can see why you are frustrated. Tell me what you are proposing to do."

"I want to attack. I want to organize a female army of amazonionites, dwarfs, elves, leprechauns and anyone else we can come up with, and attack. If we destroy Morgos, the magotite stronghold. That would take away one-third of the Kabul's power. Once we've done that, we regroup and decide if we are capable of attacking another city, maybe Gamotz, the home of the gnomes. But first I have to see if I have an army."

Ejijone was getting excited. She had received weapons training because every dwarf goes through it, but she never saw any use for the training, until now. She was hesitant to show Goglbarj her excitement, because dwarf culture didn't allow for outward bursts of excitement, so she said, "I would like you to stay with me and spend the evening in my home. We can have a nice dinner, play some dwarf games, have some conversation, but we can't talk about this subject again today. Tomorrow morning I will share my thoughts."

Goglbarj was more direct in her conversations and expected the same in return. She was confused by the princess' request, but she knew she didn't have a choice, so she responded, "Thank you for your invitation. I would be delighted to stay here tonight. And I look forward to hearing your thoughts in the morning."

"Good," responded the princess. "I will have one of my attendants escort you to your room where you can get refreshed, take a shower, lay down and rest, and we will come for you in an hour and have dinner with you. Does that work for you?"

"That would be wonderful," responded the amazonionite. With the wave of a hand from the princess one of the attendants escorted Goglbarj off in the direction of her room for the night.

The evening went on as planned and was cordial. The food and games were from the dwarf culture and the whole experience was strange and unusual for the amazonionite. But she enjoyed learning and this was a rare chance that she was given to learn about a culture that was extremely foreign to her.

After dinner and some dwarf games, Goglbarj and Ejijone drifted off to their rooms for a good night's rest. Goglbarj was restless in her excitement to learn what the princess would have to tell her in the morning.

In the meantime, Ejijone rounded up her female attendants and presented the idea to them, "Here is what the amazonionite is proposing. She wants to organize an army of female warriors from her tribes and from the dwarfs, elves, and leprechauns. She thinks we shouldn't wait to be attacked. She thinks a defensive war is a mistake. She wants her female army to attack one of the Kabul cities, like the magotites, and eliminate them thereby making the Kabul less of a threat. She thinks that the traditional defensive war leaves us vulnerable. She thinks that by weakening the Kabul it will be easier for us to defend against them if and when they decide to attack. What do you think?"

One of the attendants, Ejijtwenty, said, "It sounds like they already decided to attack, based on what you said about Giter. Maybe her plan is too late."

"It may be," replied Ejijone. "But what if we destroy their cities while they are gone?"

Another attendant said, "It seems like they're headed south first. That means that we may be safe temporarily. That would give us the time to destroy one or more of their cities. I think it's a great idea."

A third attendant said, "The men always play down our value and I'm tired of it. We train alongside of the men and in many cases we are a lot better than them. Why shouldn't we be a part of this war? I know we can make a difference."

Ejijone was surprised by the aggressive reaction of her assistants. They showed no sign of fear. It made her feel weak because she had experienced some hesitation about Goglbarj's proposal. But with the support of her friends, she now felt like, not only was this the right thing to do, but that they would actually be able to accomplish it.

"Is that how all of you feel," Ejijone asked her group of attendants. Everyone nodded their head positive so she said, "I'll tell Goglbarj that we're all in."

"Excellent," said Ejijtwenty.

The evening was uneventful and, in the morning, Goglbarj and Ejijone met together for breakfast. Goglbarj was overanxious to know Ejijone's opinion. "What is your decision about my proposal?" she asked.

"We're all in," responded Ejijone. "I talked with a group of the dwarf ladies yesterday and they're excited to make their mark. And they're excited to show the boys what they can do?"

Goglbarj was overjoyed by the news. She responded, "Excellent. That's wonderful. Can you get your warriors ready while I go to see if the elves are interested in joining us?"

"How are you going there?" asked the dwarf. "Isn't it going to be dangerous?"

"I will need to tell you a secret," Goglbarj whispered. "The wizard gave me the ability to transform into an owl and that gives me the ability to fly." Ejijone look skeptical. She wasn't ready to believe what Goglbarj was telling her so the amazonionite said, "I'll have to show you, but first we need to empty the room."

Ejijone ordered everyone to leave the room and then Goglbarj said the magic word and suddenly transformed into an owl. Repeating the process, she returned to her amazonionite form.

Ejijone was speechless. She just stared in shock. After a few moments she said, "Unbelievable."

"Pretty cool isn't it," said Goglbarj. "Now you see how I can go visit the elves."

"Go," stressed Ejijone. "We'll get ready here while you're gone. We're going to need to do it without the men finding out so it's going to be a little tricky. The men will hassle us if they see us preparing. They think we're worthless without their protection."

"We're going to be changing that," responded Goglbarj. "I'll leave you for now, but I'll return as soon as I know what the elves are going to do."

With that Goglbarj transformed herself again and then departed through a window into the morning sky.

CHAPTER SEVEN

THE KABUL SPIES

Elasti and Gido continued to be frozen in their spots, afraid to move. They knew they needed to warn the southerners, but they also knew that getting rid of the spies would be an even better solution. They patiently waited.

After several hours it became dark and the four gnome spies finally went to sleep. Elasti whispered to Gido, "Let's cut their throats, each of us cutting them at the same time."

Gido responded, also in a whisper:

"The plan you make,
         Is good for me,
If we kill them,
         We should be free."

Continuing to remain cloaked but feeling weak because of the length of time they had spent being cloaked, the leprechaun and elf approached the sleeping gnomes. Elasti went to one of the gnomes and Gido to another. They hoped to be able to rapidly cut the throats of the two and then move on to the next pair and finish them off as well.

Plans don't always work out as hoped, no matter how well planned they might have been. As Gido was attempting to cut the throat of the first gnome, he did the deed a little slower than he should have and suddenly the gnome woke up, because of the pain, and let out a shriek. Gido was able to finish the job, but he realized a little too late that he should have done the deed a little quicker.

Elasti had quickly killed the first gnome and had moved over to the second when Gido's gnome yelled out. The noise caused Elasti's

second gnome to start squirming and Elasti plunged the knife into his throat, stopping the gnome from yelling out. It was quick and clean and the gnome fell back to the ground.

However, Gido's second gnome immediately jumped up. He was the gnome who had come through the mist first and who thought he had seen a glimpse of a leprechaun. He looked around and saw that his three companions were dead. He searched around for the killers, looking in all directions, and couldn't see anyone. In desperation he grabbed his sword and started frantically swinging it around in all directions. The gnome yelled out, "I know that you leprechauns are out there somewhere. Make yourself visible so we can have a fair fight. Quit hiding out, you cowards."

The leprechaun and elf realized that they were no match for this gnome's wildly swinging sword, so they kept their distance. After a few minutes the gnome started to tire of flaying around and stopped his swinging. It was then that the elf swung his bow into position, inserted an arrow, and sent it flying into the gnome's heart.

With the deed done, Elasti asked, "Should we hide these bodies and the camp?"

Gido responded,
"We should hide,
    What we have done,
In case more come,
    Through the mist.
We also need,
    To remove our cloak,
And become visible again,
    Our energy is broke."

Elasti agreed. The two removed their invisibility cloak and, using the light of the gnome fire, the two went to work hiding the gnome bodies and their supplies in a small gully. Then they covered everything with branches and leaves. They then went deeper into the woods, found a soft area covered with leaves, and because they were extremely exhausted, they rapidly went to sleep.

In the morning they felt refreshed and Gido declared,
"We are energetic,
    And ready to learn,
We'll go through the mist,
    And see what we churn."

Elasti nodded his head and the two quickly prepared themselves for their adventure into the Kabul. "We need to tie a rope around each other's waist so that we make sure we stay together. The last time my companions and I went through this mist we struggled to stay together."

They tied themselves with the rope and surged into the mist wall that separated the Kabul from the rest of Small World. As they walked through the mist Elasti felt the same sense of confusion that he experienced the last time he entered the wall on his way to visit the dwarfs in the north. It somehow seemed longer than before, but he was sure it was just his fear of the journey that caused the strange feelings he was experiencing.

Abruptly the journey through the wall of mist came to an end and they stepped out into the desolate and deserted world of the Kabul. They knew they were there because it was so different than the world they had just departed. The lush trees and vegetation of the Southern Plains had been replaced by dry, scraggly brush and cactus. There wasn't any green to be seen anywhere. Fortunately, there was a rough trail which appeared to have been travelled on recently by a large number of individuals with large feet. "That must have been where the trolls came through when they destroyed Giter," commented Elasti.

Gido seemed confused. He started twitching and moving in jerky motions. His eyes were crossing and each eye independently looking off in all directions. His movements made no sense. He attempted to respond to Elasti's observation, but he had trouble speaking.

"I think ahhhhh think that,
        The footsteps gooooooo,
    Only in one direction like ahhhh,
        They don't mooooo."

Elasti immediately became concerned about the elf. The mist wall seemed to have a drastic effect on him. He realized immediately that Gido would be worthless as a spy if he remained in this state. Elasti decided to wait ten minutes to see if Gido snapped out of his spasms, but nothing changed. Instead it seemed to get worse and soon Gido wasn't able to utter any words at all.

"We're going back through the mist," announced Elasti. Gido seemed too far gone to give a meaningful response. The rope was still connecting the two and Elasti started to lead Gido back through the mist. There was no resistance from Gido who now seemed oblivious to everything around him.

This time the journey through the mist seemed to take forever. Elasti started to wonder if he had turned a corner and was now travelling along the inside of the mist parallel to its sides. But he persisted on and eventually he received the welcome relief of exiting the mist. He knew he was back in the southern plains area of Small World because it was green and he saw the forest where the two of them had spent the night. Gido had stopped twitching but he hadn't fully recovered consciousness. He still seemed a little bewildered and oblivious of his surroundings. After about ten minutes of him slowly becoming aware, Gido said,

"Where are we?
     I thought we went to Kabul,
This is not Kabul,
     This is where we entered Kabul."

"Yes," responded Elasti. "You were going crazy in there, so we had to leave again. I was becoming desperate to know what to do. You seemed to have lost consciousness in there."

"I remember going in,
     I saw the desolation,
I don't remember anything,
     I have hesitation,"

responded Gido. He looked up at Elasti with pleading eyes and then continued,

"Thank you for helping me,
     I feel like a fool,
I don't know how to be a spy,
     If I can't go into the Kabul."

Elasti responded, "You can't risk going back in there again. Next time I might not be able to help you. I think you will need to stay out here, and I will need to go in alone. Would you prefer to wait for me, or would you like to return to Amins?"

Gido responded,

"I will wait for you,
     Until you come,
Unless some other danger occurs,
     Then I will run."

Elasti nodded in agreement, untied himself from Gido, turned, and reentered the mist wall into the Kabul.

***

Egiforty-four and Egininety-one arrive in Amins, ready to deliver the elf king's message to the wizard. They travel directly to the council chambers where the wizard was in conversation with the council members, discussing their strategy and preparations in the event that the Kabul forces should arrive at their door.

Once they were welcomed by the council, Egiforty-four spoke up first, "The elf king is making preparations as you directed. On our way back we passed by the destruction in Giter and it was pretty bad. We saw the trail of the trolls and they went off to the north, toward the Sheere Cliffs but their trail never came back. They just disappeared. We decided not to follow their trail because we felt that reporting back about our mission with the elves was more important. We have completed our mission and now we would like to go back and investigate what happened to the trolls."

He continued, "We also discovered that Gijivure was still alive. It was his brother that had been killed by mistake when Gido snuck into his house. However, while we were there Gijivure was with the doctor. He had been bitten by a werewolf and was unconscious because of the doctor's drugs. We pretended sickness and when the doctor wasn't looking Egininety-one smothered him."

The wizard responded, "Excellent. You have performed admirably."

The wizard was about to continue his comments when, just then, to everyone's surprise, Egisix walked into the chambers. The wizard turned his attention to him and asked, "It's good to see you have returned. Do you have an update for us?"

"Yes," replied Egisix. "The king of the dwarfs refuses to make an offensive attack against the Kabul. He is getting everyone ready in case there is an attack, but he chooses to wait and let the Kabul make the first move."

"But the Kabul has already made the first move," complained the wizard. "They have already destroyed Giter. Isn't that enough of a first move?"

"I understand," responded Egisix. "But he won't change his mind. Dwarfs have a tradition of being defensive and not offensive."

After a pause, Egisix continued, "I encountered Goglbarj when I was there."

"What was she doing there?" challenged the wizard.

"She was there to meet with Princess Ejijone. She never said why. I helped her get her meeting and then I flew back here. It all seemed very sneaky. She may be planning her own attack separate from what we're doing."

"I hope not," replied the wizard. "It may defeat what we are doing."

"But we're not doing anything," burst in Egininety-one. "All the cities we have communicated with are preparing their defenses in the event of an attack, but no one is doing anything to prevent an attack in the first place."

The wizard jumped in, "We have sent Gido and Elasti into the Kabul to be spies. They have the invisibility cloak which should shield them, and they should be reporting back in a few days. Once we know what the Kabul is planning, we can make better preparations as well."

"Unfortunately, the Kabul may be down here before then," responded Egininety-one. The dwarf received a reprimanding look from Egisix causing him to back off and say no more.

The wizard continued, "We have also received word from the giants and they are going to place a guard at the location where the trolls came through for their last attack. This guard may become our best offensive / defensive weapon since the giants seem to be the best force we have for defeating the trolls."

Amaz felt the need to step in before the conversation between the dwarfs and the wizard became heated, "Everyone is trying to do their best here. The wizard has insight that goes beyond the rest of us. He has gone through this war before and we need to listen to him in spite of our frustrations with the Kabul. What I think we need to do next is three things, one is to figure out what happened to the trolls, another is to figure out what Goglbarj is doing, and the third is to hear back from our spies."

No one responded to Amaz's comments, but several nodded their heads in agreement. The wizard went on to say, "I think we know what happened to the trolls. The giants said they were attacked by the trolls and they wiped out the ones that attacked them. I wonder if it was the same trolls that attacked Giter? Can you dwarfs, Egiforty-four and Egininety-one, go north and follow their tracks to see if there are more trolls or if that was indeed the same ones."

Egisix responded, "I can do that quickly by myself. I'll fly along their tracks and see if I can see what happened to them."

"Excellent," responded the wizard.

Egiforty-four asked, "Egininety-one and I can go to the point where the trolls came out of the mist and see if the giants are there. We'll be their messengers in case there is something that you need to know."

"That's an excellent and useful idea," responded the wizard. "Why don't the three of you take off and report back as soon as you have helpful information."

***

The Kabul Prince Kakakrul was becoming worried. He hadn't heard from his spy Gijivure for several days and that was extremely unusual. He had demanded regular updates and those were not happening. He transformed himself into his eagle form and flew to the elven city of Gije to see if he could spot anything unusual. Have there been any changes in the city, like a lock down, that wouldn't allow Gijivure to contact him? Had Gijivure's betrayal been discovered? Was Gijivure still alive? The prince needed answers and he was hoping to learn some of those answers by traveling down to the city.

It didn't take long before he arrived at Gije. He started by flying over the city at a very high level. He saw farmers in the field, which convinced him that there was not a lock down. He flew lower and lower until he landed on one of the city's towers. He watched and saw nothing unusual. The city seemed to be going about its business as normal.

He continued to watch. He focused on Gijivure's house, hoping to see some activity there. It took a couple hours, but eventually he saw some people coming out of his house. He was surprised to see them carrying something. Were they stealing Gijivure's belongings? They were carrying furniture, dishes, and kitchen utensils. They were stripping out his belongings. Then it dawned on him. Gijivure must be dead and these are his relatives, evacuating his residence.

The prince was frustrated. It had taken many years for him to develop a spy amongst the elves. And now he was gone. There wouldn't be enough time to develop a new spy amongst the elves, but fortunately he also had a spy amongst the dwarfs. He hadn't used this spy recently because the focus had been on the south, but now he would need to reestablish this connection.

The prince decided to fly off toward the north to see if he was able to communicate with his other spy. He took a route that led him over the location where the trolls had entered the south when they conquered Giter. As he came close to the border, where the mist wall separated the Kabul from the south, he was surprised to see a large group of giants arriving at that location. What were giants doing there? How did they know where to go?

"These giants are becoming a major interference," he mumbled to himself. "Now I'm going to have to change the route where my troops invade the south." He continued his flight north, hoping he would be able to connect with his dwarf spy. Upon arriving in the North Groves, he circled around Hilebin wondering how he could attract the attention of his spy. He spent a long time circling, but eventually his spy looked up and noticed the eagle overhead. The spy went out into the forest, finding a place that was isolated, sat down next to a tree, and began to hum. She crossed his legs, folded her arms, closed his eyes, bowed her head, and began to hum. "Hummmmm ummmmm ummmmm," went her chant for several minutes.

The eagle landed in front of the spy and quickly transformed into his princely shape. Then he said, "Thank you for coming out to talk to me. My elf spy has been killed and I need your help."

The spy responded, "I am here for you. Tell me what you need."

CHAPTER EIGHT

AN OFFENSIVE ARMY

Goglbarj arrived near the gates of the elfin city of Gije behind the cover of a tree and immediately transformed herself from an owl into her amazonionite body. She walked through the gates and immediately became the center of attention. No one had ever seen an amazonionite before. They all thought it was simply a legend and that they didn't really exist. She was accosted by a series of questions like,

"Who are you?

Are you pretending to be an amazonionite?

What do you want in Gije?

How can we help you?"

Goglbarj responded with, "I need to talk to your queen. Can you show me the way?

The elves were eager to help and several of them said,

"We know the way,

We will show it to you,

You must follow us,

And help you too!"

Other elves stated,

"Her name is Gushe,

She is very nice,

You'll like meeting with her,

She'll be very interested in you."

"Lead the way," Instructed Goglbarj.

Two elves led her to the castle and when they arrived one of the elves instructed the guard,

"She is here,
To see the queen,
You need to lead,
Her there directly."

The guard was confused and uncertain. He had never been instructed about how to treat an amazonionite. He waved another elf over who was most likely the captain of the guard and asked,
"What do we do?
This amazonionite is here,
She wants to meet with,
The queen Gushe."

The captain of the guard responded,
"I will check,
To see what the queen,
Wants to do."

The captain disappeared for a few minutes while the amazonionite waited. The guard and Goglbarj were uncomfortable with each other and didn't speak. They just stood there fidgeting until the captain returned. He instructed,
"Follow me,
The queen wants to see,
If you an amazonionite,
Truly be."

The captain led Goglbarj into the palace and around a series of corridors. Eventually they arrived at what appeared to be the queen's chambers. The captain opened the door and Goglbarj entered the room to find about a dozen women in attendance. It was difficult to identify which of the women was the queen since no one seemed to stand out in their dress or mannerisms. Goglbarj, not afraid to speak out asked, "Which of you is the queen?"

One of the ladies at random asked,
"Who is asking?
Who are you?
Why are you here?
What do you want?"

Goglbarj responded, "I am an amazonionite warrior sent on a mission by my Elderess to speak with the queen. Are you the queen?"

Another elf lady spoke up and said,
"How do we know,
You're not here to harm,

The queen?
How do we know,
You're not a spy,
From the Kabul?"

Goglbarj, feeling slightly insulted, demanded, "I'm not here to play your silly guessing games. I'm here on an urgent mission which involves the imminent war with the Kabul. And I am only to speak with your queen, no one else. I would need everyone but the queen to leave."

A third lady spoke up and said,
"All of you leave,
So I can find out,
What this request,
Is all about."

The second lady protested saying,
"How can we trust her.
I can't even believe,
There is such a thing,
As an amazonionite.
I think she's a fake,
You may be setting,
Yourself up for trouble."

The third lady, who was now obviously the queen, responded saying,
"She seems trustworthy,
All of you exit,
So I can learn,
Her big secret."

All the ladies stood up except for the queen and slowly left the queen's chambers. Once they were gone and only the queen and Goglbarj were left in the room, the queen demanded,
"What's your big secret?
Why are you here?
The mystery you present,
Is all rather weird."

The amazonionite explained everything about her plans to the elf queen, just like she had done earlier to the dwarf princess. She hoped for a similar response. The queen was enthralled by the proposition that they organize a female army of amazonionites, dwarfs, and leprechauns and go on the attack against the Kabul. She responded,

"I know that the men,
        Prefer a defensive war,
I have always left decisions,
        Like that to stay far,
Away from my concerns,
        But I know that so far,
Their preparations include,
        Both men and women arms,
In any battle.
        Women are not treated fair,
Below the men,
        And are,
Their equals when it comes to battle,
        So separating afar,
From the men seems,
        Traitorous in war."

Goglbarj was surprised by this answer. She was always told that men suppressed women and that women looked forward to the day when men were no longer dominant. She asked, "You are saying that you won't support us? You won't join our army?"

"What I can do,
        Is talk to my king,
Who leads the elves,
        If he supports a ring,
Of women warriors,
        Then we will sing,
And join in what,
        You bring."

Goglbarj responded, "It seems strange that you would ask a man if the women can have an army. But if that is the way of the elves, then please proceed. Should I stay in town and come back tomorrow?"

The elven queen responded,
"We have a place,
        For you to stay,
I will call for you,
        When we have a say."

Goglbarj could only offer a flabbergasted reply, "If that's the way it must be then let it be so."

The queen ordered her attendants back into her chambers and then instructed one of them to lead the amazonionite to her quarters.

It wasn't long before she was again called and led back to the
queen's chambers. This time the attendants weren't dismissed and
were included in the conversation. Queen Gushe explained,

"I have instructed my attendants,
  About your plan,
And they all received it,
  They are all a fan,
I talked with the king,
  He was surprised,
He said if the women can get organized,
  He would be advised,
He said more power to us,
  And that we should be revised,
He supports us to do whatever we choose,
  A plan we should devise."

Goglbarj responded, "Excellent. Glad to hear you are joining
our forces. The plan is that we get all the female warriors together
and attack one of the Kabul cities. We should start with their
weakest, which seems to be the Magotite home of Morgos."

One of the queen's aides wondered,

"How do we get,
  The north and south troops together?
How do we communicate,
  Between the two armies?
This all started,
  Because we lost contact."

Goglbarj answered, "I have a secret weapon which allows me to
travel between the two. It is a power given to me by the wizard and
will help us stay connected. I'm planning an army from the north
composed of dwarfs and amazonionites, and an army from the
south composed of elves and leprechauns. We will hit Morgos from
two directions. It should be a quick victory."

The same elf attendant asked,

"I am concerned,
  That we are running around,
Pretending to be,
  Warriors for good,
And attacking empty cities,
  While at home,
Kabul forces are destroying,
  Our homes when we,

Should be helping,
Save our homes."

Goglbarj was ready with her answer, "Don't worry. I will use my special powers to watch their activities and movements. When I travelled here, I noticed that they were busy making preparations, but they were not on their way yet."

The same elf again spoke up, leaving Goglbarj with the impression that she must be some kind of spokesperson for the queen,

"What is this special power,
You keep talking about,
Is it something,
You can tell us about?"

Goglbarj responded, "I'll do better than that. I will show you the power that the wizard gave to me." She privately said the secret word and was suddenly transformed into an owl. The elves in the room gasped in disbelief. Goglbarj flew around the room and then landed in the same place where she had started. Then she said the magic word and was again transformed back into her amazonionite form.

The queen spoke up,

"Now I see,
That you have real powers.
I am surprised,
To see such strange flower.
I now know that,
You are not fake,
And I believe,
There is much at stake.
We are on your team,
We will prepare,
And wait for your signal,
Without a moment to spare."

Goglbarj said, "My next stop is the leprechauns. I will see if they will also join the all-woman army. Then I will report back to you about the status of the southern effort. Hopefully we will then be ready to march on the Kabul."

With that the amazonionite said the magic name and transformed herself back into an owl. Having completed the transformation, she flew out of one of the windows of the room and headed off in the direction of Amins. She knew who she wanted to meet with in Amins. She had travelled with Jesves over the Sheere

Cliffs as they travelled with the dwarfs to Amins. She was confident that Jesves would go along with her plan and be supportive.

The trip to Amins, which had previously taken several days on foot, only required a few hours by air. However, since it was late in the day, a portion of her journey would have to be travelled by night. Luckily, with the vision of an owl, traveling at night wasn't a problem.

As she approached Amins, it was becoming late at night and Goglbarj knew that she would have to wait until the morning before she could find Jesves. She decided to stay in her owl form and spend the night in a tree. As she searched for a place to rest, she found a tree that had a hole from a broken off branch. She went into the opening and decided that this would be the place where she would spend the rest of the night. This turned out to be an easy and comfortable place to sleep and she ended up getting a good night's rest.

In the morning Goglbarj finished her trip, landing just outside of Amins and transforming herself back into her amazonionite form. She entered the city and made her way directly toward the council chambers where she knew the wizard and the leprechaun leaders would be endlessly debating their future. She didn't enter the chambers but started asking the people outside of the chambers where Jesves could be found. They were quick to respond, explaining that she was in the woods with her family. Goglbarj was given directions on which route to travel in order to find Jesves.

Goglbarj headed off immediately in the direction suggested by the leprechauns at the council chambers. It was a long walk, but eventually she encountered one of the leprechaun hideout camps. Asking around she found out that this wasn't Jesves' camp and that she would need to travel another half hour before she came to the correct encampment.

The amazonionite hurried along. She was anxious to organize her own little war against the Kabul and she knew that her army would be able to conquer the magotites. Eventually she came to the correct camp and she yelled out, "Is this the camp where I can find Jesves?"

A response was yelled back to her, "Yes. This is her camp."

"Excellent," responded Goglbarj. "How do I find her?"

Jesves answered, "I'm here Goglbarj. Why have you come all the way out here? What can I do to help?"

"Come out here and talk to me," the amazonionite responded. "I need to have a private conversation with you."

Goglbarj stopped walking toward the camp and waited for Jesves to come out and meet her. When Jesves arrived the amazonionite asked, "Are you ready to go to war with the Kabul?"

"Of course," responded the leprechaun. "What are your plans."

"The men are moving too slow. They only want a defensive war. I am organizing all the women into an army focused on attacking the Kabul, which should surprise them and blindside them. I already have the support of the dwarfs, the elves, and of course the amazonionites. The plan is that there would be two attacks, one from the north and one from the south. The leprechaun and elf women would join forces from the south and enter the Kabul, avoiding the cities of Tragis and Gamotz and head straight for the magotite city of Morgos. Then, when the northern forces and the southern forces are both ready, we will attack on two fronts. Morgos should be the easiest of the three cities to conquer, but any victory would decrease the strength of the Kabul and help all of Small World."

"I agree and am extremely excited," replied Jesves. "But I am not sure that the rest of Amins will like having their defensive forces reduced."

Goglbarj responded, "I will use my owl form to communicate between the north and south forces, and I will also use it to keep an eye on Kabul activities. If the Kabul organizes an attack, we will change our strategy."

"Egisix will also be able to help with keeping track of the Kabul forces. And we now have two spies, Elasti and Gido, who have the invisibility power and who are heading into the Kabul. We have lots of people keeping track of the Kabul and we should keep in touch with each of them. Also, you may not know this, but the giants have been commanded by the Creator to join forces with us southerners. They are positioning themselves at the location where the trolls came from the Kabul into the south. The giants have been tasked with making sure that no one else comes to the south."

Goglbarj was fascinated by this new development. Would the giant females also be willing to join in her attack plan? She said, "So even the giants are playing the defensive game. I wonder how their women feel. Maybe they will also join an attack. I will check with them but in the meantime you need to get the leprechaun female forces organized. I think a good place for the elves and the leprechauns to meet would be on the South Road between the Tako Ruins and the Avol River. When do you think you will be ready to meet there?"

Goglbarj and Jesves agreed on a plan to meet two weeks out. Jesves said, "I will go to work immediately organizing the leprechaun forces and preparing them for our meeting."

"Excellent," was Goglbarj's response. "I will relay our schedule to the elves and then I will try to make contact with the giants. We may yet be able to win this war."

Goglbarj transformed herself into an owl and departed leaving Jesves to organize the leprechaun army. Then, when they were ready to depart, she went to Hiztin's camp and gave him a big hug. He looked at her confused but delighted by the hug. He didn't realize that this might be the last time he would ever see her.

Chapter Nine

The Spy

Elasti nodded in agreement, untied himself from Gido leaving him on the south side of the barrier away from the Kabul, turned north, turned on his invisibility cloak, and reentered the mist wall traveling back into the Kabul. He was nervous about his return to the Kabul because the results weren't always the same. On previous occasions, after the journey through the mist, the travelers ended up in a different place. But this time there were no surprises and he ended up in the same place as when he had travelled there with Gido just minutes earlier. He turned off his invisibility cloak in order to not overuse it and cause him to become weak.

Elasti hated this place. It gave him an ominous feeling. He could sense the evil and it pressed down on him as if it was going to smash him. But he realized the importance of his mission, with or without the help of Gido, so he pressed on. Gamotz was the closest city to the south, so he decided to head in that direction, carefully watching to make sure no one from the Kabul would be able to spot him. He found a rock rising, about the height of twenty leprechauns, and used it as a hiding place. It also served as an excellent lookout from which he could observe activities at Gamotz.

As he waited in his lookout the evening turned to darkness and he made himself a bed using the grasses and brushes that were growing on the hill. He went to sleep. The following morning he continued his watch, but it was uneventful. The city was walled and the only activities he could observe was when a gnome left or entered the city, which didn't occur very often. Around noon he decided he would move on to Tragis, the volcano city of the trolls which was also used as the headquarters base for Lord Karkus. "Maybe I'll have better luck learning something useful from the trolls," he muttered to himself.

The terrain became rougher as he worked his way north. It was hillier and at times even mountainous. He wasn't able to travel as far as he hoped, and he had to spend another evening making his bed in the hills before he was able to reach Tragis.

The following morning, when he woke up, he noticed an eagle flying high in the sky overhead. He immediately turned on his invisibility cloak but it seemed as if the eagle had spotted him because the eagle flew close to where he had made his bed. The eagle circled around a few times and then seemed to give up the search and flew off to the north. "I need to be more careful," muttered Elasti. "I'll bet that was the prince. He must have spotted me and came in for a closer look. I'm lucky I noticed him soon enough to become invisible."

He completed his journey north and when he came into sight of Tragis he found himself another lookout point from which he was able to observe the city gates. He spent the rest of the day observing the city and again found it to be fruitless. There was the occasional troll that came in and out of the city, but there were no observable military activities. He also noticed the Kabul Prince Kakakrul leaving the city, transforming into an eagle, and flying off to the south. He didn't place any significance on this because he assumed the prince was just traveling to Gamotz.

Elasti decided that since he had travelled this far he would stay an extra day and continue his surveillance of the troll city. When it was dark he removed his invisibility and bedded down for the night. Then, the following morning, he was surprised to find an army of magotites encamped outside the city gates. He wasn't sure when they had arrived. He had slept so soundly that he hadn't heard anything. He immediately turned on his invisibility, just in case anyone was crawling around in the hills. He waited and watched, but there didn't seem to be any new developments. The magotites stayed in their camp and the trolls stayed in their city.

Elasti continued his watch, not sure what the presence of the magotites meant. Shortly after noon he noticed a group of about twenty trolls coming out of the city and heading directly for the magotite camp. Elasti was shocked when he saw the tolls starting to tear up the magotite camp. Obviously, the trolls and the magotites weren't the best of friends.

About ten minutes into the ruckus several individuals including trolls and a man came rushing out of the city gates and went charging up to the rampaging trolls. Elasti couldn't hear what was being said, but he could sense that they were trying to stop the destruction.

Elasti was convinced that the man stopping the destruction had to be the Kabul Lord and that the other individuals with him had to be the troll leadership. Elasti wondered how he could keep this internal conflict going hoping that if the Kabul forces destroyed themselves, then it would be a lot easier for the Small World kingdoms to defeat the Kabul.

The yelling and screaming of the leaders brought the troll destruction to a stop, but not before numerous magotites had been killed. For Elasti it was a joyous sight to behold. He loved every minute of it. Now he was convinced that he had to stick around to see what these magotites and trolls were trying to accomplish. *What was the reason for the arrival of the magotites? What was it that the trolls didn't like about their arrival? He hoped he might get some answers, but how was he going to accomplish his goal?* Then it dawned on him. He was invisible. He could go closer and listen in on their conversations. He might even be able to get close to the lord and hear some of his conversations.

Elasti knew it would be risky to try to get close to the Lord. He felt that he hadn't accomplished his mission and that he needed more information if he was to help save his home. What he had now wasn't very useful. He needed to learn more, and going into the magotite and troll camps would teach him what he needed to know.

He decided to proceed, choosing to go to the magotite camp first and then, when the gates of the city were opened, he planned to go into the city and find out what he could learn. He was cautious to be as quiet as possible. They wouldn't be able to see him, but they would definitely be able to hear him. He even worried about them seeing his footsteps. He arrived at the camp and slowly moved towards its center. He assumed that the center was where the leadership would be camped out.

Everything looked the same. Nothing looked like a leadership encampment. Not having the type of luck he had hoped for, he turned around and started to head out of the camp. He moved too quickly and bumped into a magotite, knocking him to the ground. The creature angrily jumped up, yelling at another magotite that was close by. He couldn't see Elasti so he assumed that it was this other magotite that had knocked him over. It wasn't long before the yelling turned into shoving, which turned into a wrestling match. Each of the magotites had friends, and each of them jumped into the ruckus. It became an enormous brawl between the two magotite groups. This turned out to be fortunate for Elasti because it distracted everyone as they focused on the fight. He was able to move away quickly.

Elasti quickly maneuvered himself out of the magotite camp and went directly to the front gate of the city. He didn't want to open the gate himself because it would raise suspicion if the gate opened and cl0sed without anyone being visibly there. It wasn't long before someone came through the gate, leaving it open long enough for Elasti to slip through. Once inside he searched for the possible location of the Lord's chambers. It wasn't long before he saw the Prince enter through the front gate. He would obviously head to the Lord's chambers so Elasti was quick to fall in line behind the Prince and follow him.

The prince was too fast. He entered through the door to the Lord's chambers too quickly for Elasti to sneak in as well behind him. The prince closed the door behind him causing Elasti to be left outside, waiting for another opportunity to enter. Surprisingly he heard the prince talking through an open window. Elasti moved close to the window and was able to hear the conversation as clearly as if he was in the room with them.

"They have the giants on their side," blurted out the Prince. "I saw giants patrolling the road that we were using to get into the Southern Plains. Now we'll have to come up with an alternate route when we resume our attack."

"Giants," responded the Lord. "Those creatures are going to be a thorn in my side. I didn't expect them to be involved in this conflict. It will take two or three trolls for every giant that we try to eliminate. I was hoping we could wipe everyone out just using trolls but now it sounds like it's going to be more complicated. What else have you learned?"

"My elf spy has been discovered and has been killed so I'm going to have to rely on my less-reliable dwarf spy. It's a major inconvenience, but we don't have a choice. That dwarf spy is not as high in the ranks as my elf spy was and therefore the information is going to be less reliable. When do you plan to make another attack?"

"I was starting to put that into motion already," responded the Lord. "That's why I have the magotites out there. But the trolls and the magotites are major enemies, even though they are both on the same side. They're going to be fighting with each other the whole time."

"Unfortunately, the same can be said of the gnomes," responded the prince. "They don't get along with either the trolls or the magotites. What's the next step in your plan."

"I still want to next take out Amins followed quickly by Gije. We need to do both of them in quick succession. That will finish off the south and then we head north."

"Are you planning to send the trolls and the magotites south sometime in the near future?" asked the prince.

"Yes, but first I have to get the two to work together. According to the Murqack, the prince of the magotites, his forces aren't ready. They need more training, both in how to fight and also in military discipline. He estimates that we can't go for another month. So that would be the soonest that we would be ready to head south."

"Okay," responded the prince. "After that I assume we head north."

"That's the plan," answered the Lord.

The prince responded, "I learned that the amazonionites are now in the mix. They will probably be joining the forces in the north so we'll have them to deal with as well."

"Giants and amazonionites?" barked the Lord. "I'm not liking the sound of this. They're building up forces and becoming stronger while we have a bunch of random savages that hate each other and want to kill each other."

"That's about the size of it," responded the prince. "But I'm not ready to give up and I know you aren't. That brings me to another question. You mentioned some kind of secret weapon. What is that and how do we use it?"

"That's a conversation for a different time," responded the Lord. "Here's what I want you to do next. Go to the south and find out as much as you can about the defensive preparations at Amins and Gije. What are they doing? What are our chances? Do we do a direct attack or do we starve them out with a siege? I need to know what the best strategy is for defeating the two remaining southern cities."

"Will do," responded the prince as he turned and left the Lord's chambers.

This was the queue for Elasti to also leave Tragis and the Kabul and head back to Amins to update the wizard on what he learned. He carefully tried to follow the prince through the gate but was once again prevented because of how quickly the prince moved. He

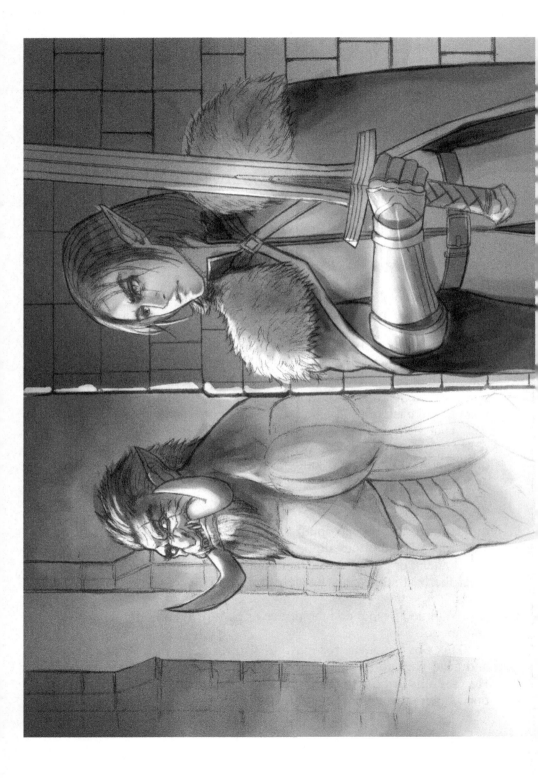

had to wait for a troll to open the gate, giving him more time to maneuver out of the city.

Eventually a troll came along who was working his way toward the gate. Elasti stepped in behind the troll, planning to make his move but as he did so the troll suddenly reversed direction and ended up tripping over the invisible Elasti. The troll let out an enormous grunt and started cursing. He started waving his arms around, trying to discover what had caused him to fall. One swing of his arm hit Elasti in the stomach and knocking him sprawling across the ground. Now the troll knew that there was something invisible which had caused him to fall and he started swinging his arms wildly hoping to once again make contact with the invisible image.

Elasti was quick. He jumped up and ran to safety several yards away from where the troll was making his search. The troll did not give up for quite some time. He was very angry and persisted in his search but came up empty. Elasti had to wait until the troll became bored with his search because he was now blocking the city's exit.

Eventually the troll gave up the search and Elasti was able to make another attempt at escaping from the city. He moved close to the gate, waiting for someone to exit. It wasn't a long wait until another troll arrived and this time Elasti was more careful, watching the movements of the troll as he exited. Luckily, since Elasti was much smaller than the troll he was able to slip out quickly, sneaking around the gate's latch frame before the much larger troll was able to swing the large gate to a close.

Elasti felt free and moved quickly back up into the hills where he had found refuge before. As he passed by the magotite encampment he heard shouting and yelling. Apparently, the ruckus that he had started earlier had still not been resolved.

As he approached the top of the hill, he was surprised to find several trolls scouting out the area and looking closely at the place where he had made his bed. He noticed that the prince was also with the trolls, trying to figure out who had been sleeping there. He heard the prince say, "That bed is too small to have been a troll. Even the magotites are bigger than that bed, and I doubt they would leave their encampment to sleep alone on this hill. Who is sneaking around our camp? Who is watching our city? Are there spies amongst us? I want you to search the surrounding hills and see if you can figure out what's going on here."

"Yes commander," one of the trolls responded as they started to move away from the top of the hill. Elasti decide that he better quickly move away himself before they noticed his movement through the brushes or saw his footsteps. He carefully snuck through the brush, thereby hiding his footprints and trying not to move the vegetation any more than necessary, heading along a parallel route to where he had observed the Gamotz.

He bedded down for the night in the same location as before overlooking the gnome city, assuming that the trolls would also stop searching during the night. He removed his invisibility cloak for the night. He also hoped that they would have lost his trail by now and would be running around the hills of Tragis with no success.

In the morning, Elasti jumped up early and finished his journey to the misty wall separating the Kabul from the Southern Plains. He badly wanted to get out of the Kabul and remove the dark cloud of doom that he felt was engulfing him in this dreary land. He removed his cloak of invisibility and rushed into the misty wall, hoping there would be no surprises on the other side.

As he came out of the other side of the misty wall he was shocked to be greeted by a dozen spears pointed at him from all directions. And it wasn't just the spears that shocked him, the biggest surprise was that they were being wielded by giants. Elasti stopped in his tracks, his mouth gaping wide open.

Gido screamed out,

"Stop and desist,
    Do not Elasti pry,
He is our partner,
    We must not fry."

The leader of the giants commanded, "Drop your spears. This is the spy that was sent into the Kabul by the wizard. We must allow him to pass."

Elasti said, "Yes. There are important updates that I need to get to the wizard."

Gido continued,

"The wizard sent,
    The giants to help few,
They are here to guard,
    Anyone coming through.
Is there any news,
    That they should know,

That you can tell them,
Before we go?"

Elasti responded, "Yes. There is one thing you should all know. The prince has spotted you here and he has instructed his father the Lord that they need to pick a new point where they should cross into the Southern Plains. He also said that they won't be ready for another month before they can return to attack the south."

"Then we giants need to spread out," responded the giant's leader. "We need to have spies that can keep a watch and be ready to inform the rest of us when they see anyone from the Kabul come through."

Elasti continued, "Also watch for an eagle. The prince spies on us in the form of an eagle."

"That we can do too," responded the giant.

Elasti turned to Gido and instructed, "Let's go. We need to get to the wizard as soon as possible with the information that I have. He will be waiting on us."

Far above them, high up in one of the trees, and eagle watched.

Elasti and Gido rushed to get down to the South Road. They felt the need to deliver the information that Elasti learned to the wizard. They were also uncomfortable around the giants, who seemed extremely intimidating because of their size.

They arrived at the South Road and headed toward the Avol Rover crossing. Unfortunately, it was starting to get dark and they had to bed down for the night. They choose to stay away from the road and bed down a little way into the forest, just in case any Kabul travelers happened to pass by.

The following day they crossed the river and travelled through the Amins Groves, hoping that would get them to Amins quicker than by continuing on the South Road.

It was dark when they finally arrived in Amins. Since the town was deserted for the most part they went to Elasti's home and the two of them spent the night there. The following morning the went directly to the council chambers to give their report. The wizard and some of the council members were already there, having heard that Elasti and Gido had returned. Egisix, the dwarf messenger, was also in the room waiting for the update.

Once in the chambers the wizard asked, "Welcome home. I am surprised but delighted that you are back so quickly. Can you give us an update?"

Elasti responded by giving the attendees a review of their spying experience, recounting all the details. Then he explained, "The Lord and the prince were talking and they said that they would have to find a new route into the South Plains because the prince had seen the giants guarding the location where they had come through the last time. "

"Interesting," said the wizard. "What else did you learn."

Elasti continued, "Apparently his elf spy is no longer responding to him and he is assuming he had been discovered and been killed."

"Apparently that's true," responded the wizard. "Anything else?"

"There is a new spy," added Elasti. "A dwarf."

"That can't be," barked Egisix. "I can't believe that a dwarf would be a traitor."

"Apparently it's true," responded Elasti. "The prince talked about his meeting with the dwarf spy, but gave no clue who it might be."

"You've given me a lot to think about," added the wizard. "Anything else."

"Yes," continued Elasti. "The most important information of all is that they are organizing for a planned attack, first on Amins and then on Gije, in about one month. The magotites were already encamped outside of Tragis and the two species were working and training together in preparation for the attack. After the attack on the south they plan to head north."

There was a gasp in the room and then complete silence. This was the news that they feared the most, and here it was, in their face.

CHAPTER TEN

THE FEMALE ARMY

Goglbarj the amazonionite was excited to learn about the giants. She didn't even consider them an option because they had been so standoffish in the past. She remembered them from her climb up the Sheere Cliffs during the journey south to Amins and how they latter had saved them from the attack of the trolls during that trip, but the giants had made a point of saying that they were not going to get involved in any battle with the Kabul. However, learning that they were attacked by the trolls in their homes changed everything. Now they were ready to become part of the resistance against the advances of the Kabul.

She used her magic name to transform into an owl and flew first to Gije in order to relay the plans of the Women Warriors, as they now called themselves, to Gushe the elf. She informed her that they would be meeting the leprechauns at the intersection of the South Road and the Kilo Pass road in two weeks' time. Then she flew off to the Sheere Cliffs, where the giants had their caves. Her ability to fly allowed her to enter the cave from the side of the cliffs. Otherwise, she would have no way of knowing how to contact the giants.

Once inside the cave she found that she was completely alone. She transformed herself back into her amazonionite form and started walking deeper and deeper into the cave, hoping at some point to encounter someone that she could talk to and explain her plan. It wasn't long before she saw a fire off in the distance and she heard voices. She knew that there had to be giants there that she should be able to talk to.

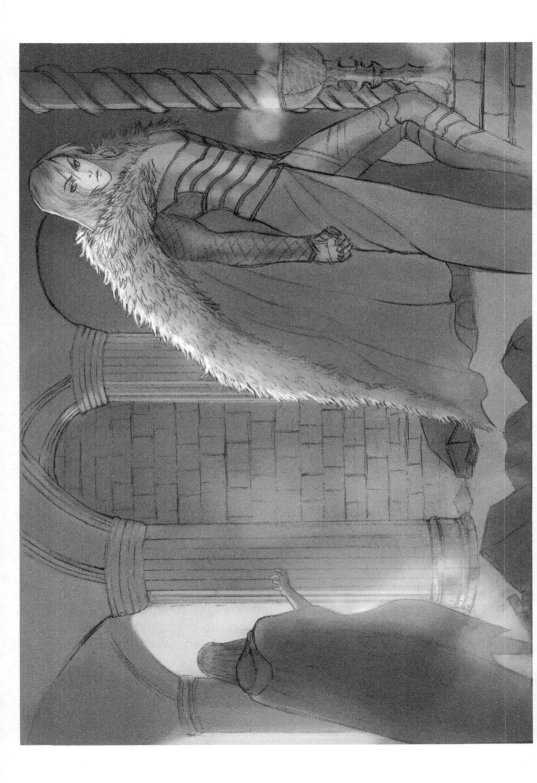

She saw the giants before they saw her and she noticed that they were all sitting around their fire, talking. It was three couples, each paired up. They were probably out on the giant's version of a date. As she approached them the male giants jumped up and pulled out knives that they had tucked in their belt.

"I'm not here to attack anyone," explained Goglbarj quickly. "I'm here to talk about the war with the Kabul, and I know that you have decided to join in this war. I am alone. I am Goglbarj, of the amazonionites and I come in peace to discuss war time options."

The giants relaxed and started putting their knives back in their belts. One of them asked, "Our leader, Giant-giant, is not here. He is discussing war strategy with the wizard. You just missed him."

"I don't want to talk to him," explained Goglbarj. "I want to talk to the leader of the giant women. Who would that be and how can I talk to her?"

One of the female giants spoke up, "That would be Giantess Annala. I will go fetch her for you, or would you rather come with me to meet her?"

"I'll go with you," explained the amazonionite. "That would be quicker. Lead the way."

The two took off, leading further and further into the caves. Eventually they arrived at a large chamber, which was obviously the center of the community. It was filled with giants, all going about their business, but when the saw the amazonionite they all stopped and stared.

Goglbarj was not disturbed by their stares and pressed ahead with her giant guide. They entered a side cave which was elaborately decorated and continued walking down to the end where there was a large door with one guard. After arriving at the door, the giant guide instructed the guard, "We have an amazonionite visitor here to meet with the giantess."

"I'll have to confirm with Giantess Annala in order to get approval for her to come into her presence. Please wait here," responded the guard.

It wasn't long before the guard returned to deliver his message from the giantess, "She is in council. You will have to wait. She will call for you when she is ready."

Goglbarj was disappointed and asked, "How long is this going to take?"

"I don't know," responded the guard. "You'll just have to wait and that's all I can tell you."

The giant that had escorted Goglbarj responded, "I'm going to return to my friends. I'm sure they are waiting for me. It was nice meeting you." Then she turned and left the amazonionite waiting outside the giantess' quarters with the guard.

After the escort had departed, the guard seemed to become brave and he asked Goglbarj, "Are you really an amazonionite? I was told that they are a child's fantasy and don't really exist."

"Yes, I'm real enough as you can see," responded a slightly insulted and irritated Goglbarj. Then she explained, "We live in the Central Ranges, which have always been our home, just a little ways north of you here, in the thick forests. We have very little contact with anyone else in Small World and that's why no one knows about us. But because of the attacks of the Kabul, we have come out to unite with the other Small World species. We can only defeat the Kabul if we all work together."

Unknown to Goglbarj, the questions of the guard were questions that the giantess had asked him to ask, and she was listening to their conversations from the other side of the door. The giantess opened the door and spoke directly to Goglbarj, saying, "I have been listening and now I have become extremely curious. Why have you come? Why are you here? Come inside so we can have a conversation."

"With pleasure," was Goglbarj's response as they crossed the threshold of the gate and entered the giantess' chambers. Once inside Goglbarj saw several attendants in the room and she requested of the giantess, "What I want to discuss with you is private."

The giantess waved the attendants out of the room and then asked, "What is it you want to tell me?"

Goglbarj explained her plan about organizing a female army that would work around the defensive plans that the wizard was suggesting, and rather engage in an offensive attack on the Kabul. She explained, "The men all want to sit back and wait for the Kabul to come to them, but I believe that we can significantly weaken the Kabul if we attack before they attack. I think we need to move forward aggressively if we are to prevent the Kabul from taking over the entirety of Small World."

"We female giants are not prepared to engage in battle," explained Giantess Annala. "We don't know the first thing about doing battle. I understand what you are trying to achieve, and I support your plan, but I don't see how we can make a difference."

"One of the biggest ways that you can make a difference is simply by being with us," explained Goglbarj. "It will inspire all the other female forces. And we can do some basic training as we move into position to attack. I would be delighted to help the giantesses prepare. But the most important thing is that all the female species of Small World are together in this struggle."

"You are very inspirational and persuasive," responded the giantess. Then she called her female attendants back into the room and she had Goglbarj repeat all the things that she had explained to Giantess Annala earlier. Then Annala asked her attendants, "What do you think?"

The giantesses that were her attendants, almost in unity yelled out, "Let's do it."

One of the attendants added, "Let's prove to the men that we are more than just their slaves and servants. Let's show them that we can make a difference in their world, not just in ours."

But not all the giantess attendants were in agreement. Some were scared about the prospect of going to war and one of them spoke up saying, "It sounds dangerous and scary. I don't think I will be very effective fighting. I may be more in the way and not helpful at all."

Giantess Annala spoke up, "I don't want anyone to go unless you are committed to the idea. I won't think anything bad about anyone that does not go. It is your own personal choice for each of you. I'm not sure I'm ready to go myself. But I think that any of you that want to go, you should definitely go and help prevent the Kabul from doing another attack on our homes here. I think their last attack was a big surprise and, even though we won, we weren't ready for an attack and we lost far too many lives. I encourage any of you that are willing to go. You will be heroes to all the giants."

Goglbarj spoke up, "We would very much like you, Giantess Annala, to be involved because it would be an inspiration not just to other giantesses, but to all the women of the different species that will be involved in our little female army."

"Then I'll do it," responded Annala. "I'll join your army. What do we need to do?"

"The southern forces, which includes the leprechauns and the elves, are meeting where the South Road meets the Tako Ruins road," explained Goglbarj. "We would like you to join us there. Then we can start your weapons and military training as we move northward into the Kabul."

"We can do that," responded Annala. "We'll meet you there."

With that Goglbarj said farewell and retraced her steps back to the place where she had entered the caves. Then she transformed into the owl shape. Her next stop would be to the amazonionite village to give them an update of what the south was doing and to prepare them to meet with the dwarfs near the Hile Desert. This will be the location from which the amazonionite forces and the dwarf forces will move into the Kabul.

Next she flew to the dwarfs to give them the same information. After getting everyone informed and prepared she flew to the South Road / Kilo Pass junction, waiting for the elves, leprechauns, and giants to combine forces and proceed into the Kabul. Goglbarj had successfully organized her own little army and possibly started her own war.

***

Lord Krakus was sitting in his chamber in Tragis, the troll city. He picked this location for is headquarters and for his home because he assumed that the trolls would be the best species in the Kabul for his protection. It was also the most central city, making it feel safer. He had a large palace in the center of the city and he lived there with his son, Prince Kakakrul. This palace had a big secret, which the Lord hadn't even shared with his son. The palace was also one of the secret entrances to the Caves of Dread, which was the dwelling place of the Kwdad, the Destroyer and the anthesis of the Creator. For every positive, there must be a negative. For every good there has to be a bad. For every joy there must be a sorrow. And the Kwdad was this negative, bad, and sorrow. He used corruption to achieve his goals, and he had successfully corrupted Krakus with promises of power and glory, and now Krakus would do anything that Kwdad the Destroyer commanded.

Krakus was sitting in his chamber when he received a message from Kwdad. The message came to his head in the form of a feeling and an impression which Krakus recognized immediately because it had happened so many times before. "Come see me," was the command from Kwdad.

Krakus stood up from his chair and walked over to a bookcase on the wall that was behind the chair. He pulled two books halfway out and pushed two other specific books partially in, causing the bookcase to swing open like a door. He walked through the door and pushed a button inside the opening causing a light to come on and causing the bookcase-door to close behind him.

Now that Krakus was securely inside the wall he pushed another button which was a light switch and which lit up a stairway that went downward into the earth with a bright red light. From the top it looked as if the stairway went down forever, but Krakus was familiar with this stairway since he had travelled it numerous times in the past. It had mirrors along the sides which gave the impression that the stairway went on forever, but in reality it twisted in a spiral and went off in numerous various directions, shifting direction several times. The directional changes didn't make any logical sense, but it didn't matter. The Lord assumed that the confused route was intentional.

After traveling down the stairs for what seemed like hours, but in reality was only about thirty minutes, Krakus arrived at a level surface. At this point he had lost all sense of direction and he had no idea in which way the cave was traveling. With the help of the red lights he followed along in the cave. There were no side caves giving no chance for confusion or loss of direction.

Eventually he arrived at a large circular cavern. The entrance to the cavern was as if you were entering the side of a ball. There was nothing inside, but it glowed red. Its floor was made up of tiles. It was the Erates that moved around and whose cracks fell away to the bottomless Lamos. After arriving at the doorway, the Lord spoke out, "I'm here Master Kwdad. What can I do to help you along on your mission?"

A voice answered him. It was a low, rough sounding voice. The voice echoed back and forth along the walls of the ball which made the voice sound ominous. However, Krakus saw no one. The voice said, "I want the power of the Creator wiped out. I feel the Protee powers. The Creator has given someone the Protee powers and that's dangerous. Remember how I told you that this war can be won in a few months. That requires that the Protee power be wiped out. Now it seems that the only way we can wipe out this Protee power is by wiping out all the individuals in Small World. The Protee power is the only power that can suppress my influence. By suppressing this Protee influence you will be left with only needing to contend with mortal enemies not spiritual ones. The Creator has given this power to someone and you must find out who that is and kill him immediately. I told you that you can have control of all of Small World in seven months and that is only possible if you

eliminate this Protee power from Small World. My command is that you place all your power and influence on identifying and wiping out this power immediately. Then conquering Small World will be easy."

"Yes, Master Kwdad," answered Lord Krakus. "How do I identify the individual who has this power?"

"I give you the power to recognize the evil Protee power. He can also be identified by his acts of healing. If you injure someone, this Protee healer will come and heal that person and then you will be able to recognize him for who he truly is. Now go out and destroy this power."

"Yes Master," responded Lord Krakus.

Kwdad continued, "I have a second mission. It would be helpful to eliminate the wizard before he realizes his true powers. He is not important enough to keep us from winning, but it will be a lot easier if he is not around."

"Yes Master," responded Lord Krakus. "We will do our best."

"Now go and do what I asked," commanded Master Kwdad.

Krakus left the Destroyer's chambers and started the long journey back to his personal chambers in the world above, back in the city of Tragis.

As he arrived at the secret entrance he peeked into his chambers through a peephole and noticed that his son the prince was standing in the room. Lord Krakus waited until the prince departed before returning to his chambers because he felt he needed to keep Destroyer Kwdad a secret just a little longer.

When his chamber was empty, the Lord pushed a lever which opened the secret door. He stepped into the room and closed the door behind him. Then he sat down at his desk, continuing with his plans as if nothing unusual had happened.

A few minutes later the prince reentered the Lord's chambers and as he entered he stopped in his tracks, staring at the Lord. Then he said, "What's going on here? Something unusual is happening. You weren't here a couple minutes ago and I have been outside your door. I would have seen you come in. Where were you? How did you disappear and reappear?"

The Lord brushed him off by saying, "I don't have time for this nonsense. I'm here and I don't know where you were and what you've been doing. I have been working on our plans for the next steps in this war and I need you to get the three species leaders together here in my office immediately."

The prince felt rejected but also knew that his father wasn't about to reveal anything, so he turned and left, looking for the leaders of the magotites, the trolls, and the gnomes.

It took about a half hour but eventually Lord Krakus, the lord of the Kabul, finally had his military leadership around him. It included King Rakadam, the king of trolls, Prince Murqack, the prince of the magotites, Duke Kaklu, the gnome leader, and the Lord's son Prince Kakakrul. The Lord challenged each of them about their preparedness for an attack on the Southern Plains.

Each of the species reported on their progress. The trolls were ready to go any time. The magotites still needed another month to prepare. And the gnomes wanted to use a couple more weeks to prepare, but they could go now if the Lord commanded.

Then the Lord explained his plan, "We need to be ready to attack and wipe out Amins and Gije but even more important is that we eliminate two individuals which alone hold the power to destroy us. If we wipe out these two, we will be able to conquer all of Small World in a matter of months. First, we need to discover and wipe out the individual who has the Protee powers, given to him by the Creator. These powers give him the ability to heal, which makes him vulnerable. We just need to injure someone, like one of the leprechauns, and then watch who arrives in order to heal them. Then we need to wipe out the person that has the healing power."

"Is that something you want me to do?" asked the prince.

"Yes," replied the Lord, "but I may need to go with you since I have the ability to discern who has this power."

"I will go out and try to find this individual," replied the prince, "then I will report back to you who this individual is and we can discuss how to eliminate him. Do you have any suggestions where he is located?"

"No idea," responded the Lord. "You will have to go to the three main species, leprechauns, elves, and dwarfs, and try each location until you find the correct individual."

"I can do that, but it will take some time," responded the prince.

"The second individual that we need to eliminate is the wizard," responded the Lord. "But that may be tricky since he can fight back, so we'll have to do something sneaky in order to get rid of him."

The prince responded, "We know where he is. I have seen him in Amins working with the council there. But I don't know how to attack him."

The Lord said, "Watch him and watch for a weakness. I'm not sure what to do there. Maybe we need to do an all-out attack and wipe out everyone there. We can do that if necessary. For now just watch him and see what you can learn. He must have some weakness that we can take advantage of."

"I can do that," responded the prince.

Then the Lord closed the meeting by commanding each of the species leaders to get ready as soon as possible. "I also want to send two small groups of about twenty gnomes, separated by about 20 days, as a kind of advance spying party down the Kilo Pass, since there's no one guarding that, to explore their preparations. Go through the Amins Groves and spy on them to see what preparations they have made. The prince will be too busy to do that and we can't have him do everything. Then send back a few gnomes to report on what you find and leave the remainder there to continue your spying. I want to do a full-blown attack on the south in two weeks and wipe out Amins and Gije. Ready or not, here we come so get ready."

The three leaders bowed to the Lord and then left the room following the prince out the door.

CHAPTER ELEVEN
THE ARMY COMES TOGETHER

Goglbarj, the amazonionite warrior, was the first to arrive at the meeting point of the southern female warriors. She flew in, landed, and transformed herself. It was early afternoon. She waited at the junction of the South Road and the Kilo Pass Trail, hoping that the three southern species, the leprechauns, the elves, and the giants, would be arriving soon. She made camp for herself south of the road with a plan to move forward the first thing in the morning.

About an hour later Queen Gushe, the elf, appeared from the west with about two hundred warriors, all armed with bow and arrow, and all of them ready for the fight.

Goglbarj greeted the new arrivals with, "I'm excited to see all of you here together. Thank you for coming."

Gushe responded with,
"We wouldn't miss,
A chance to be,
The saviors of,
Our place to be free.
Our men are wondering,
What we are doing,
I think they may,
Also be spying.
We will do,
Our best regardless,
We know this is,
Our chance to be fearless."
"We will make a difference," responded Goglbarj.

Just as they were finishing their conversation, they heard a group coming from the east. This time it was Jesves, the leprechaun hero and warrior, who was arriving with a troop of about two hundred leprechauns. She yelled out, "We are here, ready to fight and make a difference for Small World."

"Welcome. Welcome," yelled Goglbarj.

"We made it but I'm not sure that the men believed our story that we're just looking for a safe place to camp. I'll bet there's probably a couple of them spying on us right now," responded Jesves.

"That's the same thing we heard from the elves," replied Goglbarj. "I guess we'll have to work hard to earn their trust."

Introductions were quickly made between the elves and the leprechauns. There seemed to be an instant bond. They were all working together for a common cause and the normal animosity and mistrust between the two species seemed to evaporate.

All the women were a little afraid. This was something that none of them had ever done. It was all new territory. They believed in what they were doing, but their lack of experience caused a level of confusion. They trusted in their leaders and their bravery pushed them forward.

The two species went to work setting up a camp for the night. It was about two hours later when a group of about thirty giants arrived, led by Giantess Annala. They walked up to the camp, not saying a word. Goglbarj was the first to speak up saying, "Welcome to the camp of the southern female warriors."

Annala looked around as if to investigate the remainder of the people in the camp. Then she looked back at Goglbarj and smiled. "I see no men here, only women. I guess I now believe that you are truly organizing what you said you were organizing."

"Of course," replied Goglbarj. Then she went ahead and made introductions, putting everyone at ease.

The rest of the evening was spent laying out a plan of attack. Goglbarj's small army was to head up the Kilo Pass and enter into the Kabul. Once inside they were to work their way up to the north end of the Kabul where they would team up with the northern forces. Once they were all together they would surround Morgos and attack. The plan was to take the magotites out of commission and keep them from being involved in any future attacks.

The night was uneventful and early the next morning, the combined forces started their march up the Kilo Pass road. They hurried past the Tako Ruins, hoping that because it was daytime they would avoid the riposters, the creatures with fish bodies, birds wings, and rats teeth, which had devastated the previous expedition.

Luckily, they were able to pass the ruins without any encounter with the deadly creatures. In the distance they could see the mist wall that separated the Southern Plains from the Kabul. Suddenly, and unexpectedly, gnomes started appearing through the wall. The gnomes seemed utterly surprised to see the strong female army waiting for them as they came through and, rather than turning back and warning the other gnomes not to come through, they pulled out their swords and started doing battle with the female army.

The elves were in the front of the marching female warriors, followed by the leprechauns and the giants came last. The elves were quick to take their bows and made fast work of the twenty gnomes before they could even come close with their swords. They were so quick that it seemed like the gnomes were dead with two or three arrows before they had even finished crossing through the mist.

Having won this battle, the newly formed army soon arrived at the mist wall that separated the Southern Plains from the Kabul. Goglbarj, having heard Elasti's explanation of how they had to cross through the mist wall on previous occasions, instructed everyone to connect themselves together in a long chain of ropes. Then Elasti had explained how previously he had taken the lead, being the first to walk into the mist. Goglbarj was careful to be ready, sword in hand, just in case there were more gnomes waiting for her on the other side of the wall. However, once on the other side, she was disappointed to see that there was no one else there. The small group of twenty gnomes were all there was.

Traversing the mist took hours as the four hundred and thirty warriors passed through the wall in a single file, one at a time. Eventually they were all safely through and in the Kabul only to be disappointed by what they found. The landscape was a devastating nothingness.

"This place is horrible," commented Giantess Annala. "Where we are is so beautiful. Why would anyone want to make all of Small World look like this place? Lord Krakus is foolish."

Queen Gushe also chimed in saying,
"This place is dread,
How can it be,
That someone would want,
Like this to see."

The leaders had nothing else they could say or add. They simply nodded their heads in agreement. The Kabul was a place of utter devastation.

Once the army had regrouped on the other side of the mist wall, the march toward the north resumed. As they travelled north along the Kilo Pass, they were suddenly attacked by an enormous number of small, snake like lizards. At first, they didn't seem like much of a threat and were easily stamped out. But soon the number of these creatures became overwhelming, they were popping out by the thousands, and they started piling up on top of each other in the form of a wall. Often one of the creatures would climb up the legs of a warrior and bite them, causing numerous screams of pain.

In the meantime, the living wall, which was obstructing their progress forward, continued to grow taller and taller and started to grow around the sides of the travelers, encircling them. Goglbarj remembered how Elasti told the story of how the Southern Sword had saved the northward expedition in the past. But that sword wasn't available now because it was still with the dwarfs in the north.

The leaders looked at each other in fear and wonderment. Was this battle against the Kabul going to end before it even started? But then the giants pushed their way forward. Their swords were much larger and with each stroke large sections of the living wall were destroyed. Unfortunately, the walls grew back quickly requiring several of the giants to team up and together they would open a doorway through the wall. With each doorway, a group of about twenty warriors was able to dash through. This process was repeated again and again, each time with the wall filling in with these lizard-like creatures, until everyone had successfully escaped the enclosing circle of these fearsome creatures.

The injuries were plentiful but minimal. About a third of the warriors had been bitten on the legs, but none so severely that they couldn't continue to travel. Their wounds were bound, and they continued to push forward.

For a while the warriors were able to stay on the Kilo Pass as long as it continued north, but then it turned west which was not the direction that this little army wanted to go. It caused the small army to leave the trail and divert their route into the scraggly forest and the rough hillsides that seemed to prevail. They did their best to avoid getting too close to Gamotz, hoping to not be spotted.

Now that they were safely on their way, Goglbarj announced, "I need to go to the north and see how their preparations are going. I will leave the leadership of our army in the hands of the three of you and I will rejoin you once I am sure that the dwarfs and amazonionites are prepared to join us once we come close to Morgos."

She left the group, went to a place that was secluded by scrub brush and desolated trees, transformed herself into an owl, and flew off toward the north. Gushe, Jesves, and Annala took over the lead of the southern warriors and continued the march northward. They could see smoke off in the distance to the east causing Queen Gushe to send two elves to investigate and report back. When they returned one of the elves reported,

"To the east,
    We followed the smoke,
We could see,
    It was the city of Gamotz,
It is the city,
    And there is no one else."

"Excellent," responded Jesves and the warriors continued their progress. Several additional elves were sent out in all directions, especially toward the front of their movement, to watch for any potential threats.

It was now becoming late and the band of warriors needed to make camp for the night. No fires would be allowed, and the Kabul nights were cold, so they had to wrap themselves as best they could in blankets. "We weren't as prepared for this cold weather as we should have been," complained Giantess Annala.

Jesves sympathetically said, "I wish we could help but it would take three of our blankets to make one of yours and we just don't have that much to spare."

"I don't expect you to give up your blankets," responded Annala. "I'm just disappointed that we didn't do better in preparing ourselves." The giants were forced to cuddle closely together in order to share warmth. This made it a long and uncomfortable night."

Guards and lookouts were arranged, and they took turns making sure the remainder of the warriors were safe. In the morning the march northward resumed. Around mid-day they could see a volcano off to the east and the elf spies reported,

"We see Tragis city,
    With trolls moving in and out,
The gate,
    None are going very far
From the city.

Also a large encampment,
Of magotites,
    Just outside the gate.
Preparing for an attack.
    The Kabul Volcano,
Is behind the city,
        Spuing the smoke and flames."

"Magotites," expressed Jesves with concern. "Will there be any magotites left in Morgos for us to conquer?"

"I hope so," express Annala. "However, at this point, we don't have a choice. We have no way to contact Goglbarj and tell her that magotite troops are amassing in Tragis. We have to stick to the rendezvous as planned."

"Agreed," said Jesves, "I just hope we aren't wasting our time here."

Additional elf spies from front reported,
    "There are no threats,
    We can move forward."

The three leaders agreed that forward progress should be continued, and they travelled forward leaving Tragis off to the east as they headed further northward to their goal of Morgos. Another night needed to be spent in the hills of the Kabul, surrounded by guards and lookouts.

The night was uneventful and in the morning they continued their progress to the north. It was midday when Morgos was finally in sight. The warriors made camp and waited for Goglbarj and the northern warriors to appear.

***

Goglbarj started flying north toward the dwarf city of Hilebin. As she flew over the Hile desert she saw the dwarfs were already starting to collect together at the designated meeting place. However, she didn't see any amazonionites so she decided to head east toward the Central Ranges in order to catch up with any warriors that might be there. She had confidence that the amazonionites would come through, especially if it meant showing that they were more powerful than men.

Goglbarj could see a large group of amazonionites amassing on the northern end of the Central Ranges. She landed, transformed herself, and approached the amazonionite warriors. "Greetings," she shouted out. "Are you ready for this battle?"

"We're always ready," responded one of the Elderesses who was not from the same tribe as Goglbarj. "Are you the one organizing this crusade?"

"I have organized a large army of female warriors who are ready to defend Small World from destruction," replied Goglbarj.

"What kind of cooperation did you get from the other species?" continued the Elderess.

"We have a lot of cooperation," replied Goglbarj. "We have two hundred elves, two hundred leprechauns, and I have an additional surprise. We have thirty giants who are all coming from the south and are already in the Kabul."

"Giants!" exclaimed another of the Elderess. "How did you manage that?"

"It's a long story," responded Goglbarj. "I'll tell it to you some night around a campfire. I also noticed the dwarfs are getting together at the Hile desert and we need to get over there and join them."

"How do you know about the dwarfs?" asked the first Elderess. "I suppose that's another long campfire story."

"Right you are," commented Goglbarj.

Then a third Elderess asked, "Are you sure these dwarfs are willing to work with us? I really don't trust them and I don't want them attacking us in the middle of the night when we're sleeping."

Goglbarj responded, "I have three species who are weary and afraid, all of them are working together for a common goal. The leprechauns, elves, and giants don't typically like each other, but they're all happily working together right now and the biggest reason they're working together is because they are all unified under the bond of womanhood. They would normally have no desire to be together, but they have connected through the common goal of conquering the Kabul and of course proving to the men that they are capable of holding their own in a battle. If they can work together, then we can work with the dwarfs!"

"We will do our best and try to lay our prejudices aside," responded the third Elderess.

Goglbarj responded, "I have been working with the dwarfs for the last couple weeks as we struggled to get to Amins and make plans for defending the Southern Plains. You will find that they are a reasonable lot and excellent fighters with their axes."

With that the march to the Hile Desert began. As they approached the edge of the Central Ranges it was becoming dark and the amazonionite warriors made camp for the night.

When morning came, they continued their march and about noon the following day they could see the dwarf camp off in the distance at the edge of the Hile Desert. A couple hours later, with Gijivure in the lead, the amazonionite Elderesses were introduced to Princess Ejijone of the dwarfs. The northern army of female warriors had been united.

Gijivure explained to the entire army, "We are united as a female force. This war is no longer just about defeating the Kabul and its evil Lord's intentions to take over all of Small World. It has also become a battle of whether the male approach of a defensive only war is adequate, or if an offensive attack would make a difference. We have now created a female army who is on the attack. The southern army is already in the Kabul and includes two hundred elves who are excellent bowwomen, two hundred leprechauns who are excellent swordswomen, and thirty giants who are swordswomen with excellent strength. We will enter the Kabul ourselves and be joining forces with them as we plan an attack on Morgos, hoping to weaken the Kabul by taking away one of their armies. We five species are united in our belief that we can make a difference in this war! We will succeed!"

A cheer went up amongst the dwarfs and amazonionites. After the cheer died down Gijivure continued, "Have a good night's rest tonight. Tomorrow early we will cross into the Kabul and join the southerners in our attack on Morgos."

Another cheer went up.

CHAPTER TWELVE

"What do you mean they were all killed," barked Duke Kaklu, the gnome leader. He was still in Tragis waiting for further instructions from Lord Krakus.

"We sent a second spying expedition down the Kilo Pass, as ordered, and after we crossed through the mist wall that separated the Kabul from the Southern Plains we found the dead bodies of the earlier spying expedition. A large group has killed our spies and then travelled through the mist wall. They are somewhere here in the Kabul," reported one of the gnome spies from the second spying expedition.

"What did you do?" challenged the duke.

"We came back to report their deaths to you and to tell you we have an invading party here," replied the spy.

"You are telling me that we have no spies in the south?" repeated Kaklu.

"Exactly," replied the spy. "Actually, we are reporting back what we learned in our spying."

"Clever," replied Kaklu. "And you were worried about getting killed yourselves."

"We wouldn't be able to report much if we were killed."

"I need to report this to Lord Krakus right away," responded the duke.

The duke departed and went directly to the lord's chambers. He approached the door and asked, "I need to speak with you immediately. May I come in?"

"Yes," responded a grumpy lord, acting as if the visit was a disturbance.

The duke approached the Lord's desk and explained, "Our first group of twenty spies have been killed and the second group claims that a large group of southerners have invaded the Kabul and are now somewhere in our lands."

"Impossible," complained an exasperated Lord. "They wouldn't dare invade us." He had never considered the possibility that they could actually be invaded. He only saw himself as the aggressor and never considered the possibility of the reverse happening. "This is challenging. I'm no longer able to be in touch with Prince Kakakrul because I commanded him to not return to me until he had completed his mission. I could really use his ability to fly in order to investigate this report. I'll have to consider my options. Leave me and come back with the other leaders in ten minutes so we can discuss this situation."

The room was quiet for the ten minutes while the Lord considered his options. After that King Rakadam, the king of trolls, Prince Murqack, the prince of the magotites, and Duke Kaklu, the gnome leader, all arrived at the Lord's chambers. The lord had the duke explain what happened to the spies, then he added, "We have invaders, and we have no idea where they are located so we need to send out search parties in all directions to see if we can locate them."

The duke spoke up and said, "We are ready to go invade the south right now. We are angered by the deaths of our spies and we want to go south and wipe out Amins. We have enough people and enough strength to accomplish our goal. We want revenge."

To everyone's surprise Lord Krakus said, "Go!" Then after a pause he said, addressing the king, "Send a group of twenty or so trolls with them and go wipe out that city, including their pesky wizard."

"Yes lord," responded King Rakadam and Duke Kaklu at the same time.

Then Prince Murqack spoke up, "What about us? We magotites can help!"

"You told me you weren't ready," responded Krakus. "Get ready and then we'll put you to work too! In the meantime, I plan to use your men as spies. I want you to send out groups of five to ten in every direction and to every corner of the Kabul until we know who these intruders are and what they are planning."

"Excellent," responded Murqack. "We can do that."

"Now go," commanded Krakus as he dismissed the leaders to do their assigned duties.

The magotites were quickly organized into groups of ten and sent off in every direction of the Kabul with instructions that if they see anything or anyone that doesn't belong in the Kabul they were to report back immediately without confronting them.

Duke Kaklu, the gnome leader, hurriedly traveled back to Gamotz to organize an army that would be ready to move on the Southern Plains and head directly to Amins. It would take him the rest of the day and into the next morning to get back. Then he planned to move out with his army immediately the following morning.

The troll leader King Rakadam spent the day organizing a select group of twenty trolls he would be able to send out to Gamotz on the following day to join the gnome army. The trolls were sent out the following morning. They were able to travel faster than the gnomes and were able to make the trip to Gamotz within a day. Then, the following day, the army moved out heading for a different route, other than the Kilo Pass or the route taken by the first invading army. They needed to travel into the Southern Plains. The Kabul army was ready and was off to accomplish their planned destruction and revenge.

***

Prince Kakakrul, using his eagle form, flew north toward the dwarf capital Hilebin. He was flying over the city, hoping to be spotted by his dwarfish spy, when he received a call from the spy. The call was in the form of a humm, which he could hear and feel as a vibration, even from long distances. However, he was surprised that the humming was calling him from somewhere south of the North Groves.

The message from the spy occurred when the spy crossed her legs, fold her arms, closed her eyes, bowed her head, and began to hum. Ejijtwenty, the first assistant to Ejijone, said "Hummmmmm ummmmmm ummmmm," much like a chant for several minutes, and the prince was able to hear it.

The prince headed off in that direction, flying over the Hile Desert, when he heard the humming again. It was coming from the Kabul, which was very confusing. Why would someone call him from inside the Kabul?

He continued his flight toward the Kabul and on into the Kabul heading along its west edge. Then he heard the hum again and suddenly and unexpectedly he found himself flying over the top of a large army which seemed to include forces from the north the east, and the south of Small World. It seemed to include forces from all parts of Small World except the Kabul itself. It didn't make sense. Where did this army come from? It seemed to appear out of nowhere. And what was their intention?

He waited for a repeat of the hum. It seemed to have stopped. Perhaps his spy had been discovered. Just as he was about to give up and fly to his father in Tragis to tell him about the troops that had amassed in the Kabul, the hum started up again.

The prince was able to follow the sound and soon discovered his spy hidden away behind some brush far to the west and away from the rest of the army. He landed in front of the spy and quickly transformed himself into his prince form. Then he walked over to the spy and asked, "What is going on here? Where did all these troops come from?"

Ejijtwenty replied, "The amazonionite organized an invasion force which includes only women from all the species of Small World including the leprechauns, the elves, the dwarfs, the amazon-ionites, and even the giants. It's quite a large army. They have invaded the Kabul and their first target is Morgos."

"Where do a bunch of women come off thinking they can take on the Kabul?" challenged the prince.

Ejijtwenty was enormously offended at the sexist remark, but she wasn't surprised. She had very little respect for the Kabul prince. She fought back with, "I think you're underestimating their abilities. The amazonionite has them convinced that rather than be defensive, like the men of their species tend to think, we should be on the offense. Your reaction already proves that they have outsmarted you by their actions with their invasion of the Kabul, and now they are going to outbattle you by their strategy."

"Don't be stupid," barked the prince. "They don't stand a chance against our training."

"I don't think I'll be giving you any more updates," barked the dwarf as she stood up and started to walk away.

"You'll regret this," barked the prince as he transformed himself back into his eagle shape and flew off to Tragis to warn his father the Lord.

The flight to Tragis only took him a couple hours. He landed outside of the city, transformed himself back into his princely shape, and entered the gates of the city. He went directly to his father's chambers and walked in. Before he could say anything, his father spoke up, "I'm glad you're back. I need your help. We've been invaded and I need to find out who these invaders are. I need you fly out immediately and see if you can find them."

The prince was surprised and asked, "How do you know we were invaded?"

The lord responded, "The first group of gnome spies were killed and a second group of gnome spies found their bodies and discovered the tracks of a large group that had moved into the Kabul. I have commanded a gnome army to go down and destroy Amins. They have left and are being joined by twenty trolls. Amins should be destroyed soon. That will teach them to come and invade the Kabul."

The prince explained, "My dwarf spy is fortunately a member of the invasion and she called me. I spoke with her and she told me what was going on. There is an army of all female warriors camped and ready to fight slightly to the west of Morgos. It includes about two hundred elves, two hundred leprechauns, two hundred dwarfs, three hundred amazonionites, and thirty giants. They are a large army, but they are one hundred percent women, so it shouldn't be any challenge to our forces."

"Why an invasion?" asked the father.

"They think their men are too passive because they want a defensive war, and the women want to be aggressive and take on an offensive war. They think they need to attack us."

"What do we do?" asked the lord.

"Send the magotites home. The invaders are going to attack Morgos first. Let's give them a surprise. We have about ten thousand magotite warriors outside our city gates. Send them home and they should be able to take care of those women. It shouldn't even be a challenge for them."

"Excellent," remarked Lord Krakus. "Go inform Prince Murqack, the prince of the magotites, that Morgos is being invaded and that I have ordered him to go home and quell the invasion."

"Will do," remarked the prince as he left his father's presence.

After passing the instructions on to Prince Murqack, Prince Kakakrul returned to his eagle form and flew off in the direction of Amins. Since his father had ordered an attack on the city, he wanted to check there first, hopefully still before the attack, to see if he could identify the Protee power and the wizard. He needed to make sure they were eliminated.

The prince planned to observe the attack and watch who administered the healing power. Then he planned to come in and attack the person that exhibited that power. That should put an end to the Protee powers, if it was there in Amins. The second assignment, of wiping out the wizard, should have been easy since the wizard looked different and therefore was easily identified.

The prince flew to Amins and landed in a tree just outside of the city. He observed the city for a short period of time. He was comfortable that there had been no attack on the city so he flew up the South Road until he arrived at the Avol River crossing. He knew that the invading Kabul army would have to pass over this river so he made himself comfortable in a tree from which he could watch any activity at the river, and he waited. He wouldn't have to wait too long.

CHAPTER THIRTEEN

THE ATTACK ON MORGOS

With all the five Small World species united in the hills and woods to the west of the magotite home city, the five leaders came together to plan an attack on Morgos. They had all spent a restful night and it was now early morning. They were alert and eager to move forward with the creation of a plan. Goglbarj, the amazonionite, started the discussion with, "What do we name ourselves?"

Jesves suggested, "How about SWIFT? 'The Small World Integrated Female Team'?"

Goglbarj responded, "I like SWIFT, but the other part seems a little wordy. Are the rest of you leaders okay with that name?" The leaders nodded in agreement, not really concerned by what they called themselves. Then she said, "We are now called the Swift Army."

The rest of the leaders again shook their heads in agreement. Then Goglbarj continued, "Now that you have all met each other and become acquainted with each other's capabilities, we need to discuss how we should organize this attack. I will set forth a proposal and I would like your feedback. I think we should surround Morgos and attack from all sides simultaneously. That should force a quick surrender."

Jesves, the leprechaun, suggested, "I have thought of a different approach. What if a small group of our smallest and weakest warriors make a pretended attack on Morgos. The magotites will laugh at us as we attack. Then what will happen is that this small group will run away, drawing the magotites out of their stronghold, chasing after us at which point the rest of our army will sweep in and wipe them out."

Queen Gushe, the elf, jumped in on the discussion,
"How about a combination,
        Of the two suggestions?
After the leprechauns,

Draw the magotites out,
We have a group,
    Ready to attack them,
But we also have,
    The city of Morgos,
Surrounded with hidden warriors,
    Who swoop in,
After the magotites,
    Have left their stronghold."

Princess Ejijone, the dwarf, then took her turn, "This plan of attack is getting better all the time. I suggest that after we have conquered Morgos, we take over the city and make it a stronghold for our little army. Then we can plan our next attacks in the safety of a walled compound."

Giantess Annala commented, "I'm ready. I like the plan. The giants move the fastest so we will travel around to the east side of the city and attack from that side. Let's do it!"

Gushe added,
"I like it.
    We elves will take,
The south side,
    Of the city."

Ejijone said, "Then the dwarfs will take the north."

Goglbarj commented, "I see we are a team of great thinkers. We've come up with an excellent plan. The amazonionites will support the leprechauns on the west side and together we'll wipe out the magotites who are lured out of the city. Then we will attack the city from the west, hopefully gaining access through the gates to the inside of the city."

"When do we attack," asked Annala. "We're ready right now. We have a full day ahead of us and I think we should get going before the magotites have time to discover us and make plans. We should catch them off guard."

"Then let's go," said Goglbarj. "The elves, giants, and dwarfs should leave immediately and sneak around to their positions on the north, south, and east of the city."

Jesves added, "I'll get a group of about one hundred leprechauns ready for the initial attack."

***

Ejijone asked, "Let's set a time for the attack. I suggest three hours from now. We should all be ready by then."

Goglbarj responded, "In three hours it is. Does everyone agree? Today we take over our first goal, the city or Morgos."

"Yes," responded the various leaders in unison. Everyone departed to organize and prepare for the attack.

The elves, dwarfs, and giants departed almost immediately. They had to identify clandestine routes, hoping that they would not be spotted. The giants followed along with the elves around the south side of the city, doing their best to stay low so they wouldn't be spotted.

Unfortunately, the elves and giants encountered a small group of about fifty magotites who were returning to Morgos from Tragis. A battle immediately ensued but the arrows of the elves, who were in the lead, made short work of the magotites. Sadly, a couple of elves lost their lives to the magotite swords and several more were injured. The elves woke up to the fact that the magotites weren't going to be as easy to defeat as they had hoped.

The three hours passed quickly, and it was time for the small leprechaun army to attack. However, since the amazonionites were better with the bow and arrow, a dozen amazonionite warriors were mixed into the front of the leprechaun army. The plan was adjusted so that the amazonionite bowwomen would shoot flaming arrows over the west wall of Morgos, thereby angering them even more and making it more likely that they will come out to attack the small leprechaun-amazonionite army.

The initial attack went as planned. The leprechauns attacked and the amazonionites shot arrows over the wall into a surprised city of magotites. There weren't very many guards on the top of the wall, so the Swift Army was not noticed until there were several buildings burning inside the city. The magotites never imagined that anyone would be brave enough to actually attack them, so they never took the guarding of the wall seriously. Smoke could be seen rising above the walls of Morgos.

It wasn't long before magotites started appearing on top of the west wall in large numbers. The magotite bow skills were poor. Very few had experience with the bow and arrow. It wasn't long before the gates of the city swung open and magotites started rushing out of the city, swords in hand, running towards the leprechauns. They didn't wait for the leprechauns to run off in

retreat. They came out long before the planned retreat even occurred.

The leprechauns were suddenly involved in the fight of their lives. Amazonionite warriors, still hiding out of sight far behind the initial attack army, came rushing to the aid of the leprechauns. As the battle ensued more and more magotites came pouring out of the city. All the remaining leprechauns and amazonionites also arrived to help in the fight.

It started looking bad for the female army when, almost out of nowhere, the dwarfs and elves came to the rescue. They were diverted from their initial plan to attack the city from the north and south and came to the aid of their leprechaun companions. The tide of the battle turned, and the Swift Army started shifting their attention to the open gates that the magotites had been pouring through. Elves and dwarfs, in unison, started rushing through the gates, only to find the city practically deserted.

In the meantime, the giants had also pushed their way through a set of east gates and were now successfully in control of the city. It was as if a major portion of the city's population had deserted the city.

The magotites were defeated. Since they were maggot-eaten dead animals brought back to life by the Kabul Lord so that he could use them for his evil designs, there were no children. There wasn't even the distinction between male and female. The Swift Army felt no remorse in wiping them out completely, or so they hoped.

After the destruction of all the magotites that were in Morgos, the army reconvened in the city, shut and locked the gates, and posted guards on the walls. The leaders got together for a status meeting to discuss what they should do next. Goglbarj was again the first to start the meeting by saying, "Congratulations to everyone on a swift victory. But I feel that somehow that wasn't the end of the magotites. There must be more of them somewhere and I fear that they may be on their way to attack one of our cities."

"That will give the men something to do," responded Jesves. "What do we do next?"

Goglbarj responded, "I think our work for today has been completed. The question becomes, 'What do we do next?' Do we attack Tragis or Gamotz? And which one should we attack first?"

Gushe responded, "I suppose it would make the most sense to attack Gamotz, even though that's at the completely opposite end of the Kabul. The gnomes would be easier to defeat than the trolls."

Annala suggested, "Why don't we split up and attack both cities at the same time?"

Goglbarj answered with, "I don't think we're strong enough to split up. I'm not sure we're a match for the troll city, even if we are in full force. The trolls are our staunchest enemy."

"Then what do you suggest?" asked Annala.

"I don't have an answer," replied Goglbarj. "I think we should sleep on it and reconvene in the morning when we've had a chance to think about it. At this point, all I was focused on was defeating Morgos and I haven't thought past that point so I need your help with ideas."

"That's probably a good idea," suggested Jesves. "My head is still full of the battle we just fought. Let's go out and take care of our dead and wounded and then sleep on what to do next."

"Agreed," responded both Ejijone and Gushe.

The meeting was dismissed, and each leader went their way to work with their species, helping them rejoice in their victory, minister to the injured, and morn those that were lost. Each species had their own way of morning, and the dwarfs, who had lost twenty members, were the most unusual. The started humming which reverberated into different pitches and tones. To the remainder of the species, their morning seemed almost freakish.

The giants escaped without any losses. Their battles were minimal. By the time they entered the city it had emptied out of the west gate attacking the leprechauns.

The leprechauns had the biggest losses, losing twenty-five members, and the elves lost ten. Each of their funerary rituals were quiet and respectful.

After the wounds were mended and the dead were buried or burned, everyone went to sleep, leaving a few guards on the tops of the walls as lookouts.

It was about two in the morning when a cry went out from the guards, "We're being attacked. An army of Kabul forces are coming to attack us here at Morgos!"

The magotite army of about ten thousand creatures, that had been stationed at Tragis in preparation for the attack on Amins, was now wildly charging toward their home city. They had learned about the warriors that were planning to attack Morgos, and they were now out for revenge at the audacity of such an attack.

The screams and yells of the guards quickly awoke the entire Swift Army who came charging out from wherever they were sleeping. Goglbarj yelled out commands, "Seal the gates and make sure they are secure. Giants, you need to guard the gates. Everyone that is good with the bow and arrow, which includes elves and amazonionites, get to the top of the walls! The rest of you need to be ready, swords in hand, in case any of the magotites are able to break through anywhere."

The entire Swift Army was frantically scurrying around, preparing for the onslaught. They wanted to get into the fight, but they knew that keeping the gates closed and battling the enemy from the walls was the best strategy.

The guards yelled out, "There are thousands of them. It looks like they are all magotites. We don't see trolls or gnomes."

The warriors waited. They knew the attack was brewing but there was nothing else they could do to prepare.

As the magotites started to come into range the arrows started to fly off the walls of Morgos striking the creatures down in rapid succession. However, the horde of magotites was so large, there were so many, that the arrows seemed to have very little overall effect. The horde just ran over the top of the dead bodies of their fellow magotites and charged on ahead to the walls of the city.

The magotites were brutal, not caring about each other, almost to the point of being obsessed. They would pile each other's bodies on top of each other, using the dead or live bodes as a stairway to climb up to the top of the wall.

The screams of the Swift Army warriors, calling for help, caused troops to come to the tops of the walls and, using their swords or axes, they would beat down the magotites who were fighting to get over the top of the wall.

The battle raged on for hours. The stream of magotites was endless. Hundreds and then thousands were killed at the walls of the city but eventually a few made it over the wall and did battle with the warriors on the top of the wall, thereby allowing more magotites to come over the wall, and then even more came over. Soon the stream of magotites filled the top of the wall and they started spilling over onto the main grounds of Morgos.

The Swift warriors made quick work of the magotites, but the volume of them made it difficult and often the warriors were fighting two or even three magotites at the same time. The large number of magotites gave the creatures the advantage of being able to kill the occasional Swift warrior, as the battle raged on.

The Swift warriors knew that their lives were in danger, and they fought the way no warrior ever fought. They fought for their world, and for their lives. They knew that they had to fight harder than they had ever fought if they were to live long enough to see another day. The gruesome creatures desperately pressed on with their aggressive attack.

CHAPTER FOURTEEN
THE ATTACK ON THE SOUTH

The gnomes were fired up. The southerners had killed their spy party and they wanted revenge. Now that the Kabul Lord had given them the go-ahead to attack Amins, they were madly pushing forward. They had the support of a few trolls, twenty to be exact, and the two species each hated the stench of the other. The trolls thought the gnomes were useless, and the gnomes resented the arrogance of the trolls. But here they were, forced to be together in their attack on the south.

They had been warned to not cross over into the south using the route that the previous invasion party had used because it was being guarded by giants. They also wanted to avoid the Kilo Pass because that was where their spy party had been killed. They decided to cross through the mist wall that separated the south from the Kabul at a location halfway between these two previously used routes.

The Kabul army arrived at the mist wall shortly after mid-day and came to a halt. No one wanted to be the first to cross through the wall because they feared the southern troops on the other side. "You go first," commanded Duke Kaklu, the leader of the gnomes.

However, the trolls had heard the rumor that Prince Kakakrul had seen giants guarding the other side of the mist wall and they refused to be first. They simply stood their ground and stared at the duke as if they didn't understand a word he was saying.

The duke barked at the trolls even louder, "You go first. You are bigger and stronger and have a better chance against anyone guarding the other side of the wall. You move out and break through and after you have cleared the way we will come through."

Again the trolls stood motionless in defiance of the duke's commands. They felt no allegiance to the gnomes and were not interested in the duke's commands.

The Duke decided on another strategy. "I need ten gnome volunteers to go through the wall, spy out what they see, and then return and let us know what it's like on the other side." He pointed at the first ten gnomes that he saw and said, "You ten are the chosen ones. Go!"

The ten hesitated, not eager to follow the duke's command, and then they slowly, in unison, marching in a straight line, barged through the wall.

It was only seconds later when three of the gnomes returned yelling, "There are giants on the other side waiting for us. They have killed our companions and we escaped because they were busy killing everyone else."

"Then we can't cross here," barked the duke. "Let's move a few hundred paces to the west and try again."

The combined gnome and troll army followed the command of the duke and moved off to the west. Then they tried the same strategy again, sending ten gnomes through the wall. This time only four returned, again screaming that there are giants on the other side of the wall.

"The giants can't be everywhere," complained the duke. "Let's change our strategy. Let's break up into three groups and simultaneously go through the wall in three different locations. We'll take one group through a couple hundred more paces to the west. A second group should go through a couple hundred paces to the east of the first place we went through, and a third group should go through a couple hundred paces beyond that point. We'll wait for a signal from me and all charge through the wall at the same time. The giants may get a few of us, but they can't be everywhere and get all of us."

Gnomes and trolls were broken up into the three groups and each was sent off to the location they were assigned to. It took half an hour before everyone was in place and ready to go through the wall. Then, when each group had given the signal that they were ready, the duke gave the signal to move forward.

On the other side of the wall, the giants were spread thin with only a few giants every hundred yards. They were ready, but maybe not for the large onslaught that the gnomes and trolls had planned.

As the Kabul army came crashing through, the giants were overwhelmed. They fought hard in the three locations where the Kabul attacked, and the remaining giants rushed to their rescue, but it was impossible for a few giants to contain an army of thousands of gnomes supported by a few trolls.

The battle raged on, but most of the gnomes simply charged through the giant line and rushed into the southern plains, without even doing battle. Each giant was quickly subdued by the combination of a troll or two and about twenty gnomes. They didn't stand a chance. About fifty giants were killed. Even though the Kabul army lost most of their trolls and about a thousand gnomes, they still had a few trolls and about five thousand gnomes left for the attack on Amins. It was a bad day for the Southern Plains.

The duke regrouped his gnomes and the remaining trolls about halfway to the South Road. Once they were all regrouped, he led the march toward to the South Road. It was getting late in the day so he ordered his army to camp for the night. He instructed, "We had a good day today, defeating the giants. We're going to have about three or four more days of traveling. We're going to cross the Avol River which can only be crossed by a few individuals at a time, so it will take at least a day just to get everyone across that. Then we have another day's march to Amins. However, we need to stay on the alert. The giants might come back with reinforcements."

***

The remaining giants that had survived the attack along the mist wall, felt devastated. A large number of giants had fallen and had to go through the burial ritual, which would take at least a day. Additionally, a group of three giants were sent off to report to Giant-giant what had happened. The Kabul army was on the move and reinforcements were desperately needed to stop their onslaught.

The giant in command of the small army that was defending the south side of the mist wall commanded, "I need three of you to hurry back to our home in the Sheere Cliffs and inform Giant-giant that we need immediate reinforcements. Tell him what has happened and that there is a large gnome army in the Southern Plains and we're not sure where they're heading. In addition, I need the another three of you to go directly to Amins and warn them that they might be under attack."

"What about Gije?" asked one of the other giants.

"We better send three of you there to warn them as well but I'm pretty sure the Kabul army is heading to Amins because they came out near the east end of the Kabul."

Then one of the traveling giants asked, "If the army is heading for Amins, aren't we going to encounter them when we try to cross the Avol River bridge?"

"That's true," responded the commander. "They might be there already. You definitely need to avoid them."

One of the commander's assistants chimed in, "There is a spring about halfway between the bridge and the Sheere Cliffs, which is the source of the Avol river. We all know that the river runs in both directions, both north and south, and that the source is that spring. I've never been there, but I have heard that there is a way to cross the Avol river at the spring. It's dangerous, but it may be a better option than encountering the Kabul army."

"That's an excellent idea," commented one of the travelers. "We will work our way to the Avol river and then head upstream, from whatever side of the spring we're on. That way we should be able to arrive at the spring and take our chances crossing the river at that point."

"Go," commanded the giant commander, and the six giants that were heading to the east side of the river departed. Then he identified three more giants and sent them on a similar mission to warn Gije. However, these three would have to cross the Avoli River and they had to be careful to avoid a possible crossing by the Kabul forces, if they were indeed headed for Gije.

The six giants that were traveling together toward the east travelled in a straight-line east with a plan to come to the Avol River as quickly as possible. Giants move three to four times as fast as any of the other smaller Small World species, so it only took them a couple hours to arrive at the river.

At the point where they encountered the river, the water was flowing southward, which meant that the spring would be toward the north. They started moving in that direction, hoping that the spring would indeed be a place where they would be able to cross the river.

An hour later they arrived at the spring. It was like a fountain with water shooting out of a small mound that looked a lot like a small volcano. Surrounding the volcano shaped spring was a small moat. The water flowed out of the spring, down the volcano, and into the moat. From the moat, which was on the top of a small hill, the water flowed either to the north or to the south, depending on how it came off the volcano. Then, from there the flowing river of water became the Avol River. The southern section of the Avol River flowed past the South Road and on into Alice Lake. The northern portion of the Avol River flowed over the Sheere Cliffs where they formed a large waterfall, and then these waters flowed into Mar Lake, the home of Marmaroplis which was the city of the mermaids.

"This will be easy," said one of the giants. "The river flows around both sides of this volcanic fountain and is only half as wide on each side. We just need to jump onto the volcano, walk around to the other side, and then jump off the volcano to the eastern side of the river. We should be able to get back to our giant caves before it gets too dark."

"Right you are," responded another one of the giants. "This would still be too far for any of the other species to get across, but we giants should be able to get across with a good run and a jump."

One of the other giants did exactly that. He ran and jumped and soon found himself on the volcano, having jumped over the moat on its west side. Then he walked around to the east side of the volcano and jumped over the moat on that side. The other giants followed and all six soon found themselves on the east side of Avol River.

From here the giants split up into two teams of three. The one team went northeast to their home at the Sheere Cliffs while the other team of three went southeast toward Giter, hoping to get through the Amins Groves and on to Amins to warn the leprechauns of the pending attack.

The three that traveled to their home made quick work of their trip and arrived in the evening, even though it was late. They went directly to Giant-giant's home and approached the guards. One of the threesome asked, "Can we speak with Giant-giant? It's extremely urgent. It looks like there will be an attack on the south."

The guard responded, "He's not here. He travelled to Amins to talk with the wizard and he's still there."

The threesome, discouraged by the news, realized that the other team of three would soon be in contact with Giant-giant and would be able to update him. Instead they went to the great hall and announced to everyone, "We were attacked by the Kabul forces. They have invaded the Southern Plains. They have killed many giants. We think they are headed for Amins and we need to rush to help them. We don't want our warriors to have died in vain. We will leave in the morning to help stop the invasion. Are there any volunteers who will join us?"

Dozens of giants jumped up and yelled out, almost in unison, "We will join. We don't want our homes to be attacked by those disgusting trolls. We want to protect our homes and the Southern Plains, as ordered by the Creator."

"Let's all meet here in this room immediately after the morning meal and we will charge off together."

With that the giants sat back down and continued their conversations; however, the atmosphere had shifted dramatically from one of gaiety to one of seriousness. They knew they were going off to war, and that the war had already cost many giant lives. The next to die might be one of them.

***

The three giants that were heading for Giter, and then on to Amins, ended up spending the night just north of Giter. They kept watch to make sure that they were not overtaken by the Kabul forces. The night was uneventful and in the morning they travelled through Giter, viewing the utter destruction, and then went on into the Amins Groves. They knew that cutting through the groves would be a shorter trip than using the South Road, and they knew that they had to get there as soon as possible. Additionally, they assumed by cutting through the groves there would be less chance of encountering the Kabul Army.

It was the afternoon of that next day that they finally arrived in Amins. As they walked through the city, they immediately noticed Giant-giant with several other giants surrounding him. They went directly to their leader and one of the three arriving giants explained, "We have just come from the mist wall that separates us from the Kabul, and we have experienced a devastating attack. Several trolls and thousands of gnomes came through the wall in a large mass and attacked us. There were just not enough giants there to handle the attack and most of our team was killed. There are still a few giants left guarding the wall, but not enough to hold off another attack. The Kabul forces that have broken through are probably coming here to attack Amins but we're not sure. They may also be going to Gije. We couldn't follow them because there wasn't enough of us left and we felt we should come and warn you.

There were also giants sent to Gije to warn them, and to our home on the Sheere Cliffs to warn them."

"How distressful," responded Giant-giant. "We were overconfident in our abilities to ward off any attack. This has shown us our weakness. We are not invincible. I will have to pass this news along to the wizard and we will have to develop a strategy."

The arriving giant stressed, "It has to happen quickly because the attacking army may be here as soon as this evening or possibly tomorrow."

"Giant-giant turned to two of his aids and said, "I need you to travel immediately and quickly to the cliffs and round up as many giants as possible. We need their help to fend off any attack that is on its way to Amins.

"We'll head off immediately," responded the aide.

Then turning to the arriving giants he said, "The situation is understood." Then he walked off to the Amins council chambers and beckoned the leaders to come out to talk, since he wasn't able to fit under their low ceilings.

The lead giant explained the situation to the council members and the wizard. A panicked look came upon all their faces. "We were thinking we had a couple months before any attack might occur," an Amins council member blurted out. "Now you're telling me it may happen in the next day."

"It sounds almost certain," responded Giant-giant. "I have sent for more giants to come and help us, but I am not sure they will arrive soon enough to make a difference."

Hiztin, who was now also considered to be a member of the council because of all his experiences in traveling to the North Groves and back, jumped in and added, "We also have excellent leprechaun warriors, however Jesves, along with several hundred of our best female warriors, have just disappeared. It's completely strange. I haven't seen them for over a week. Why would all our bravest women just disappear?"

Amaz suggested, "Maybe they are doing some special training. I'm sure they'll appear when we need them." Then, turning to the wizard, he asked, "What do we do?"

The wizard jumped in, "Empty the city and send everyone to find refuge in the Amins Groves. Organize small defense groups that will attack any Kabul forces that try to enter into the Groves. We cannot defend the city. We don't have the forces to do that. If the giants weren't able to defend the mist wall, what chance do we have here. We need to forget the city and just worry about the lives of your people. Go now and get everyone to safety. The best thing for me to do is to go back to the Tako Ruins. The scrolls that I already have talk about and describe other tools and weapons that might be available, and I need to make sure I have discovered everything that might be able to help us."

The council members scurried around the town warning everyone and encouraging them to leave the city as soon as possible. There already were dozens of leprechaun camps throughout the Amins Groves and the remaining citizens were encouraged to join them as quickly as possible.

The city was quickly emptied, the leprechauns heading to one of their camps, the wizard heading through the Amins Groves toward the Avol River and the Tako Ruins, Egisix flying north to update the dwarfs on the latest Kabul activity, and the giants hiding out along the eastern edge of the Amins Groves, waiting to see the expected onslaught of Kabul forces coming down the South Road.

High above in the top of the trees, an eagle could be seen watching.

CHAPTER FIFTEEN
THE SWIFT WARRIORS

The army of female warriors known as the Swift warriors knew that their lives were in danger, and they fought the way no warrior ever fought. They fought for their world, and for their lives. But the stream of magotites coming from Tragis seemed endless. Every warrior had killed more than their share of these fearsome creatures, but they continued to pour in against the walls of their home city Morgos. The Swift army wasn't sure how long they would be able to hold out against this never-ending onslaught.

The warriors knew that they had to fight harder than they had ever fought if they were to live long enough to see another day. However, the magotites' charge on Morgos was a desperate attempt to save their homeland.

Goglbarj, of the amazonionites, and Queen Gushe, leader of the elves, used their entire team of archer warriors on the top of the walls, shooting down magotites as much as possible before they reached the walls. Any that reached the top were greeted by the swords of Jesves' lepelves or the axes of Ejijone's dwarfs. And any of the magotites that made it past these warriors and were able to enter Morgos were quickly dispatched by the giants and then thrown back over the walls of the city joining the other dead magotites outside of its walls.

The battle raged on for hours. The Swift warriors were becoming exhausted. There seemed to be no end in sight, and if exhaustion overtook them, they were destined to fall prey to the magotites' attack and die. But these warriors weren't ready to give up. They were determined to succeed in spite of the fact that they were embattled by the entire magotite army and would have to defeat them entirely by themselves.

The battle raged on. The warriors were awoken at two in the early hours of the morning, and it was now six in the evening. They had never worked so hard. In spite of being on the verge of exhaustion, they continued when suddenly a cry went out from one of the amazonionite warriors, "I can see the end. The magotite forces are nearly at an end."

The warriors were rejuvenated by this message and seemed to receive a second burst of strength. There was a new fierceness to every swing of the sword or stroke of the ax. This would all come to an end soon and they would be victorious.

One hour later the end did come. The magotites had run out of bodies to sacrifice. The pile of dead magotites outside the city walls was so high that any additional attackers only needed to walk over the tops of the dead in order to reach the top of the wall. But when they arrived, an ax or a sword would be anxiously waiting there for them.

The battle raged on for another two hours, until eight in the evening, and then it abruptly ended. The stream of magotites had come to an end. There were no more.

"We're through," yelled out Goglbarj. "We've completely wiped out the magotite army."

A cheer went up and everyone, no matter if they were leprechauns, elves, dwarfs, amazonionites, or giants, was jumping up and down with excitement. Today they were all companions. Today species didn't matter. Today everyone gave out cheers, hugs, and slaps on the back. Today the Swift army had made a difference. They had reduced the Kabul forces by one third and they deserved to be extremely proud of their accomplishment.

Goglbarj, Jesves, Ejijone, Gushe, and Annala congratulated one another with emotions of exhaustion, excitement, and relief, all mixed together. "We have accomplished the impossible," responded Jesves.

"We have indeed," agreed Ejijone.

Goglbarj added, "Now we take care of our injured, then get a well-deserved good night's rest, and in the morning we take care of our casualties."

Giantess Annala added, "We also need to get out of here soon because the smell will be terrible. We will need to discuss what our little army is going to do next. Do we go home or do we attack another city? And which city?"

Goglbarj responded, "I'm glad you brought that up. That will give us something to think about tonight."

The giants didn't suffer any losses and the amazonionites lost five warriors, elves only suffered ten, but the leprechauns and the dwarfs, who had the most direct hand to hand contact each lost about thirty warriors.

Most of the surviving warriors had minor, superficial wounds which were easily bandaged. Some had more serious wounds which took stiches and more elaborate bandaging. Most warriors felt fortunate that their wounds weren't more serious. After the bandaging they all went to bed hoping to recover their strength and energy.

The night was uneventful. Everyone was extremely exhausted which helped some fall asleep immediately. However, some of the other warriors were so hyped that they needed to spend some time winding down before they could fall asleep. The stress of such a violent battle, something very few of them had previously experienced, made it difficult for most of the warriors to calm down.

Eventually morning arrived and the warriors started busying themselves with burying their dead. While they were busy doing that, Goglbarj, Jesves, Ejijone, Gushe, and Annala, the leaders of each of the species, met together to discuss what they should do next. As usual Goglbarj, the amazonionite, started the conversation asking the question, "As I see it, we have three choices. One is that we give up, disband, and go home. Another is that we go all the way to the south circling around Tragis, and attack Gamotz. And the third is that we attack Tragis. Does anyone see another option?"

Annala the giant suggested, "We could break up and attack both Tragis and Gamotz simultaneously."

Gushe the elf responded,
"We can't give up,
        We've done so well,
We can't split up,
        We work together well,
I think Gamotz,
        Is the next step best,
For us to quit,
        We can't just rest,
We are fearsome,

We've Morgos wiped,
We've avenged Giter,
And now we're hyped."

Goglbarj was excited by Gushe's response, "I love that. We have proven ourselves as a fighting force. We should press on now to continue toward our goal of weakening the Kabul's forces. And I agree that Gamotz should be the next target since it is the next weakest target in the Kabul."

"Let's start the march as soon as the last rights have been performed on our dead," suggested Jesves the leprechaun. "This place is already starting to stick from the bodies of all the dead magotites, who were already dead at one time before we killed them again."

"Agreed," said Goglbarj. "We should retrace our route through the mountains and brush of the Kabul hillsides and work our way down to Gamotz. Let's spy them out first before we attack and see what we're up against. I will send some of my amazonionite friends to hurry ahead and spy out the situation and then get back to us."

"Excellent idea," responded Jesves.

The meeting of the Swift leaders broke up as each of them returned to their species and explained the plan. Then they started organizing their warriors together in preparation for the march southward.

Goglbarj went to her own amazonionite Gogl tribe and decided that she would use them for the spying mission on Gamotz. She approached her Elderess and asked, "We need to send a small group of amazonionite warriors ahead of the main group. They need to go to Gamotz and spy out the situation down there. We don't want any surprises. Would you take about four or five warriors and go down and do that. And if there is anything to report, that you think we should be aware of, can you send someone back to us and let us know?"

"Of course," responded the Gogl Elderess who was still hyped about the success that they had achieved on the previous day. We'll head out right away."

About one hour later, the entire Swift Army was ready to depart on their journey south. The warriors were excited about their victory against the magotites and they were feeling like they could accomplish anything. They felt like they were on top of the world and that their strength and power would soon bring about the freedom of all of Small World, free from the domination and influence of the Kabul.

It was already midday, but no one wanted to spend another night in Morgos. The smell of the magotites was growing intense, and the idea of camping out in this city was uncomfortably gross as well. The march began knowing that they would probably need to spend the next couple nights camping out in the hills of the Kabul.

The first half day of the march was uneventful. And the night campout was also without incident. There was always a guard posted, just in case there were any Kabul spies searching for them, but no one was spotted.

The second day of the march was also uneventful. At one point they could see Tragis and the Kabul volcano off in the distance, but the magotite camp that they had seen previously was no longer there. There was very little activity in and out of Tragis. The city seemed deserted, however the smoke of chimneys from inside the city made it obvious that there was life inside the walls of the city.

It was just as they were passing Tragis that the amazonionite spies that had been sent ahead to check on Gamotz returned to the warriors in order to report what they had learned. The Elderess started the conversation with, "Gamotz seems almost deserted. There seems to only be women and children in the city. The army must be on the march, probably southward, because we didn't see any marches northward."

Goglbarj shared the information with the other leaders and then suggested, "We should take over the city, just like we did in Morgos. Once we are inside, we'll use their walled defenses to protect us when the gnome army returns."

"Agreed," said a couple of the other leaders in unison.

Then Goglbarj instructed the Elderess, "Go back and continue your watch. We'll probably have to camp out one more time and then we'll get there in the morning."

"Will do," responded the Elderess as she and her small group turned and headed back south to spy on Gamotz.

The remainder of the day was uneventful and eventually night arrived. The Swift warriors made camp and were soon fast asleep.

The night was again uneventful. The following morning arrived and the warriors broke camp just as the guards came rushing in to say, "Our camp has been spotted by some Kabul spies. We successfully were able to shoot down two of them with arrows, but another two escaped our grasp. They were heading back towards Tragis, probably to warn the Kabul Lord."

"We need to move fast," responded Goglbarj. "We need to get inside Gamotz quickly in case the Kabul Lord sends his troll army after us."

A new sense of urgency surrounded the camp. They started their march, charging just a little bit faster than before.

Goglbarj assigned a group of three amazonionite warriors to stay behind and keep a watch on Tragis in case an army is sent after them. They were to report any activity out of Tragis heading south.

Then Goglbarj instructed the other leaders, "We need to head toward the southeast. We need to get to Gamotz as quickly as possible."

Without comment the direction of the march was shifted and the army moved directly in the direction of Gamotz. They weren't going to develop an elaborate attack plan. They relied on the comments of the spies that the city was mostly abandoned so they hoped to be able to simply walk through the city gates and take over. But they were in for a surprise.

It was several hours of travel, and it was starting to become late in the afternoon, when the Swift army finally started getting close to Gamotz. It was no long a city off in the distance, they were now close enough that they could hit the city walls with an arrow. But, to everyone's surprise, instead of the warriors shooting arrows into Gamotz, arrows started flying at the Swift warriors.

Just as they were about to charge the city gate, the spies who had been left behind to watch Tragis came rushing up to Goglbarj yelling, "There is a troll army coming from Tragis and headed directly toward us!!!"

***

Prince Kakakrul was frustrated. Nothing seemed to be going as planned. He had flown to Amins and landed in a tree just outside of the city. He had observed the city for a short period of time and confirmed that there had been no attack on the city. He also watched for the wizard and for this mysterious individual who had this Protee power, but he saw nothing that indicated either of them was there. He hoped that the attack against Amins, which was about to occur, would take care of both of these individuals and solve the problem for him. He flew up the South Road, watching the entire way for the Kabul Army but saw nothing of them. Eventually he arrived at the Avol River crossing where he knew the army would have to pass. He found himself a comfortable perch on the top of a tree and waited.

The wait wasn't long before off in the distance the prince could see the arrival of the Kabul army. But to his shock and utter dismay, when it was time for the troops to start crossing over the river, a battle started up. It was a battle between the trolls and the gnomes. The gnomes thought they should cross the river first and the trolls thought it should be their privilege and right. The gnomes yelled out, "The trolls are idiots. They're big fat stupid idiots who can't tell their head from their butt. And they smell like their butt."

Not surprisingly, the trolls took offense and came at the gnomes with their swords, demanding, "Take it back or we'll wipe out the lot of you right now?"

The gnomes responded, "I'm surprised you know which end of the sword to hold, you're all so stupid."

The trolls fought back with action. They took up their swords and with one stroke they were able to decapitate four or five gnomes.

The prince couldn't allow his troops to kill themselves right there before his eyes so he flew down to the west side of the Avol River crossing, transformed into his princely form, and yelled out, "Stop this right now! What's the matter with you? We're here to wipe out the Southerners, not each other."

The trolls, surprised at seeing the prince, stopped their slaughter and stepped back. The lead troll said, "We're sorry. These gnomes provoked us. They're just evil and dirty."

"I don't care who started this," responded the prince. "You're both responsible." Then he commanded the trolls, "Now throw these dead gnomes in the river and then get across to the other side using the pull boat."

The trolls were happy. They were going to get to cross first. They quickly threw the dead gnomes in the river and watched them float downstream to Alice Lake. Then they jammed themselves onto the boat and pulled themselves across the river using the rope that was connected to a tree on each side of the river. It took several trips because the trolls were heavier. After the trolls were across, the gnomes started to pull themselves across. They were able to send twice as many gnomes across as trolls, but since there were so many gnomes, it would take the rest of the day and most of the following day before all the gnomes were across.

The prince spent the night in a tree, feeling it was safer than on the ground with these crazy trolls and gnomes. He was concerned that they might start fighting again and kill him by accident.

The following day, after all the Kabul forces had successfully crossed the Avol River, the troops started marching on the South Road towards Amins. As they passed Giter, and saw the devastation and destruction of the city, they let up a cheer. However, they didn't get very far past the city before it was night and they camped out in the grasslands on the north side of the South Road. It was a beautiful night and the grasses gave them a comfortable bed.

Tomorrow would be a big day. Tomorrow they would destroy Amins and eliminate the leprechaun species forever. Amins will look like Giter. And the eagle watched from high up in a tree from the south side of the South Road, overlooking the Kabul forces with excitement.

CHAPTER SIXTEEN

RETURN TO THE TAKO RUINS

The Wizard of Havinis departed from Amins heading northwest through the Amins Groves. He wanted to take the shortest route to the Avol River crossing on his way to the Tako Ruins. He knew there were more spells that he could use, he had read descriptions of them. However, by using the scrolls he already had he didn't have sufficient information about how to execute these additional spells. The destruction of Tako, which occurred during the Lifefight Wars, contained a library of scrolls and a temple. He had found the scroll library and made a quick survey of what they contained, but he now felt as though he had missed something important. Additionally, there were scrolls in the temple which had not yet been discovered. He needed all the information possible to make sure he was making the best decisions available and that he could protect the Small World from its imminent destruction.

As he travelled through the groves he encountered numerous leprechaun encampments. Each barraged him with questions about the possible attack on Amins, and he was hesitant to answer any of them. All he could say was, "The Kabul forces are on the march. We're not sure where they are going first but Amins may be their next target."

The leprechauns were destressed by this news, but the wizard felt he must be somewhat honest or they might do something stupid, like returning to Amins.

The wizard pushed ahead and soon reached the western edge of the groves. Off in the distance he could see the trolls and gnomes amassing themselves on the east end of the Avol River pull-boat crossing. He decided to stay hidden in the groves until the Kabul troops had passed. He would have to use that same pull-boat to cross the river on his journey along the South Road to the east. He would have to camp out for the night, and possibly spend a second night, in the groves, waiting for all the troops to have travelled far enough away on their journey to Amins to make it safe for him to pull-boat his way across.

He waited, knowing full well that by the time he returned Amins would most likely be a wasteland of destruction similar to what had happened to Giter. But he hoped that the leprechauns would survive, because they were safely tucked away in the same groves that he had just passed through.

The day passed slowly, waiting for the Kabul forces to continue on their destructive journey. It was the second day before the wizard finally felt as though he could depart from his hiding place in the Amins Groves and head in the direction of the Avol River crossing. He was careful to constantly check the South Road in both directions making sure there were no surprises. Being on his own created a need for him to be extra cautious. If the Kabul forces spotted him he would be unable to outrun the trolls or the gnomes. He wasn't able to move that fast in his old age and using his staff to hobble along.

The wizard had worked his way to about one hundred yards from the crossing when, to his shock and surprise, he saw a group of about ten gnomes charging in his direction. He was desperate, uncertain what he should do in order to avoid destruction. He knew all of Small World depended on him. In frustration and confusion, he rushed to the river and, in an act of foolish desperation, jumped in, uncertain what would happen to him and where he would end up.

He attempted to float on his back as the rushing river pulled him along southward. As he floated, he looked up into the sky. He could see an eagle circling above and he immediately knew how the gnomes had discovered his presence. The eagle had to be the prince. He must have dispatched the gnomes.

The movement of the river was so fast that the gnomes weren't able to keep up. A couple of spears were thrown in his direction, but they never came close and ended up being pulled along by the river's flow, just like the wizard.

The wizard thought about what was happening to him and he became afraid. Would this river end up pulling him all the way into the Lamos? He knew that the Avol River connected with the Avoli River, and he knew that if he were to get pulled into the Avoli River, there would be no hope for him. The Avoli was even faster moving than the Avol. It was down in a steep canyon with cliffs on both sides. There would be no escape.

The wizard could see that the gnomes were no longer chasing him. He tried to work his way toward the west bank of the river in the hope that maybe he could get out of the river before it was too late. If he could get to the west bank he would successfully have avoided the Avol River pull-boat crossing. He was certain that the gnomes would be there, guarding that crossing in case he was able to get out of the river. That would no longer be an option. If he was going to make it to the Tako Ruins, it would have to be because he reached the west bank.

Suddenly the river came to an abrupt halt and he found himself floating in Alice Lake in the midst of dozens of dead gnome bodies. The current had slowed down substantially but it was still pulling him slowly toward the west and he knew that he would eventually end up in the Avoli River if he didn't get out of the water immediately. He fought and pushed himself toward the north shore with all the energy he could muster. But his energy ran out. He was drained. He couldn't go any further. He was never considered to be muscular or exceptionally strong, and now he had achieved the limit of his abilities. All the traveling, and fighting the Avol River current, had completely drained him. He knew he had lost the battle. He would end up in the Lamos. He started to sink down in the water, down to his doom and to his utter failure.

***

The Kabul Prince Kakakrul, still in his eagle form, had identified someone traveling toward the Avol River crossing. He was confused and asked himself, "Why would anyone travel alone in the Southern Plains knowing that the Kabul Army was around? Don't they realize that the Kabul is about to destroy everyone and everything in the south? Could this possibly be the wizard? Or the individual with the Protee powers? Or maybe this is a spy?"

The prince didn't hesitate. He immediately went to the Kabul forces and informed them to send a group of gnomes to kill this person. Whoever he is, his journey couldn't be good for the Kabul and the best thing to do would be to immediately wipe him out.

The prince watched the gnomes chasing this unknown individual. Then, to the prince's surprise, this individual jumped into the Avol River. The prince thought, "That was a stupid move. Now he'll get sucked into the Lamos. But I guess that's as good a way of getting rid of him and any other. Whoever he is, he's gone now."

The prince and the gnomes returned to their army. The prince continued to remain in his eagle form so he could observe the destruction of Amins from above. The prince found himself a perch high above the city and waited for the arrival of the full Kabul forces. It wouldn't be long now. Amins would be wiped off the face of the Southern Plains.

***

The wizard sunk deeper and deeper into the water and then, to his sudden surprise, he hit lake bottom. He wasn't more than five feet deep in the water. He stood up and found that about one-fourth of his body was above water. He received a sudden spurt of energy, realizing that he may now be able to save himself. He walked toward shore and with the last spurt of energy he could muster he slowly walked onto the shore. Then he collapsed.

He rolled over on his back, checking to see if that eagle was still up in the sky, but he saw nothing. He was relieved to know that he had not been followed. Perhaps the eagle assumed that he had fallen into the bottomless pit of the Lamos. Whatever the reason, he was delighted that the eagle was gone.

After a few minutes, the wizard fell asleep and wouldn't wake up again for about three hours. When he finally woke up he had to look around and try to remember where he was. He had temporarily forgotten what had happened to him, but it all came back to him soon enough. He stood up and started walking due north. He realized that eventually he would come across the South Road, somewhere between the Avol and the Avoli Rivers. A couple hours later he successfully found the road, but now it was late in the afternoon, too late to go to the Tako Ruins. He remembered the risk of the riposters. Riposters had fish bodies, bird's wings, and rat's teeth. They were flesh eating and vicious, but they only came out at night. traveling there at night was suicide so he made camp for himself in the forest south of the road.

The following morning the wizard woke up and carefully surveyed the surrounding area. He didn't want to have another encounter with Kabul warriors. Once he had convinced himself that it was safe, he left the woods and started walking west on the South Road. It wasn't long before he reached the branch in the road that headed north along the Kilo Pass. This was the route he would have to take in order to get to the Tako Ruins.

He moved quickly down this road because he wanted to get into and out of the ruins before the riposters had a chance to attack. As he arrived at the ruins, he went directly to the library where he had found the scrolls that he had utilized to cast spells on Goglbarj, Egisix, Elasti, and Gido. But these scrolls also hinted at the possibility that there were other spells and these spells might be useful in saving Small World. The wizard knew it was possible that he was just wasting his time, but he had to know for certain. He pushed ahead.

He opened up the chamber that contained the scrolls, and started to go through them one at a time. It was a slow and laborious process because he had to read the description of each scroll before he could decide if he should take it with him. In the end he found three more scrolls that he felt might be helpful. But by now he had used up the entire day and he knew he needed to get away from the ruins before the riposters came out for their nighttime feeding.

The wizard made his way east of the ruins, back into a thicket of woods, far enough away to be out of the reach of the riposters, and he set up camp for himself. He planned to use this campsite for each of the next few days while he continued to search through the ruins.

The following day the wizard went directly to the temple, which was on a mound on the west end of the city. The temple was a large, four-sided pyramid with a large interior chamber. The temple was partially in ruins, and badly overgrown by trees and other vegetation. It had been the pride and joy of the Great City Tako. Within the temple were several walls with crypts that numbered twenty high and one hundred across. As the wizard fought his way through the entrance of the temple, breaking away the vegetation that blocked his path, the first thing he saw was the large number of crypts. Surrounding the room with all the crypts, and guarding it were six glowing ghosts. The wizard approached these ghosts and explained, "I am the Wizard of Havinis and I have been awaken to help Small World survive from a second attack by the Kabul. They are once again initiating the Lifefight Wars, hoping to dominate this world. Would you have any wisdom and insight on how we can prevent their domination of our world?"

The ghosts looked at each other, then back at the wizard and explained, "We are the Shadow Warriors who lost our lives in the previous Lifefight War. There are hundreds of us, in the tombs all around this temple. We can share our experiences with you, but what would be the most valuable is for you to go to the Creator. He knows about the evil that inspires the Kabul. He can tell you how to defend yourself against the evil and how to defeat the Kabul forces."

"Tell me how to meet with the Creator," requested the wizard. "We will show you the way," responded the ghost.

"Would you be able to fight with us against the Kabul forces?" asked the wizard.

"We can no longer fight," responded the ghost. "We can only guide you."

"Do you have any additional scrolls that have spells and which might help us?" requested the wizard.

"I will lead you to the scrolls," responded the ghost. "To meet the Creator you will need to enter Mirror Pond close to Giter and you will be pulled into the mudwumps' caves. They will bring you to the Creator."

"Going back to mirror pond is dangerous because the area is overrun by Kabul forces," explained the wizard. "Is there another way to enter the mudwumps' caves?"

"Yes, but it is more complicated," explained the ghost. "We will need to contact the mudwumps and have them come to the surface to get you. We will work on contacting them while you search the scrolls. Follow me to the scrolls."

The ghost led the wizard to the temple scrolls. He was extremely excited to view these scrolls because he was certain they would contain the secrets that he was searching for and he found several scrolls that showed promise. He immediately started reading them looking for ideas that might help him save Small World. Unfortunately, he became so engulfed in the scrolls that he didn't realize how late in the day it had become until one of the ghosts came back to fetch him and explained, "It is too late for you to leave the temple. The riposters are already flying. We can hide you in a tomb for the night. Can I help you get into one of our tombs?"

The wizard was surprised at how late it had become and responded, "Oh no! I can't leave or I'll get killed. I feel I must accept your invitation. Please show me the way."

The ghost led the wizard to the area of the crypts and pointed at one that was slightly opened. Then the ghost said, "This crypt is my tomb. You can crawl in here. It has a handle on the inside so you can pull it closed. I will come in the morning and let you know when it is safe to come out."

The wizard was extremely uncomfortable having to spend the night in a tomb, but he knew he didn't have a choice. Any other option involved the riposters and he had already seen the damage they can cause. The crypt was in a wall. It was a three foot wide by three foot high hole that was about six foot deep. It was about two yards off the ground. The wizard pulled open the door to the crypt and crawled in feet first, struggling because of how far it was off the ground. For some reason he assumed the crypt would be empty but instead he encountered the skull and bones of the owner of the crypt. His first reaction was to want to escape the crypt, but again he realized he didn't have a choice. He would have to spend the night lying next to the bones of the ghost that had brought him here.

The wizard pulled closed the crypt's door. He found himself in total blackness, trying to sleep without the aid of a pillow. He slowly became comfortable with his situation and resigned himself to his predicament. He searched for, found, and pulled the skull of the ghost over, laid it on its side, and used it as his pillow. He decided that he might as well sleep because that was the only choice he had.

Morning came around sooner than expected. The wizard was awoken by the sound of the ghost yelling out, "You can open the crypt and come out now. I hope you enjoyed sleeping on my head."

The wizard pushed open the door to the crypt and slowly crawled out. He ached in places he didn't know could ache, after sleeping on a cold rock surface all night. And his pillow wasn't very comfortable either. Once he had escaped the crypt he said, "That was a miserable night. I'm sure glad that is over with."

"It was the best we could do under the circumstances," responded the ghost.

"Thank you for helping me," responded the wizard, afraid that he might have offended the ghost.

The ghost went on to say, "We have sent a message out to the mudwumps but since they can't communicate we don't know if they will come to get you or not. For now you can continue looking at the scrolls. We should know soon enough if they are coming."

"That's perfect," responded the wizard as he proceeded to return to the scrolls so he could review the ones he hadn't yet considered.

He spent the next couple hours rummaging through the scrolls. He had discovered a couple that he found extremely interesting and he decided to take them with him. As he was going through the last of the scrolls he was suddenly knocked to the ground. He felt his side where he was hit and it was encased in mud. "What's that?" he demanded.

"The mudwumps are here to take you to the Creator," responded one of the ghosts. "It's time for you to leave."

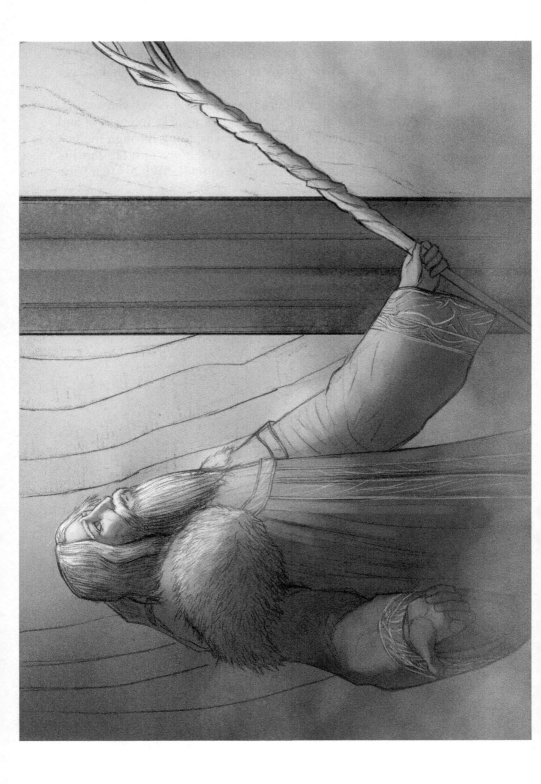

CHAPTER SEVENTEEN

THE CREATOR

The Kabul Prince Kakakrul was monitoring the progress of the Kabul army as it marched down the South Road toward Amins when he received a message from his dwarf spy. The message was in the form of a humm, where the spy crossed her legs, folded her arms, closed her eyes, bowed her head, and began to hum. Ejij-twenty, the first assistant to Ejijone, said "Hummmmm ummmmm ummmmm," much like a chant for several minutes, and the prince was able to hear it.

The prince rushed back up into the Kabul, heading toward Morgos where his spy had last communicated with him but then, when she repeated the humm he realized that the call was coming from somewhere around Gamotz. He circled around, looking for his spy, and finally spotted her in a brush on the east side of Gamotz. He landed, changed himself to his princely form, and walked up to her.

"I thought I wasn't going to hear from you anymore," questioned the prince.

"I had a change of heart because it looks like we might get captured and become prisoners of the Kabul and I want to make sure you'll help me escape," replied Ejijtwenty.

"Of course," replied the prince, willing to say whatever she wanted in order to get the information he needed. "What news do you have for me?"

"We wiped out the magotite army at Morgos. We may have eliminated the entire species, but I think your father the Lord would be able to create more if he needs them. Right now we're attacking Gamotz and it seems deserted of any military gnomes. There only

seems to be women and children there. Once we've taken over the city, we'll use it as a fortress, just like we used Morgos, and ward off any gnomes as they try to return home. That's the update. There are no plans beyond that. Nothing else has been shared but I think that's because nothing else has been planned."

The prince was speechless. After a short pause he asked, "You really think you wiped out the entire magotite army? How many of the creatures did you actually kill?"

She responded, "Maybe ten thousand. They just kept coming and we had control of the city so we were able to use the fortress for protection. They kept trying to climb the walls and we just hacked them down as they came up. It was an awful slaughter. The bodies were piled so high that you could almost walk over the wall by walking up the ramp of bodies. Our group of women are planning on doing something similar to the gnomes as they start returning."

The prince's mind was reeling. He wouldn't dare give this information to the gnomes or else they would just turn around and head back home. He would just have to wait until they had destroyed Amins and Gije. Then he would share this information with them so they could return to their homes and put an end to this pesky female army.

"Thanks for the information," responded the prince after about ten minutes of thoughtful quiet.

"What are you going to do?" asked the spy.

"I have no idea," responded the prince. "But it won't be pretty."

"Don't forget to take care of me," responded the spy.

"Of course," responded the prince even though he had no intention of doing anything for her. To him she was just another casualty of the conquest of Small World. And as for the gnomes, as long as they do their duty conquering Amins and Gije, and possibly Hilebin if he can get them to bypass Gamotz on the way north, then the whole species of gnomes can be wiped out for all he cared. Good riddance. Just give him the victory and control of Small World.

The prince changed back to his eagle form and flew off toward the South Road to see how his army was doing in their conquest of Amins.

Sitting on a branch, not far from where the prince and Ejij-twenty were meeting, sat an owl.

***

The wizard got up from the ground and tried his best to wipe the mud off his left side. One of the ghosts explained, "The mudwumps have arrived and you need to go with them."

A different ghost explained, "It's time for you to leave. Just follow this mudwump and he will take you to the Creator."

The wizard grabbed a couple of the temple scrolls that he thought might prove to be helpful. Then he turned and started following behind the mudwump. The two went outside of the temple and headed in the direction of a small hill. Then suddenly and unexpectedly the mudwump crashed into the side of the hill and seemed to dissolve into the mound. But, to the wizard's surprise, a tunnel opened up behind the creature and gave access for the wizard.

At first the wizard stopped, slightly hesitant about entering this strange cavern created by the mudwump. It was lower than the wizard so he had to bend over in order to enter the cave. However he knew he had to move forward so he proceeded to enter. He was no more than a few feet past the entrance of the cave when the dirt started closing in behind him. It closed as if it was a door. The wizard reached back to touch the newly formed wall and found it to be as solid as the sides of the cave.

As they continued to progress through the cave, it continued to close in behind them. Eventually they arrived at a large cavern. The wizard was thankful because he could now stand up. Up to now crawling through the cave had given him a severe backache and a pain in the neck. It felt wonderful to stretch.

The wizard looked back at the cave that he had just travelled through and it had entirely disappeared. It had become a solid wall like any other wall in the cavern.

The mudwump he had been following crashed into him in what seemed like announce. Apparently, the wizard had become too distracted by his surroundings and was no longer following the mudwump like he was supposed to, and this was the creature's way of letting him know he was to continue following him.

They wound around through a menagerie of caves, going up and down, making numerous turns. Sometimes the caves were too low for the wizard to stand up and other times the caves were quite large. The entire time the caves were lit by a strange orange light, the same orange light that the wizard had seen Bydola carry. The wizard recalled how Bydola had explained that he had received the healing powers from the Creator, and this must be the same location where Bydola had travelled to when he was pulled into Mirror Pond.

Finally they arrived at an enormous cave with smooth walls and no decorations. They stepped into the cave and then the mudwump immediately departed. The entrance closed behind the mudwump leaving no trace of where the door had been. The smoothly polished rock surface of the cave glowed in an orange light that filled the entire room. It was a strange mysterious light. The wizard could look directly at the light and not have his vision affected. In the center was a large, cubic, polished rock floating and slowly spinning. The wizard assumed that this was the seat of the Creator.

"Welcome my friend," came what sounded like a calm, gentle, elderly voice. The voice seemed to emanate from all directions of the cave at once.

The wizard found it difficult to form words. He had so much he wanted to ask, but found himself too captivated to talk. "You need me," spoke the Creator. "I am the one called the Creator, but some know me as the God of the Rainbow, and others call me the God of Light. And I have many other names with the various species in Small World. In the past there has been a balance between good and evil. That balance with the destructive evil has given safety to the southern and northern inhabitants. However, that balance has been disrupted and the evil now wants to throw out the good and rule everything. The evil has manifested itself in the Kabul. The Small World has hopes to defeat the Kabul, yet you know very little of what's at risk. Lord Krakus has found power by aligning with the root of all evil, Master Kwdad who is also known as the Destroyer. Only Krakus communicates with this master of evil and Kwdad has given the lord the power to recognize the Protee powers that Bydola has received from me. He plans to eliminate Bydola and thereby eliminate the Protee from Small World."

The Creator continued, "I am proud of the many species and what they are attempting. I am proud of their strength. Unfortunately the power of evil needs more than merely high-spirited and strong willed leprechauns, dwarfs and amazonionites for the Kabul to be defeated. You need to track down and eliminate this supreme evil or Small World will be defeated."

The wizard asked, "How will I find this evil source? How will I recognize it when I see it?"

"I will be giving you messages in your mind that are intended to be helpful and to give you direction. You have not experienced this

in the past, but I am giving you this ability now using the Protee power. This is the same power that I have also given to Bydola."

The Creator continued, "I will be able to read your thoughts. If you want to communicate with me, just think as if you're talking to me, much like a prayer. Think your thoughts and I will try to respond. I may not always respond, and that just means that I don't care which way you go, so don't bother me with trivial nonsense. Only ask for my help if it is vital to your mission of saving Small World. Now go, find, and eliminate the evil that exists in the Kabul."

"How do identify this evil?" asked the wizard. "Will I be able to recognize it when I see it, or will you be giving me messages that tells me it is right in front of me? And then, once you've told me that the evil is in front of me, what do I do to eliminate it?"

"You will be directed in all of this," replied the wizard. "The access cave that will lead you to the evil which is Kwdad is in the Lord's chambers behind a hidden wall that is behind his desk. You must go there, get into Kwdad's cave network, find him, and eliminate him. Otherwise this evil will reoccur again and again without end."

"You've given me no small task," responded the wizard.

"I also give you the Protee power of light. In order to produce light you need to say your secret name which is Raviump. Touch a stone and say the phrase, 'By the power of the Protee, I Raviump turn this stone into light.' The stone will start to glow. You will need this power when you search for Kwdad."

"Thank you," said the wizard.

"Only you can do this task," responded the Creator. "Now go! And beware the eagle."

Magically the door opened and the mudwump was at the door waiting for the wizard in order to lead him back to the Tako Ruins.

They started their journey, reversing their way through the tunnels. It was just as slow and uncomfortable as the previous journey. After about an hour the wizard received his first telepathic message from the Creator. The Creator said, "Your visit to me has taken the most of the day and now it is late. It would not be good for you to return to the surface. By the time you get there the riposters will be active. You must stay in the mudwump cave for the night. They know that they need to give you a place to stay for the night. They will get you close to your exit point and then settle you in. Tomorrow morning they will return you to the Tako temple and

you can resume your search of the scrolls, but don't spend too much time at it. The key for you is the elimination of the evil known as Kwdad. And you now have all the tools and power you will need in order to accomplish that objective."

"Thank you again," thought the wizard and he hoped that the Creator heard his message.

He continued to follow the mudwump through the tunnels for another hour. Then, without any hint that they were coming to the end of their journey, the mudwump turned into a cave which had a raised platform on it. After the wizard entered, the mudwump left and suddenly the door closed. The wizard was left in the dark.

"This is strange," said the wizard, "but it's better than sleeping in a crypt with a bunch of bones."

He decided to test his new powers and, touching the stone shelf, he said, "By the power of the Protee, I Raviump turn this stone into light."

Immediately not only the shelf, but the entire room lit up with the orange light that he had experienced throughout his time in the caves. He sat on the shelf amazed at himself and at the power he had been given. Eventually he laid himself down and went to sleep.

The morning came and the wizard was awaken by the opening of the door to his chamber. The awakening was so sudden that it left him a little groggy. He slowly came around and discovered the mud-wump guide waiting for him at the door. He stood up and started walking toward the mudwump who moved away. They were off, with the wizard rushing to keep up with his mudwump guide.

It wasn't long before they were again working their way through a cave that seemed to be creating itself as they moved forward, and closing itself behind them as they passed. It was a little unnerving for the wizard because it felt a little like a tomb. They were in a hole in the middle of the earth with no sense of how deep they were in the ground.

However, the wizard had no choice. He had to push ahead. He wanted to get out of this hole as quickly as possible because it was starting to freak him out.

Suddenly, and abruptly, they exited the cave in the exact same place where they had entered it the previous morning. There, waiting for him, was one of the temple ghost Shadow warriors that he was dealing with previously. The ghost said, "Welcome back. I hope your visit with the Creator was successful."

"Very much so," responded the wizard. "Thanks for taking such good care of me. Now I better finish going over the scrolls so I can leave here before nightfall."

"Of course," responded the ghost. "Follow me."

The wizard spent the remainder of the day looking through the scrolls and selecting another one that he thought would have useful information. He kept careful watch on the sun. He didn't want to be stuck in that crypt another night. He wanted to make sure he left the Tako Ruins before sunset.

At the end of the day the wizard returned to his camp in the woods on the east side of the Tako Ruins. He was disappointed to find that some animals had rummaged through his belongings and had stolen some of his food. But that was to be expected since he hadn't attended to his camp for the last two nights.

After he cleaned up the mess, he decided to stay in that camp for the night. However, sleep was difficult to achieve. He now had been given the responsibility of a nearly impossible task. And he was filled with questions. How was he going to get to Tragis and still be alive? How was he going to get into the city? How was he going to get into Lord Krakus' chambers? How was he going to find the secret access door to the tunnel the led to Kwdad's cave? And how was he going to battle Kwdad and eliminate him in order to bring peace to Small World? He felt it was extremely unfair that he should be given this mission. He felt like he was now tasked with saving the entirety of Small World by himself. The peace of Small World depended completely on him. Why had they crossed the swords and brought him out of his hibernation, only to be cruelly tasked with something that he knew was impossible. He wondered if he would be able to come out of this mission alive.

CHAPTER EIGHTEEN

THE ATTACK ON AMINS

Prince Kakakrul returned to the South Road and followed it until he caught up with the Kabul army. It was halfway between Giter and Amins when he finally found them. He watched in his eagle form from high up in a tree on the west side of the South Road. He was beside himself with excitement about the destruction that was about to be unleashed.

The prince knew he had to keep any information about the destruction of Morgos, and the current invasion of Gamotz, a secret or it would change the level of motivation felt by his warriors. He, in conjunction with his father, wanted control of Small World and wanted to be rid of the species that wouldn't support that control. For Kakakrul, that could also include the elimination of the magotites and the gnomes. If, over the next couple days, Amins and Gije could both be destroyed, then the dwarfs should be an easy target as well. He hadn't even tapped into the full strength of the troll army, and they were the best weapon that was available to him. They could finish off the dwarfs all by themselves.

The prince was conflicted by the assignment that his father had given him. He would watch the destruction of Amins and see if he could identify the wizard and the individual with the Protee powers. With any luck, the army would eliminate them and his task would be completed. He decided he needed to watch the attack as it unfolded in order to see if anyone stood out as being either of these individuals.

About three hours later the Kabul forces rounded the bend and could see Amins in the distance. The gnomes became fired up and excited. They started yelling and running waving their swords in

the air like a swarm of wild banshees. If anyone would see these wild gnomes coming in their direction, they would be sure to run.

The trolls continued at their same pace. They weren't excited at the sight of the city. They knew that this would be an easy slaughter and they would wait till the gnomes were done, then they would do any cleanup that needed doing.

The gnomes came crashing into the city and started burning everything in sight. But they were disappointed by the lack of leprechauns. There were only a few stragglers to be found and they were easily dispatched. But the gnomes enjoyed themselves in their destruction.

The gnomes destroyed everything, including the statue in the fountain in the center of the city, and all the houses and workshops. Then they burned the council building to the ground. The gnome leader Duke Kaklu, yelled out, "Where are you cowards? Where are you leprechauns? Come out here and fight. We've destroyed your city. Have you no respect for yourselves. You're just weepy, whiny wimps. Get a little backbone. Show yourselves."

Those were his last words. Seemingly from nowhere four arrows suddenly found themselves in Kaklu's chest and he dropped dead on the spot. Kaklu's second in command Klakaly, screamed out, "You cowards. You have to be sneaky and attack from a hiding spot. Come out here and fight one on one. Send your women out here. They're probably braver than you are." Little did he know that his prophecy was coming to pass and that it was the women who were simultaneously invading Gamotz and taking over the gnome homeland.

There was a pause and then the threats continued, "You can't hide out in the forest. We're going to burn the Amins Groves to the ground, just like we did your city. Then you won't have a choice but to come out here and fight."

The Gnome captain ordered fire to be set in several places all along the edge of the groves. But he didn't know that the Amins Groves' trees were living trees.

***

Bydola, Elasti, Hasko, Hiztin, and dozens of leprechauns were sitting in the Amins Groves, high up in the trees, watching the destruction of their homes. It was all they could do to restrain themselves from charging out there and doing battle with the gnomes, but they were so badly outnumbered that they knew it would be suicide. However, when the gnome duke started his rampage, several of the leprechauns, who were expert bowmen, lost their restraint and let the arrows fly.

Then, when the gnomes threatened to burn the groves Bydola whispered, "Pass this message along. These trees don't allow themselves to be burnt. We learned this when we were heading northward towards the dwarfs. Stay where you are and watch what the trees do."

"That's crazy," whispered Hasko. "You're telling me that these trees put out fires?"

"Exactly," responded Elasti. "Just watch."

The gnomes started the fires by collecting the remains of some of the Amins buildings and piling them up under the trees on the edge of the Amins Groves. The old, dried lumber from the burnt buildings lit up easily. Soon the flames reached skyward and started to singe the bark and the branches. And then it happened. The trees reacted just as Bydola predicted and the lower branches from the trees swung down in a loop crashing into the fire piles and blasting them back at the gnomes.

Many of the gnomes screamed in pain as their clothes and skin started to singe and burn. Gnomes are selfish creatures and instead of helping to put out the fires that were burning on their companions, they feared getting burnt themselves, and they ran away from their burning companions and just let them burn. A large number of gnomes were killed, not because they were attacked by the leprechauns, but because they were attacked by the trees.

***

Klakaly was extremely upset and yelled out, "Forget the fires. Cut the trees down!"

Several gnomes scurried around finding saws in the leprechaun tool sheds. Most of the sheds had been burnt but the metal saws were still findable and usable. The gnomes came at the trees and started sawing at the base, but before they could cut more than a couple inches into the trees, branches again started falling and they gave the gnomes a hard crack on the side of their heads. Many of the gnomes were killed instantly and several more were badly injured.

Klakaly, seeing that he was losing the battle with the trees, yelled out a command, "We're done here. We've destroyed the city of Amins! We're not here to do battle with a bunch of trees. These leprechauns are too cowardly to come out here and fight. They're hiding behind the protection of these trees so we can't get close to them."

Just then the Kabul prince swept in, changed to his princely form, and barked, "Forget the trees. Forget trying to burn them or cut them down. Charge into the forest and attack the leprechauns. They're hiding in there in camps. Get in there and destroy them. I want the leprechaun population wiped out and I want it to happen right now!"

Klakaly added, "You heard the prince. Charge into the forest and wipe out the leprechauns."

The gnomes, letting out a cry, and in mass, again like a band of screaming banshees, charged into the forest.

The trees knew that the leprechauns were their friends and that these gnomes, who had tried to burn them and cut them down, were indeed their enemies. As the gnomes and trolls charged through the forest, the trees moved themselves and their branches so that the leprechaun camps were hidden from the view of the Kabul forces. The gnomes and trolls charged through the forest like madmen for hours, assuming that eventually they would find these mysterious leprechaun camps, but they were unsuccessful. They backtracked and repeated their search, but all their efforts were unsuccessful. Eventually, after hours of running and screaming, they burst out of the west side of the Amins Groves, close to Alice Lake. Not one leprechaun had been found or harmed other than the few that had not left the city earlier and were killed during the Amins invasion.

They were again met by the prince who had taken on his eagle form long enough to travel from Amins to the west side of the groves. He changed back to his prince form and walked up to the gnome leader.

"That was crazy," complained Klakaly. "How could our entire army have missed all the leprechauns, unless they weren't in the groves at all."

"There is the possibility that they had some kind of invisibility spell, or that they found refuge in a cave, or that they left the area around Amins altogether," responded the prince. "I am going to fly

around the area and try to find them. I want you to organize the troops and start a march toward Gije. Go back to the Avol River crossing and get everyone across to the west side of the river. Then continue along the South Road until you get to the Albo Pass which is the point where you head south. I will stay here for a little while and do a search for the leprechauns and then I will catch up with you and join you for the attack on Gije."

"Yes, my prince," responded Klakaly and he went to work organizing his troops and instructing them on the next part of their war against the Southern Plains.

***

The Kabul prince was frustrated. Not only were they not able to wipe out the leprechaun species, but the wizard and the Protee power carrier were nowhere to be found. No one was killed. He wanted Amins to be flowing in blood, but that didn't happen. Instead, it was a bunch of stupid gnomes that were killed. Of course, the city was burnt to the ground, but the leprechauns were still alive and well. Where were they? How were they able to avoid the entire Kabul army?

The prince headed back to Amins in his eagle form. He wanted to solve this mystery. As he flew overhead over the city he could see leprechauns slowly coming out of the forest and surveying the destruction that had been reeked on their homes. They had been in the forest all along, but where were they? Why wasn't his army able to find them? Are there hidden caves? Does the wizard have some kind of invisibility spell that he uses on them?

The prince continued to circle around, hoping to see something that would give away who the wizard was or who the Protee power holder was. Unfortunately, no one was injured and so no one needed to be healed. The prince decided he was going to injure someone and see if that would draw out the healer. He would sneak into the leprechaun city and attack someone, bringing them close to death. Then he would watch to see what happens. He had a plan for finding the Protee healer, but he was frustrated because he wasn't sure how to draw out the wizard.

The prince started to carry out his plan. He flew down to Amins, landing in a location where no one could see him, and converted himself into his princely form. He waited for some unfortunate leprechaun to come close to him and then he pounced.

The poor leprechaun was caught totally by surprise when the prince jumped out at him and stabbed him in the stomach. It happened so quickly that he didn't even have time to scream before he fell to the ground. But this didn't give the prince what he was hoping for. He wanted other leprechauns to come to the aid of the injured so that he could watch for the healer. Not getting the desired response, the prince yelled out, "Help! He's been hurt. Come and save him."

Then the prince snuck away and quickly changed into his eagle form. He flew high into the sky and watched as several leprechauns ran over to help their injured friend. Several more leprechauns started running around, looking for the attacker which they were unable to find. This caused the prince to chuckle because he had so successfully eluded them.

From there on it all went exactly as the prince had planned. They carried the injured leprechaun to the central fountain while another leprechaun ran off into the forest, assumedly to bring out the Protee healer. Soon the healer arrived at the fountain and put his staff into the fountain transforming it and cleansing it. Then they laid the injured leprechaun in the fountain while the Protee healer performed another ritual with his staff. There were several flashes of orange light and then the previously injured leprechaun stood up as if nothing had happened to him. His clothes were still cut but there was no more wound.

The prince had become so completely impressed by watching the healing process that he had entirely forgotten to plan his attack against the Protee healer. Before he realized what was happening, the healer had disappeared back into the forest. But it hadn't been a total waste of time. The prince now knew who the healer was, and he would come back later to eliminate him. He would pick a time when the healer wasn't the center of attention; when there weren't so many leprechauns around and then he would eliminate him.

Unfortunately, the prince didn't see anyone that looked like a wizard. He thought to himself that maybe the wizard wasn't in Amins anymore or maybe the individual that was dragged away in the Avol River and who was now in the Lamos was in fact the wizard and that problem had taken care of itself.

The prince knew that he wasn't going to see the healer again that day so he decided to depart from Amins and fly back to the Avol River crossing where the Kabul forces were working their way towards Gije.

It took a few hours but soon the prince was flying over the river crossing area where the Kabul forces were actively trying to work their way across using the pull boat, which was the only way available to cross the Avol River. He perched up in a high tree and just watched for a few moments.

The prince knew that the journey to Gije would take a couple days so he decided to leave his Kabul Army alone on their journey and he would go and check on the battle that was raging in Gamotz.

The prince flew off toward the Kabul. He would come back in a couple days to join the attack on Gije and to hopefully eliminate the threat of the Protee healer.

CHAPTER NINETEEN

THE ATTACK ON GAMOTZ

The Swift army was finally close enough to Gamotz to hit the city walls with arrows. But, to their surprise, instead of the warriors shooting arrows into Gamotz, arrows started flying at the Swift warriors. And there was more bad news. The spies that had been watching Tragis came rushing up to Goglbarj yelling, "There is a troll army coming from Tragis and headed directly toward us!!!"

"Hurry," yelled Goglbarj. "We need to get inside the city! There's a troll army coming after us!"

The arrows coming from Gamotz were few and fairly random. It was obvious that this was not the effort of a focused military. This was done by just some random gnomes wildly shooting at the Swift women.

The female warriors pushed ahead and used shields to protect against the arrows. Then, unexpectedly, the flow of arrows from the city walls abruptly stopped. The warriors were encouraged and charged at the gate.

Before the Swift Army arrived at the gate the door that was within the much larger gate opened and an unarmed gnome stepped out. Goglbarj approached the gnome and realized that she was a female. The gnome asked, "I see that you are a female army. Are there no men among you?"

"None," replied Goglbarj, waiting to hear more about the gnome's request.

At this point the other Swift Army leaders had caught up with Goglbarj and they were all listening in on the conversation.

"All our men are gone," continued the gnome. "They have gone to destroy Amins and Gije. And we know that you are here to destroy us. But we heard that a troll army is headed our way and we hate the trolls even more than we hate you. If you will come in and help us defend against the trolls, we will allow you the safety of our city."

Goglbarj asked, "The trolls are coming to attack us, not you!"

The gnome answered, "They won't stop with you. They know that our men are gone, and they will come crashing into our city and take advantage of our women and kill any that won't cooperate. They will claim that abusing our women as their reward for protecting our city. It's happened before and it will happen again. We don't stand a chance. We will give you the protection of our walls if you help us against the trolls."

Goglbarj, knowing that the Swift Army would need to fight the trolls either way, and knowing that it would be easier to fight them from behind the walls of the city, responded, "That would be excellent, and we would appreciate the protection, but you must realize that if your male army returns we are also going to fight them, especially now that we know that they may be in the process of destroying our own homes."

The gnome answered, "We will fight one battle at a time, but you must know that if you are killing our men, we will be fighting against you. But for now, we need your help and protection against the trolls so bring your army inside and help us make a plan."

Normally Goglbarj would wait and get the opinions of the other leaders before making a decision as important as this one. She took a look at their faces, then turned back to the gnome and said, "We accept. Open your gates and let us in so we can put warriors along all of the walls."

The gnome turned, returned through the door that was in the city gate, and then the giant gates slowly started to swing open. The Swift army rushed inside the city. The gates were closed and sealed with several beams while the Swift archers were sent to the tops of the walls, preparing and waiting for the troll onslaught.

While all the preparations were being made, the Swift Army leaders continued their conversation with the four Gnome spokespersons. Goglbarj went through the introductions, introducing herself, Jesves, Queen Gushe, Princess Ejijone, and Giantess Annala. Then she said, "This is very strange. We came her to attack you and take over the city of Gamotz, but instead we are now working with you to protect the city."

Another of the gnome leaders said, "We trust you, because you are all women, more than we trust the other men of the Kabul. I know this is hard to understand, but that is the truth of the situation. We are especially very afraid of the trolls. They hate us and are extremely brutal to us. The female bond between us is stronger than our bond with the Kabul."

"I think I understand," replied Jesves. "Within the various species in our army there is also a great deal of mistrust and suspicion, but we have learned to bond together and fight together, and we have been very effective against the magotites. I'm just worried what's going to happen when the gnome men return home and find your city taken over by our army. We will be forced to fight them, and you will be forced to help them and fight against us."

"Our only response is that we need to fight one battle at a time, and right now the pressing battle will be with the trolls," responded the same gnome.

"We better get ready," responded Goglbarj, as the Swift warriors separated from the gnomes.

"We can't trust them," responded Jesves talking about the gnome women in a whisper. "You know they are planning to betray us."

"I agree," said Ejijone, "but I also agree that we need to fight this one battle at a time and if we have trolls coming after us we stand a better chance in here than we ever would out there."

"Let's get ready for the trolls," said Goglbarj and each of the Swift leaders went off to check on their warriors.

The Swift army, side by side with the gnomes, stood ready for the troll attack. It took another two hours before they could see the trolls coming around the end of the Sheere Cliffs and heading towards Gamotz from the northwest. "Here they come," yelled one of the amazonionite warriors on the wall.

It took another hour before the trolls were within shooting distance of Gamotz. Their weapons were primarily clubs, spears, and axes, with very few archers, which gave the Swift Army bowwomen a distinct advantage. As the trolls came within shooting range, the Swift archers were quick to put several arrows into each troll, felling them before they could do any harm.

There were about two hundred trolls and they were almost as tall as the giants. The tops of their heads nearly reached the tops of

the city walls and they could reach over the wall and grab one of the warriors if they were allowed to get close enough. But if they did reach up, it became the job of the dwarfs to use an ax and they hacked off the troll's arm.

The battle raged on. Often the archers would hit the troll but wouldn't cause enough damage to keep him from coming ahead. Additionally, the lengthy battle with the magotites had seriously reduced the supply of arrows, causing them to sparingly use their remaining supply. As some of the archers started running out of arrows, the dwarfs came up with a plan. About twenty dwarfs snuck out of the back door of the city, ten went around each side of the city, and worked their way to the front where the battle was raging. They were fortunate that the trolls didn't notice them at first. The trolls were too busy battling the Swift warriors on the tops of the wall to notice the short dwarfs coming around the side walls.

When the signal was given, the dwarfs started throwing their axes. They would throw their axes to each other on opposite sides of the battling trolls, cutting off the legs of the trolls on the way, cutting them halfway between their ankles and their knees. Each throw would cut at least one leg and, if they were lucky, two or three legs would be cut. The opposite dwarf would catch the ax and then throw it again in return. The trolls started falling over, screaming with pain.

The archers on the tops of the walls, held back and only shot at the trolls that made it past the battling dwarfs. Unfortunately, it wasn't long before the trolls in the back of the attacking line noticed the dwarfs and they charged directly at the dwarfs. Throwing axes at these trolls wasn't as effective because there wouldn't be a dwarf on the other side to retrieve and return the ax. However, if they didn't throw their ax, but rather held on to it waiting for the troll, they would get battered by a troll club before they could get a hit on the troll. The reach of the troll was much longer than that of the dwarfs.

In the end, the dwarfs were extremely successful and had eliminated about seventy of the trolls, while the arrows of the archers brought down about the same number. That left about the same number still raging toward the city.

It had been several hours of battling trolls and this came after the long day of battling at Morgos, which was followed by the long march to Gamotz, it had left the Swift warriors drained. Of the original twenty dwarfs that went out to battle, only five were able to escape the trolls' attack. Of the original archers, only about half still had arrows. Fear started to set in with the Swift warriors. They could see that so far they had been extremely successful against the trolls but they could also see that they still had a long way to go before the day's battles were over.

It was at this point, when the warriors were feeling frustrated, that the giants took it upon themselves to take over. They knew they were badly outnumbered with only thirty giants available to do battle, but they felt that they hadn't done their fair share, always staying in the background, and this was the point where their help was desperately needed. They opened the front gates of the city and charged out, shields and swords in hand.

Since the giants were taller and bigger than the trolls, it was a fearsome sight to see them charging at the trolls and the trolls, in confusion, became scattered, unsure what they should be doing. It was almost too easy for the giants to rampage through the remaining trolls and take them down one after another. Several of the trolls turned and started to run, but the giants knew that if any escaped, they would go back to Tragis and then there might be more trolls coming to Gamotz.

The thirty giants routed the remaining sixty trolls, killing them with almost every stroke. Then they chased down the escaping trolls and eliminated them as well. Sadly, four of the giants were killed, taken down because three or four trolls would gang up against them to accomplish their deed.

As the giants returned inside the city walls of Gamotz, a cheer went out celebrating the victory over the trolls. Everyone had worked hard, and everyone had done their share, and in the end the Swift army had accomplished the goal of taking over Gamotz and fighting and winning an impossible attack from the trolls.

The day was drawing to a close. It had been another long day for the warriors and they still had wounds to bind and warriors to bury. The amazonionites had the most casualties loosing thirty warriors while the leprechauns and the elves only lost ten.

The dwarfs lost the fifteen lives that had gone outside the city walls, and only one other. No one was sure how it happened, but somehow Ejijtwenty, the dwarf spy, was found dead. And it looked like someone from her own team had committed the murder. She had been hiding out in one of the gnome houses and one of the gnomes came to Goglbarj to inform her of the dead dwarf. Ejijtwenty's throat had been cut and she lay dead in a pool of her own blood. How she had been killed, and by whom, and why, remained a mystery for the entire Swift Army. But they were too focused on the possibility of a future troll attack to investigate the murder at this time.

Other than that no other dwarfs were lost, and the giants lost four. There were about forty gnomes who also lost their lives in the battle. The warriors went about accomplishing their medical and funeral tasks with respect and reverence.

It was a long night, but the warriors rested well. They were exhausted and needed a good night's rest, uncertain what the future had in store for them. Luckily the night was uneventful.

The following day the Swift Army leaders got together to discuss what they should do. It was Goglbarj who again started the conversation with, "As I see it, we have three options. One is that we feel successful and go home. Another is that we stay in Gamotz until the gnome army returns and we battle them whenever that happens. And the third option is that we attack Tragis."

Queen Gushe was quick to speak up,

"Giving up is not a plan,
　　We are too good to resign, that's bad,
Attacking Tragis is suicide,
　　Fighting trolls out in the open is mad.
　　We stay in Gamotz,
　　We rebuild our fate,
Make lots of arrows,
　　We wait."

Ejijone jumped into the conversation, "The queen is right. We have the risk of betrayal by the gnomes that are here, but we're not ready to quit nor are we ready to attack Tragis. Is there another option?"

Goglbarj spoke up jokingly, "The dwarfs and elves agree on something. That's amazing. We have two votes for staying. What do the giants and the leprechauns say?"

Giantess Annala spoke up and suggested, "I agree with staying until we're completely ready. But I think there is another option and that is that I am going to send one of my warriors to our home to bring in more support. We giants were very successful against the trolls and more of us will help a lot if we decide to attack Tragis."

Jesves agreed, "Let's stay here and prepare and depending on how many additional giants get recruited we can decide later if we feel strong enough to attack Tragis."

"Sounds like we have a plan," commented Goglbarj. "But let's keep a close eye on these gnomes and if we see anything suspicious let's warn each other right away. Let's not get careless. I'm positive that there has to be some plan that they've brewed up to get rid of us. We've served our purpose as far as they are concerned and I'm sure they want us gone, or even better, dead."

"Agreed," said Jesves, as the leadership group broke up and went about their tasks.

Giantess Annala went to her bravest warrior, Analoop, and instructed her on her task to go to the Sheere Cliffs and try to round up more warriors. Analoop asked, "Are we still female only or can we bring some of the men along?"

Annala responded, "If men come along, they will try to steal all the credit. I'd prefer that we keep it female only."

"Yes, my queen," said Analoop as she departed through the front gate on her mission.

Analoop left Gamotz and headed southeast knowing that she would need to cross the Avol River if she was to return to her home. She ran most of the way, hoping to get out of the Kabul before nightfall. She arrived at the mist wall and quickly crossed through it. However, to her surprise, after she crossed through she encountered three giants on the other side, with spears pointed at her.

"Where did you come from?" asked one of the giants.

"We have an army in the Kabul," responded Analoop. "We have conquered the magotites and wiped them out completely and now our army has taken over the city of Gamotz. We are there in full force, waiting for the return of the gnome army. Then we plan to wipe them out as well."

"But you're a girl," responded one of the other giants.

"Very observant," said Analoop. "And we're winning the war while you guys are sitting around staring at a mist wall."

The three giants back off and one of the asked, "Where are you headed?"

"Home," was her answer. "I'm rounding up more female warriors so we can win this war."

"There's a faster way," suggested one of the giants. "You don't need to go all the way down to the pull boat in order to cross the river. You can go to the spring from which the river originates, and you can get across there."

"Thanks for the idea," she responded. "How do I get there?"

"Go due east and you'll run into the river," answered the same giant. "If the river is flowing south, go north, and if it's flowing north, go south. Eventually you'll run into the spring and you can jump across there."

"Thanks," said Analoop as she started off running due east as directed.

Night came quickly and Analoop had to make camp. It was an uneventful evening and in the morning she continued her journey. She soon found the river, and that led her to the spring. She jumped across at the spring and she was well on her way back to her home on the Sheere Cliffs.

Chapter Twenty
The March to Gije

The prince left his Kabul Army working its way towards Gije and flew off toward the Kabul. He wanted to check out the information given to him by his spy and see if the attack on Gamotz had been successful. As he flew over Gamotz he was surprised to see that the Swift Army was indeed inside the city walls. They had conquered Morgos and now they were in possession of Gamotz. It was too much for him to accept. *How could a weakly trained group of female warriors conquer two of the three major cities of the Kabul. How could they overpower an army of ten thousand magotites?* Conquering Gamotz was easier to understand because all the gnome warriors were down on the South Road on their way to Gije. But it was still unbelievable that this band of women were able to accomplish so much with so little experience and training.

The prince started flying further north toward Tragis so that he could report to his father Lord Krakus. As he started his flight, he noticed a band of two hundred trolls marching southward. He assumed they were heading for Gamotz. He said to himself, "Apparently they know about the attack on Gamotz and have sent trolls to help out. I'm sure this band of trolls will have no trouble kicking those women out of Gamotz."

The prince landed outside of Tragis, transformed himself, and entered through the city gates. He went directly to his father's chambers, hoping to give him an update.

As he entered the chambers the Lord immediately asked, "Did you get rid of the wizard and the Protee healer?"

"Not yet but I know who the healer is and I'm watching for an opportunity to get rid of him," replied the prince. "I have no idea who or where the wizard is. I'm still watching for him but I think he left Amins. He doesn't seem to be anywhere around there."

"I need both of them eliminated," shouted the Lord. "They will become the thorn that keeps us from succeeding." Then after the pause he asked, "How are the gnomes doing?"

"They've wiped out Amins, but the inhabitants seemed to have disappeared into the forest, and the forest trees seem to be alive. They put out a fire that we tried to start, and they won't let us cut any of the trees down. Somehow they are hiding and protecting the leprechauns."

The Lord was getting angrier by the minute, "So there are still leprechauns! The reason for wiping out Amins was to get rid of the leprechauns, not to just make a mess of their city!"

"I understand," said the prince. "Right now they are on their way to destroy Gije. Then we will go back to Amins and see if we can't finish what we started earlier."

"You do that," demanded the Lord, "and finish the task of getting rid of the wizard and the healer."

"Do you have any ideas about how to capture the leprechauns?" asked the prince. "The gnomes and trolls that were down there searched the forest and could not find them. I think the trees are hiding them. How do I break the spell that is protecting these pesky creatures?"

"That's probably the wizard's doing," responded the Lord. "You have to get rid of the wizard! That's the key. As long as he is around, he will be using his spells to prevent us from accomplishing our goals."

"Understood," responded the prince. "And I suppose you know about the female warriors that have invaded the Kabul. They claim to have destroyed the magotite army and they are now in possession of Gamotz. They were able to conquer the gnome city because all the gnome warriors are at war down south."

"Yes," replied the Lord. "I know about them and I sent a band of two hundred trolls down there to solve the problem. They should be arriving there now. Those invaders should be eliminated in the next couple hours."

"Good," responded the prince. He didn't want to say anymore because his father was already pretty angry. Then, after a pause, he said, "It's late and I'm going to spend the night here. Then I better get back to my army on the South Road and see how the attack of Gije is going."

"Report back to me in a few days," commanded the Lord. "I want to hear that you've accomplished your mission."

"Will do," responded the prince as he departed.

The following morning the prince transformed back into his eagle shape and departed. First he headed north to see if the story of the magotites was true. He found it to be exactly as described by his spy. Then he turned to head south toward Gamotz to see if the trolls had wiped out the warriors that had invaded the city there. To his utter disappointment he found that the field in front of Gamotz was strewn with troll bodies. Inside the city walls he found dwarfs, leprechauns, elves, amazonionites, giants, and as a total shock, he also found gnomes walking around. The prince barked at himself out loud, "What the heck? The gnomes are helping the enemy. What's that all about?"

The prince considered going back and reporting what he had learned to his father so he could send another army of trolls to Gamotz. But then he reconsidered the idea because he remembered how angry his father had gotten and how he insisted that the prince not come back until the wizard and the Protee carrier had been eliminated. "There will be time for taking these intruders out after we conquer Gije."

The prince flew over the South Road and saw the Kabul Army was about halfway between Giter and Gije, and that they still had about a half day of traveling to do, so he flew on to Amins with the hope that he would be able to spot the wizard or the Protee carrier.

He circled over the city of Amins for about one hour, watching the leprechauns as they slowly started to clean up the mess and re-build their city. He didn't notice anyone or anything unusual. After the hour he saw several individuals come out of the forest and he immediately recognized one of the individuals as the healer. He watched carefully to see where the healer went. He hoped for the opportunity to find the healer isolated so he could sweep down and attack him by surprise.

He patiently waited, but the healer always seemed to be in a group. He was never isolated. The prince waited for another hour. He wasn't going to miss this chance to accomplish one of his assigned missions. Then it happened. An opportunity presented itself. Bydola, the leprechaun that had received the Protee powers from the Creator including the power to heal, entered what was left of a burnt out building without anyone else joining him. He was by himself.

The eagle swooped down and landed behind the partial wall of the building on a side where no one could see him and transformed himself into his prince form. He pulled a knife from his belt. He watched the healer until his back was turned. Then the prince jumped through a hole in the wall and attacked, stabbing Bydola in the neck and several times in the stomach.

Bydola fell to the ground, unable to move. He let out a loud groan but wasn't able to scream because of the cut to the neck. He had clung to his staff as he fell, hoping to brace himself with it, but to no avail. He lay on the ground, slowly bleeding away his life.

The prince returned through the hole that he had used to enter the structure where he had attacked the healer. He transformed himself into an eagle and started to fly upwards, but he moved slowly, wanting to watch Bydola and make sure he was dead. But that was a mistake. His slow rise caused Hiztin to notice him and he quickly let an arrow fly in the prince's direction. The arrow travelled through the left wing of the eagle, causing it to shriek in pain. Luckily for the prince, it didn't affect his ability to fly. The arrow had travelled completely through the wing. But it gave him a considerable amount of pain.

Back on the ground Hiztin let out a yell, "The eagle. It's the Kabul prince here to do his evil."

Several more arrows were shot at the prince by various leprechauns, but the eagle had now climbed quickly to the point where the arrows were no longer able to reach him. The prince made his escape, assuming he had accomplished the mission that was given to him by his father. He had eliminated the Protee healer.

***

Hiztin, Hasko, and Elasti knew that this was trouble. If the prince was here, something bad must have happened. They rushed into the structure where Bydola had been attacked and found him lying on the ground unconscious and bleeding away the remainder of his life. They quickly grabbed him up and ran over to the central fountain, which they knew had been purified the previous day. They slowly lowered him into the fountain, placed his staff in his arm, and waited. They weren't sure what, if anything would happen.   They   weren't sure how the Protee powers worked. All they could do was hope for the best and pray.

After about five minutes Bydola groaned and Elasti tried to talk to him saying, "Bydola, how do we make this healing power work?"

Bydola groaned again and said, "I'll try. Only I can do it." Then he mumbled some words. The three companions couldn't understand what the words were, they were whispered so quietly that they were inaudible. But then, to everyone's surprise, the flash of orange light occurred and seemed to travel up and down Bydola's body.

Bydola wasn't cured instantly. At first he slowly escaped his drowsiness and regained full consciousness. Then he began to talk, and he asked, "What happened?"

Elasti, who was closest to him, responded, "The Kabul prince attacked you."

Bydola seemed to understand. He clung onto his staff and again mumbled some inaudible words. Then there was another flash of the orange light and suddenly Bydola seemed to be back to normal. He had healed himself, to everyone's relief and happiness.

***

The prince was in pain from the arrow that had passed through his wing. He dropped off and landed on the ground just after he had passed over the Amins Groves. He transformed himself into his princely form in order to inspect his damaged body. It was his right arm that had been pierced. There were no broken bones, but the arrow had penetrated the flesh of his upper arm. He was bleeding badly from both the entry and the exit wounds. He now questioned his actions. Why did he delay his escape, giving the leprechauns a chance to shoot at him? He was extremely angry and swore out loud, "I'm going to make sure every leprechaun is eliminated before I'm through. One way or another their species is going to be completely wiped out."

As he mumbled to himself, he ripped off a piece of his shirt sleeve. It was easy to rip because it had already been torn by the arrow. Then he tied the ripped piece around his arm covering the wound on both sides of his arm using his teeth and his second arm to pull it tight. It seemed to slow down the bleeding but it didn't completely end the blood flow. He knew he would have to catch up with the Kabul Army and have the gnome doctor look to see if he could prepare a better bandage.

The prince converted back into his eagle form and flew off toward the northwest to try to catch up with his troops. He was starting to get weak and he feared that he might faint and fall out of the sky so he rushed his journey as much as possible.

The prince successfully arrived at the front of the swarm of Kabul troops. They didn't march in any disciplined fashion. They travelled as a merged mess forming into a jumbled mass of noisy bodies.

The prince landed off to the side, in the trees, converted himself to his princely form, and then yelled out, "I need the gnome doctor urgently."

Klakaly, who had taken the reins as leader of the gnomes after the death of the duke, looked over and saw the prince stumbling out of the forest. He ran over to the prince and saw that he was bleeding badly. "I'll get you help," he said then he instructed the prince, "Sit down and wait here."

A short time later Klakaly returned with the doctor in tow and the doctor went to work gluing the wounds together with tree sap. The pain was so intense that the prince fainted and lay on the ground as if dead. Then the doctor tied a better bandage around the prince's arm. The flow of blood had been stopped. But the prince was now too weak to move on his own.

Klakaly went to the trolls and explained, "The prince has been badly wounded. He is nearly unconscious and needs to be carried. Can you have someone bind him to their back and carry him so we can continue on our journey?"

"I can do it," responded one of the larger and stronger trolls. A harness was created which looked a lot like a carrier that would hold a baby. It was strapped to the back of the volunteering troll, and the prince was strapped down and tied to the troll's back. Since the prince was less than half the height of the troll, it looked a lot like the troll was carrying a small child on his back.

Having successfully taken care of the prince, the march to Gije was able to resume. Soon they would be passing the Kilo Pass which led to the Tako Ruins. Then they would be crossing the Avoli River bridge. At that point it became dark and they made camp on the west side of the river.

The following day saw the Kabul troops energetic and excited. They knew that they would be arriving on the Jove Plateau and be

within shooting distance of Gije. The attack on the elf city may not be able to start until the following morning, but they would be there and they would be ready.

The prince had regained consciousness but was still extremely weak. He was embarrassed to have to be carried by a troll, as if he was a weak small child, but he had no other choice. He wanted to be there when the army arrived at Gije. He was just as excited to see this attack begin as everyone else in the Kabul Army.

The march continued and soon turned south when they encountered the Albo Pass. After that they started a slow single file march up the winding path that would get them to the top of the plateau.

After arriving on the top of the plateau they set up a temporary camp while they waited for everyone to arrive. Because of the single file march, it would take several hours for everyone to arrive. Then, as the last of the Kabul Army arrived at the top, they would again be ready to resume their march to Gije.

It was becoming late in the day and the troops were becoming weary, but they insisted on continuing their march until Gije was visible in the distance. The sun was just setting when they could finally see the spires of the city off to the southeast. They let out a cheer, again screaming like wild banshees. Their target was in sight. Tomorrow would be the day of their victory over the elves. Tomorrow they would wipe out the entire species. Tomorrow would be incredible.

Or would it?

Didn't they remember that this was where the last Lifefight war was lost?

Did they know about the werewolves?

Chapter Twenty-One

The Battle at Gije

Analoop the giant rushed across the Southern Plains just south of the Sheere Cliffs on her way to her home. She arrived in the early afternoon and went directly down into her network of caves. She knew how to find most of the giants. It would be in the central meeting hall, which was an enormous cave where most of the giants hung out and which served as the center of her city.

Once she arrived, she stood on the central platform, which was used for speeches and for entertainment. Then she yelled out, "I have news of the war." The giants that were in the area started to quiet down and she repeated her call. The large population of giants that were in the area started to converge on the central platform. They were anxious to hear Analoop's update.

Once everyone had quieted down, Analoop gave the details of their exploits. She explained how the females of the various species had banded together to form their own army and how they had conquered the magotites and conquered the city of Morgos. Then she explained how they travelled to Gamotz where they did battle with the trolls. She explained how they were now in control of Gamotz but they were worried about future troll attacks, and about the return of the gnomes to their home. Then she pleaded, "We need more warriors. We need your help if we are to maintain Gamotz and possibly attack Tragis, the last stronghold of the Kabul and the home of Lord Krakus."

Someone in the audience yelled out, "How many giants have been killed?"

"Four," she replied.

Someone else said, "Only four. That seems impossible."

"The other species that are supporting our cause, and which are part of the Swift Army, have taken the brunt of the deaths," responded Analoop. "They have been extremely aggressive and are great warriors. We owe them a lot and that's why I've been sent her to get more recruits. We need your help and support."

"Our warrior men have all travelled to the South Road to find the Kabul warriors," someone else yelled. "The only men left are our elders and our youth."

"I'm not looking for men," emphasized Analoop. "I'm look for the bravest of our women. This is a female army that has conquered Morgos and Gamotz. And it will be a female army that will continue the destruction of the Kabul. Are any of you women brave enough to join an all-female army composed of the best warriors in Small World?"

"Yes we are," cried out several voices in the group.

"Please round up as many of you as possible," instructed Analoop. "Tomorrow morning early we will all head out to the Kabul. We will finish this war."

Early the following morning, about one hundred female giants had amassed in the central meeting place with weapons in hand. They were ready to be led by Analoop back to the city of Gamotz and to war with the hordes of the Kabul.

***

After Wizard of Havinis had been given the responsibility of a nearly impossible task he was filled with questions. How was he going to get into Lord Krakus' chambers? And how was he going to battle Kwdad and eliminate him in order to bring peace to Small World? He felt that he was now tasked with saving the entirety of Small World by himself and that the peace of Small World depended completely on him.

He headed due north, following the Kilo Pass trail and after a couple hours he encountered the mist wall that separated the Southern Plains from the Kabul. This was his first encounter with this mist wall and he was concerned that his new Protee powers would be recognized. But he knew he didn't have a choice. The mist wall completely surrounded the Kabul and at some point he was going to have to cross through it.

As he approached the wall he was stopped by a pair of giants who asked, "Who are you and what are you doing here?"

"I am the Wizard of Havinis and I have been tasked with a spy mission in the Kabul. I need to cross through this mist wall and enter into that dreaded kingdom. I assume you are the giant guards who were assigned the responsibility of protecting the Southern Plains from invasion."

"Correct," responded the giant. Then he said, "Proceed."

The wizard continued his march, walking straight into the wall. He travelled through the wall for what felt like an eternity to him, but eventually he exited the wall, walking out into a forbidden and desolate wilderness. But he knew that his journey had just begun.

He continued on the Kilo Pass road for a few hours when suddenly he encountered an enormous number of small, snake like lizards. At first they didn't seem like much of a threat and were easily stomped out. Then the wizard remembered the story that Elasti had told of encountering these creatures and he knew that he didn't want to be trapped by them. He remembered that soon the number of these creatures would become overwhelming and that they would start piling up on top of each other in the form of a wall. Realizing that he wouldn't have the power to do battle with these creatures on his own, he turned and ran southward, back the way he had come, until he felt he was safely far enough away.

Having escaped the creatures, he turned west into the forest and on to higher ground. Then he circled around and once again headed north. Several hours later he once again encountered the Kilo Pass. He crossed over the Pass and continued north. After another couple hours he could see Gamotz off in the distance to the east. Not realizing that Gamotz was now safely under the control of the Swift Army, he carefully continued sneaking north until he was once again out of the sight of the city.

At this point it was becoming dark and he knew he had to make camp. He parked himself in a cluster of trees and decided that he would spend the night there.

The following morning he continued his march northward, hoping he would come into sight of Tragis before the day was over. Then he would spend his second night in view of the troll city. *But then what? How would he get into that city without being recognized as an intruder?*

He decided that after he had accomplished his goal of arriving at a point where he could see the city, he would then spend a day going through the scrolls that he had brought with from the Tako

Ruins. Maybe there was a secret there which could help him accomplish his assigned mission.

Eventually he arrived at his destination. He found himself an excellent place to camp out, and then buckled down for the night. He thought he was safe. But then he noticed, walking up behind him on the same path that he had just arrived on, was a dark, black figure. It didn't look human. It seemed to walk on its arms rather than on its legs. Was this some type of magotite abortion? Had someone spotted him? Had someone been watching him? He did his best to remain concealed and quiet. Would he be discovered?

***

The elven city of Gije was in an uproar. The Kabul Army had been spotted off in the distance and they knew that tomorrow there would be an attack. The elfin lord Gimans called a meeting at the town square, "Remember my elven warriors that the Lifefight war was won at the walls of our city last time, and it will be won again at the same place this time. You are all trained and know what to do. Seal the gates. Line the walls with archers. Prepare for any breaches into the city by guarding the streets with swords and knives. We are ready! We are trained! Tomorrow we will win!"

Then he issued a further command, "Bring all our non-warriors down into the caves under the city. The women and children are our future. Our female warriors have deserted us in our time of need and we have no idea what has happened to them, but the remaining women, children, and aged members of our community must be protected. Bring them to the caves and seal them in so they will not be discovered by our enemies. Today we will win but the battle of the day goes to our warriors. It is up to them to save our city. And I will stand side-by-side with them to protect our heritage."

Everyone worked quickly to follow the instructions of the king. Soon the city was as ready as it would ever be and in spite of the fear that the presence of the Kabul forces instilled, the elf warriors felt they were up to the challenge.

***

Their target was in sight. Tomorrow would be the day the Kabul Army would wipe out the entire elf species. Tomorrow would be incredible.

The prince was in much better shape. After being carried up on the plateau by his troll, he was finally able to get out of his baby-carrier. He was still sore from the arrow through his arm, but he had regained a lot of his strength and he was walking around on his own. He felt embarrassed and stupid about being attacked. It was a foolish and vain error that caused him to be shot and he swore he would never be that stupid again.

The prince tried his shape shifting to his eagle form. He wanted to make sure he was still able to make the change. He wanted to see what the elven city of Gije's preparations were and if there would be any surprises. As he flew over the city he saw nothing unusual. The elves had not developed any special weapons. The Kabul attack on Gije should go smoothly with no surprises. The elves had not found a way to hide out the way the leprechauns had done. They were all there and ready to be slaughtered.

It was getting late so the Kabul Army made camp. It was an elaborate process, and the army was tired because of their long marches from the previous days, so they quickly hunkered down. It wasn't long before snoring and farting could be heard throughout the camp.

Around midnight they struck. There was only about twenty of them, but they attacked the Kabul warriors with fierceness, biting as many gnomes as possible. Fifty gnomes had been bitten by the werewolves before the gnomes even knew what had hit them. Then there was a lot of screaming and yelling which woke up the entire camp.

The werewolves weren't frightened off by the noise or by the resulting attacks against them. They continued biting and scratching their way through the camp and the gnomes struck back with swords and spears, killing the werewolves as quickly as possible. After about one hour of battle the twenty creatures had been killed, but not before about one hundred gnomes had been bitted and therefore infected. However, they didn't realize that they were infected. They didn't understand the danger of a werewolf bite. They thought they were wounded and just need to be bandaged up. They weren't willing to miss out on the battle against the elves on the following morning. This bite wasn't going to stop them. They didn't realize that it would be a couple of days before the infections would transform them into the hideous creatures that they had just battled.

As if one attack hadn't been enough, just as they were finished bandaging up the wounded, and were starting to again lie down for the night, there was a second attack. This time it was by only five werewolves. This time the gnomes knew what to do and the five were quickly killed, but not before another twenty gnomes were infected. This had become a dangerous night for the Kabul forces from an unexpected enemy.

Guards were set up around the camp, making sure that there were no more attacks. But the rest of the night was uneventful. The morning would come soon enough and the excited band of Kabul warriors looked forward to the attack on Gije.

The next morning found the entire camp waking up early, ready for the onslaught. Even the warriors that had been attacked by the werewolves were anxious for the fight. They showed no signs of weariness or exhaustion.

The gnome leader Klakaly organized the gnome and troll forces together which didn't mean much because they would just be attacking in mass like a wild horde. The prince came forward for their orientation and preparations and addressed the army by saying, "We must win this battle. This will recover our rightful leadership over the entirety of Small World. Leadership rightfully belongs to us. It is our inherited right and it was stolen from us in the Lifefight War, which was lost on this very battlefield. But we are now ready. We are now better prepared than ever. We will no longer be ruled over by these miserable species. Today is our day of victory!"

A loud cheer went up and swords, shields, and spears could be heard clanging together. The noise was so loud that it was heard all the way to Gije, which was the intent. They wanted to drive fear into the hearts of the elves.

Then the command was given by Klakaly, "Attack!" And the Kabul forces ran madly toward the elven city, always screaming like wild banshees.

Because of the distance between the city and the camp, it took a half hour of running before the Kabul Army reached the city walls. But their excitement did not waver. The elf archers were ready and they let a shower of arrows fly. Unfortunately, the gnome archers were also ready and they fired back with arrows that were ablaze. The elves, in their effort to protect their citizens, had left no resources to put out the flames from the arrows that stuck bundles of hay, or the straw roofs of the buildings. It wasn't long before it seemed like the entire city of Gije was ablaze.

Warriors made futile attempts to put out the fires, but they were also badly needed on the walls shooting the attacking army. Their efforts had very little effect. The town would soon be a pile of burnt-out rubble.

Then came the trolls. They were always last because they let the gnomes do their best and then the trolls came in to clean up the mess. The trolls were about the height of the walls, so it was easy for them to reach over the wall and grab the elf warriors and throw them to the ground where the gnomes would finish the job.

The elves did their best shooting at the trolls, and were often successful, especially when they targeted the eyes. The arrows in the eyes would go directly into the brain and cause instant death. But the trolls recognized this strategy and protected their eyes with their hands and, although their hands ended up looking like the back of a porcupine, they were still able to make it to the city wall and do considerable damage.

Eventually two of the trolls were able to break down the gates of the city allowing the gnomes to swarm in. Once inside, the battle became fearsome and the elves stood very little chance. The remaining warrior elves were butchered and the remainder of Gije was decimated. It was burned to the ground. There was little left to allow anyone to recognize the splendor which had once been the glory of the elven kingdom. Now it was the center of celebration for a horde of Kabul forces, delighted over their victory.

Then it started to rain, and the rain poured down in torrents. Soon the streets of Gije were flowing in water one foot deep. The rain fell as if it was tears from heaven, drowning the city and attempting to wash away it's disgrace. The rains were so strong that the bodies of the dead, both gnomes and elves, were washed away toward the downslope of the plateau to the west, and were washed off into the Lamos.

The Kabul forces, what was left of them, returned to their camps where they would be able to find shelter, since any shelter that had existed in Gije had now been destroyed.

The prince met with the gnome leader and said, "We have won a great victory today. You should be very proud."

"Yes but we lost about half our army in the process, and we only have three trolls left," responded Klakaly. "We have paid a great price."

The prince cared very little about the cost of gnome lives. He was thrilled to see Gije destroyed. His only comment was, "Now we must do the same to Hilebin!"

Chapter Twenty-Two
The Attack on Hilebin

Lord Krakus was still on a rampage. He had lost his entire magotite army, which he had planned to use against the dwarfs. And he was becoming too impatient to wait for the gnomes and their efforts against Amins and Gije. Win or lose, their armies would most likely be decimated. He called for King Rakadam, the king of the trolls. As the king entered, the lord said, "I need the dwarfs wiped out and you're the only one that can accomplish that for me."

"What do you need me to do?" asked the king.

"I need you to form an army of as many trolls as you can and go attack Hilebin, and then after that's done, finish off Hilebon as well. I need both of them wiped out and I would like the entire race of dwarfs wiped out if at all possible. Can you do that for me?"

"Of course," replied the king. "I'll get on it right away. Do you want me to include the magotites or the gnomes?"

The lord responded, "The magotites have been wiped out and the gnomes have probably also been decimated. You're all that's left. It will have to be a troll army that eliminates the dwarfs."

"Should I round up the trolls that are running to Gamotz, or should I leave them there?" asked the king.

"Leave them," responded the Lord. "We need that city protected as well in case of another invasion. You don't need them do you?"

"No," responded the king. "I have about five thousand trolls that I can use for an attack on the dwarfs and that should be more than enough to eliminate those pesky dwarfs."

"Good," said the lord. "Go to it then."

The king left and immediately started rounding up his troops. Once he had them all together, he instructed, "We are given the opportunity to wipe out the dwarfs. They have been a thorn in our side long enough and it is now our opportunity to eliminate them. We will be leaving first thing in the morning and we will go directly to Hilebin. Then, after destroying that city we will do the same to Hilebon. Now go and prepare."

A cheer went up amongst the trolls. They were excited to finally have the opportunity to attack the dwarfs in mass, feeling that it was the only way they could possibly be successful. The time had come and they were ready.

The following morning the trolls started their march northward. They were able to move at close to three times the speed of any of the other creatures in Small World, except the giants. It only took a couple hours before they started coming close to Morgos, but the smell could be experienced long before they could even see the city. As they approached, they could see the mass of rotting bodies, piled high against the walls of the city. Even for the trolls, who weren't the cleanest of creatures, this smell was intolerable.

They rushed to get past the city. Soon they were approaching the mist wall at the northern edge of the Kabul. They would need to travel through this wall on their way to the dwarf homeland. When they reached the wall they were cautious and nervous. This was an unknown and new experience for them. Would they be safe? They had heard of many strange occurrences at the wall and this made them uncomfortable.

The king encouraged them to move forward even though he was also somewhat hesitant. They charged into the mist and came out on the other side, right at the edge of the Hile Desert. A couple of the trolls stepped into the desert to see if they could pass through it, but they were immediately attacked by the sand squirrels who clamped onto their feet and wouldn't let go. Unfortunately, the trolls fell over and the sand squirrels were quick to clamp onto their hand, and in one case, his cheek. The trolls screamed in pain, but there was no one that would help them. None of the trolls knew what to do. They just left the two unfortunate trolls to fend for themselves while they started their march westward and around the Hile Desert.

Eventually the troll army successfully worked their way around the west side and came to the edge of the Hile Groves, which was the home of the dwarfs. They stumbled into the groves hoping to get some indication of where they should be traveling in order to get to Hilebin. The troll king commanded, "Spread out wide and we will march through the forest, searching everywhere until we find a trail or some indication where the dwarf city is located."

The trolls made one straight line across of trolls, each about ten feet apart, much the same as a search party, and they started marching through the groves. They had to walk slowly because of the denseness of the trees. They knew that eventually they would find the dwarf hideout known as Hilebin.

***

Dwarfs who guard the perimeter of the Hile Groves came rushing into Hilebin yelling, "We are being invaded by an army of trolls." The report was immediately brought to the Dwarf King Egione's attention. He knew that there was always a possibility that this could happen so he commanded his military leader, "Hide the women, children, and elderly in the trees. Have the warriors prepare for the attack using their ax throwing abilities. They may destroy our city, but we can't let them destroy our people. Send a messenger to Hilebon and tell them to do the same."

"Yes king," responded the military commander as he departed the king's chambers.

Then the king commanded his guards, "Remove everyone from my chamber and close all the doors."

The king laid down on the floor and began to hum, "Hummm-mmmm, Hi Ho, Hummmmmmmm." He repeated this pattern several times.

Then the king heard a voice, "We hear you oh king. What is it you want to know?"

"I want to warn you that there are evil forces that have entered the groves. They plan to destroy our town and our people. They are also a danger to the forest and they may try to start a fire."

"We see them," responded Treeclap, the leader of the trees in the Hile Groves. "Are you sure they are enemies of the groves? They are just walking through it peacefully."

"You will see a change in their behavior when they find Hilebin. I just wanted you to be prepared."

"What do you want us to do?" asked Treeclap.

"Drive them out," responded the king.

"We will do that if we see any evil activities," responded the tree, wanting to stay neutral and in a defensive mode.

The dwarfs hurried their preparations along and soon they were ready. Their non-military were all tucked away and hidden, and their military were ax ready. Soon the battle would begin.

***

The troll king had heard about the ax throwing skills of the dwarfs and he decided to keep his trolls spread apart so that the dwarfs wouldn't be able to strike more than one troll at a time, giving the other trolls that surrounded him a chance to identify and eliminate the dwarfs.

The five thousand trolls continued their march in what seemed like an extremely disciplined straight line which stretched nearly the entire way across the Hile Groves. They were amazed that they hadn't seen even one dwarf, but the trolls were unfamiliar with the stealthy skills of the dwarfs.

The march went on for about two hours before anything was sighted. Then a cry could be heard from one of the trolls, "I see a dwarf home." It was a small home built into the side of a tree.

"Stay in your line," shouted the troll king as he marched over to the home to investigate. It was indeed a dwarf home so the king commanded, "Burn it out!"

A torch fire was lit, and the torch was thrown inside the small house, too small for a troll to enter. Then the march continued. Occasionally other troll houses were found and they were similarly torched. The process continued for another hour and the trolls were starting to become disgruntled and discouraged. They wanted to kill dwarfs. They wanted to destroy a city. They didn't want to burn the occasional house.

Just as the troll discouragement was coming to a peak, the cry went out, "We've found the city! We've found Hilebin."

The trolls came to life and everyone wanted to join in the fun of destroying the city. But where were the dwarfs. There was no one to kill. Suddenly, and unexpectedly, a troll cried out in pain and fell to the ground. His foot had been cut off just a short way above his ankle. Then another troll cried out, experiencing the same pain. Then another, and another. Soon it seemed like the trolls were dropping like flies.

The king yelled out, "Find those dwarfs and destroy them."

The trolls started to scramble around, looking for the dwarfs. "Found one," could be heard from several directions. The fate of any dwarf that was found was certain. The trolls would make quick work of them. But the chopping off of the troll legs continued, in spite of the loss of dwarf lives.

"Come out your cowards," yelled the troll king. "Quit hiding and sneaking around."

The battle raged on. The dwarfs knew they didn't have a chance in a one-on-one battle with the trolls. They had to be sneaky. They fought the only way they knew how; by throwing axes and cutting off troll legs.

Many of the trolls continued their destruction of the city. Many dwarf homes were burnt to the ground. However, when a dwarf home was inside of one of the trees, the fire never seemed to catch the tree on fire. It seemed to burn out the furnishings inside the house and then quit burning shortly afterward before it could affect the tree. But that didn't discourage the trolls. They continued trying to start fires, even if it took several attempts.

After an hour of fighting between the trolls and the dwarfs, the battle was getting weary. The trolls had lost about two hundred of their warriors, not dead but unable to fight because their legs had been cut off. Similarly, the dwarfs had lost over one hundred brave warriors because there were so many trolls that it was difficult to hide from them all and still wield their axes.

Hilebin was destroyed. The troll king commanded, "We've done as much damage as we can do here. Let's rebuild our line and march on to Hilebon."

"What about our injured trolls?" someone asked.

"Leave them here and we'll come back for them," responded the king. "We'll pick them up on our way back." That command was the equivalent of a death sentence and everyone knew it. Any troll left behind would be quickly dispatched by any of the dwarfs that were still around. But the king's command was always to be followed so the trolls reformed their line and restarted their march in search of Hilebon.

It was getting late in the day, but the king wanted to get the destruction of both cities competed before making camp. He thought it would be safer for his trolls if the dwarf cities were eliminated.

The troll march continued on. It was only about a half hour later when Hilebon was discovered at the far east end of the troll marching line. The trolls immediately set out destroying the city but they were frustrated because once again there were no dwarfs to kill.

Then a dwarf attack started, with axes flying and feet being cut off. This time the trolls were alert and immediately started finding and killing the dwarfs that were responsible. The losses on both sides were again great but the trolls felt as if they had accomplished their goal of wiping out the two dwarf cities and ridding themselves of the pesky dwarfs. In the end the trolls lost three hundred and the dwarfs lost two hundred and fifty. Neither species was decimated as the trolls started to work their way back towards the southern border of the Hile Groves.

As they approached the edge of the groves, the troll king commanded, "Set up bonfires in several locations along the edge of these groves. I've decided that I want to burn down the groves so that any dwarfs that we might have missed will get burned out."

They set up over a dozen bonfires just to the inside of the southern edge of the groves and lit them on fire. The fires blazed higher and higher. Then suddenly, when the fire started to scorch the bark on the trees, and when it started to burn some of the branches, the lower branches of the trees started to flay about. They would smack the bonfires so hard that the burning embers would fly up in the air and towards the trolls, setting many of them on fire. It was so unexpected that the trolls weren't ready to react.

Soon the bonfires were scattered and burned out, not having accomplished their purpose of starting the groves on fire. The only thing that caught fire was about thirty trolls, who were screaming in pain as they tried to extinguish the flames.

The king commanded that they try again, and a dozen fires were started. This time the trolls stood far enough back from the bonfires that when the embers were battered by the tree branches the trolls weren't close enough to be set on fire. But again, the effort was futile. The trees prevented the forest fire that the bonfires were intended to start.

The king of the trolls commanded, "We have accomplished our mission. We have destroyed the two dwarf cities and we have killed as many of the dwarfs as possible. Now it's time for us to return home to Tragis and defend our own homes. We will see if the Lord has any more commands for us.

CHAPTER TWENTY-THREE
THE RETURN TO AMINS

The Kabul forces, what was left of them, that had just decimated Gije, were now on a march northward. The plan was to cross over into the Kabul, march to the north end of the Kabul, and then attack the dwarfs. As the Kabul forces were making their way down the single file path that took them off the Jove Plateau, the prince decided to change back to his eagle form and check on his assigned mission of wiping out the wizard and the Protee power wielder. The prince had instructed Klakaly, the gnome leader to proceed to the Kilo Pass and to use it to cross into the Kabul. "I will catch up with you along the way," said the prince. "I'm still searching for that pesky wizard. I need to eliminate him at some point."

"Understood," replied Klakaly. "What about the leprechauns? We never killed any of them."

"We'll just have to worry about them later," responded the prince. "I think the dwarfs are our next target."

The prince flew off toward Amins to confirm the death of the Protee healer, and to see if he could spot the wizard. The flight took a couple hours since it required a trip across the full width of Small World. However, he eventually arrived in Amins. He wasn't quite back to full strength and so along the journey he occasionally had to perch on the top of a tree for a while and rest. Eventually he made it and he flew over the top of Amins looking for the two individuals that he was assigned to eliminate. He searched for the body of Bydola, the Protee healer, but he couldn't find any sign of him. He assumed that Bydola must have been buried or perhaps taken into the forest for some funerary ritual.

The prince waited and watched for several hours but saw nothing that looked like a wizard. In frustration he flew off toward the north, hoping to report to his father. It was several hours before he finally arrived in Tragis. He again was forced to stop often to rest.

As the prince travelled over Gamotz he was disappointed to see that the Swift Army was still in control. He couldn't believe that a troll army couldn't defeat them. The only thing he noticed, which was new, is that there seemed to be more giants there than before. He wondered where they came from. Why hadn't he noticed them last time? Or are these new arrivals.

When he landed in Tragis he shifted back into his prince form and went directly to his father's chambers to report his progress, "I've killed the Protee healer, but I can't find the wizard anywhere. I don't think he's in Amins anymore. I'll keep watch, but he's somewhere in the south. I just have to find him."

"Excellent," replied the prince. "But it's important that you find him so keep making it a priority. What's the progress of the army?"

"They've wiped out Gije and killed all the elves," responded the prince. "They're on their way north to attack the dwarfs."

"I already sent trolls to wipe out the dwarfs," inserted the Lord. "No need to send the army there. Send them back to Amins. I want those leprechauns wiped out."

"Excellent," said Kakakrul. "Maybe that will draw out the wizard as well. I'll leave right now and change the direction of their travels." He liked this idea because the gnomes wouldn't know that their home had been captured and they would stay in touch with the battle at hand. He also didn't want to mention to his father that Gamotz was still dominated by the Swift Army because he thought it might cause the Lord to change his mind about allowing the gnome army to return to Amins.

The prince left his father's chambers, changed into his eagle shape, and flew north. He decided he was going to check on the progress of the trolls in their attack against the dwarfs. The trip took several hours but eventually he was in the groves. It wasn't hard to find Hilebin because of the smoke that was rising from that part of the groves. He flew over that section of the groves and saw that the town of Hilebin had been destroyed. He also noticed that the trolls, which were easy to spot because of their size, were on the move in a straight line, apparently searching for Hilebon.

Feeling satisfied that the dwarfs were being taken care of, the prince decided to take the long trip back down to the South Road where he was sure the remainder of his gnome army was still travelling. This trip took a day because he was still extremely weak. He had to make several stops, sometimes sitting and resting for several hours at a time. He made sure his nights were spent under the protection of the Kabul forests.

Eventually the prince flew over the Kabul mist barrier and started following the Kilo Pass toward the South Road. He could see the Tako Ruins off in the distance and his army just starting their journey along the Kilo Pass. He swooped down, close to the front of the marching troops, but off to the side so he wouldn't be noticed, transformed himself, and marched out to meet Klakaly, the gnome leader. He waved his arms to get the gnome's attention. After getting together, the prince instructed the gnome, "The trolls are already attacking the dwarfs. We're no longer needed up there. We have been instructed to return to Amins and to try to wipe out the leprechauns. We didn't finish our job there. We need to return to the South Road, cross the Avol River, and go back into the Amins Groves, find the leprechauns hiding place, and wipe them out."

"Gladly," responded Klakaly. "We weren't looking forward to a march to the complete opposite end of Small World. And we were also frustrated with our failure to wipe out the leprechauns."

The gnome leader turned and started commanding his troops to take the east connecting road that led back to the South Road. He commanded, "We are going back to the leprechauns so we can finish the job there."

A cheer went up in the troops. Wiping out the leprechaun species was something they took delight in.

The army made their way back to the South Road, shortly before nightfall. They had heard about riposters but they never took the claims seriously. They didn't realize how fortunate they were to have escaped a riposter attack. They didn't realize that there was something much worse that they were still going to encounter.

It was now their fourth night on the road after the defeat of Gije. They made camp on the South Road, halfway between the two rivers, and bedded down for the night.

It wasn't long after nightfall that the entire camp was awoken by a series of loud howling noises. Then screaming could be heard causing the entire camp to be in a panic.

Torches were lit from the numerous campfires and they were brought to the locations of the screaming, but the noise didn't stop. However, they could see what was happening. A large number of the gnomes had been transformed into werewolves. They were attacking the gnomes that hadn't been transformed, which caused the screaming.

Gnomes and trolls started killing the werewolves with swords and spears. However it seemed futile since there were now a new large number of gnomes that were bitten, and they knew what their fate would be in just a few short days.

It was a frantic sight. Gnomes and trolls running around with torches, being attacked from any and all directions. Gnomes started screaming in a panic, not knowing what to do and trying to find a place to hide, but no place was safe.

The trolls took it upon themselves to start killing not just the werewolves, but any gnomes that were bitten. That night over two hundred gnomes were killed before Klakaly or the prince realized what was happening and they were able to put a stop to it.

The prince was furious, "We don't need anyone to defeat us! We'll defeat ourselves."

"What do we do," challenged Klakaly. "Do we lock these gnomes that are turning into werewolves in a cage every night? And how do we keep track of them?"

"Every night," explained the prince, "before we go to bed, we tie up the werewolves against a tree. Those gnomes that have been bitten know who they are, and they are to voluntarily come and be tied up. If they don't get tied up, and they become werewolves, we kill them. The first few nights we post extra guards to watch for and kill any gnomes that change into werewolves."

"Why not just kill all of them right away like the trolls were doing?" asked Klakaly. "I sure don't want to risk being bitten."

"Because I'm thinking we can use them," responded the prince. "What if we have all the werewolf types camp out in the middle of the Amins Groves. In the nighttime they will transform and then they will go out chasing down and killing leprechauns."

"Incredible idea," responded the gnome leader. "Then we have leprechaun werewolves, and the leprechauns will start killing each other off as well. I love it."

"Make it happen," commanded the prince and the gnome leader went off to command how they would control the gnome werewolves. In the end there were only about forty gnomes who had the werewolf venom in them. The remainder had been killed by the gnomes or trolls.

The following day the march continued, and they arrived at the Avol River pull boat crossing. That crossing would go a little quicker this time because there were fewer warriors. However, it still took the majority of the following day before the entire army was across.

Once across, and after another good night's rest, the army headed due south, trying to get as close as possible to the Amins Groves. As planned, the gnomes with the werewolf venom, proceeded to go deep into the groves and made camp as close to the center of the groves as possible.

The remaining army camped outside of the groves. No attack was planned. They decided to wait and see what happened with the gnome werewolves. If they were successful in finding and infecting the leprechauns, then the leprechauns would take care of wiping themselves out without risking any more gnome or troll lives. But it would also be disappointing because the gnomes wanted badly to be able to wipe out the leprechaun species.

For the prince what was important was identifying the wizard. According to his father, eliminating the wizard was critical if they were going to win the war and take over domination of Small World.

While the gnome army was settling in for the night, the prince transformed himself into his eagle form and flew over the Amins Groves to inspect Amins, just in case the wizard was visible. As he flew over the city he noticed that the leprechauns had started rebuilding their homes. Several had their walls set up and they were working on their roofs. The city was coming back to life.

The prince was frustrated. He wanted the leprechauns eliminated, not reestablished. He wanted them gone. Soon Amins would look as if there had never been an attack at all. Soon the leprechauns would be back to normal without having lost hardly any lives.

The prince didn't see anyone that looked like a wizard. In frustration he decided to stay on top of a tree and spend the night there. He didn't want to be in the gnome camp in case the werewolves attacked the camp. He preferred to continue observing Amins, just in case someone interesting, like a wizard, appeared.

***

Amaz, the council leader, and Bydola, the Protee healer, had taken over the shared and combined role as the leaders of the leprechauns. They had instructed the leprechauns to venture out of their Amins Grove hiding places during the day in order to work on reconstructing their homes in Amins. Then, during the night, they would return to their camps in the groves. They continued hiding out until they had rebuilt their homes and until they felt safe from any additional Kabul attacks.

The leprechauns felt fortunate that they had not lost many lives during the Kabul attack on Amins. They didn't want to take any chances that would risk lives if there was a future attack.

It was approaching nighttime and the leprechauns had all returned to the safety of their camps. They were grateful for the protection the trees had given them and they rewarded the trees with nurturing and care, especially paying extra attention to their younger trees.

The night started as any other and it seemed like it was going to be uneventful, when the leprechauns were awaken by the active rustling and movement of the trees.

Amaz and Bydola quickly came together and Amaz asked, "What do you think it means? Is there another attack under way, perhaps this time through the Amins Groves coming from the west?"

Bydola responded, "We have guards posted along both the east and west borders of the groves. Last night one of the west guards reported that a group of about thirty gnomes came into the groves and set up camp in the middle of the groves. This didn't seem like a serious threat and so I had spies posted in the trees around their camp in order to watch them and to report back about any activities. It was a little confusing why such a small group of gnomes would come into the groves. They also reported that a large camp of gnomes and trolls were outside of the groves on the west side."

Amaz suggested, "Maybe that large group has decided to march through the groves during the nighttime."

Bydola continued, "It appears that the trees are once again protecting us. But protecting us from what? I don't see masses of gnomes parading through the groves which is what we would expect to see if they were on the march."

Just then one of the leprechauns that was assigned to be a guard of the small gnome camp inside the groves, came rushing into Amaz's tent. He was injured, having been bitten by one of the werewolves. He yelled, "The gnomes that have the camp inside of the groves are all werewolves. The gnomes must be planning to infect leprechauns as much as possible with the venom, hoping we will infect and kill each other off."

"So that's their game," responded an angry Amaz. "Round up a group of warrior leprechauns and kill off the werewolves."

Then Bydola added, "Don't be afraid of being infected. I will heal anyone that's been bitten tomorrow and we will foil the plans of the gnomes and the Kabul prince. Go forth bravely and kill the werewolves so we won't have to deal with them again tomorrow night."

The leprechaun warriors were quickly dispatched and, after a long night of searching and killing the werewolves, the threat was eliminated. All the gnome werewolves were discovered and eliminated.

Amaz commented to Bydola, "We may have rid ourselves of the werewolves, but we still have to deal with the gnomes that are camped on the west edge of the groves."

"Understood," responded Bydola. "Hopefully the trees will once again be our saviors. Let's make sure none of our companions go out into Amins. They need to stay under the protection of the forest until we are sure that the Kabul Army has once again departed."

The following morning there were nearly fifty leprechauns that required Bydola's Protee healing powers in the central fountain of Amins. As soon as their healing was completed, they quickly returned to the safety and protection of the groves.

***

The following morning brought more frustration for the Kabul prince. He flew over Amins and there was still no wizard to be found. Instead, what the prince found was a parade of healings going on at the central fountain of Amins. Wasn't this the same healer that he had killed? Or was there more than one healer? He waited for an opportunity to swoop down and rid himself of this healer, but the opportunity never came. There were always too many leprechauns around for him to solely mount an attack. And he was still sore and weak from the last time he had attacked a healer.

The prince flew back to the gnome camp on the eastern edge of the Amins Groves, converted himself to his princely form, and approached Klakaly. "What have we heard? Did the werewolf trap work?" He hadn't connected the healings as a cure for the werewolf venom. He thought that the healings were just for the injuries, but he hoped that the venom was still active and that there would be a horde of leprechaun werewolves coming up in one of the following nights.

"We don't know yet," responded the gnome leader. "We're still waiting for the gnome werewolves to come out and report."

"What would they report?" asked the prince. "Aren't they oblivious of what happened during the time they were werewolves?"

"That's true," agreed Klakaly. "I guess we just wait and see what happens. The problem is that we would have to wait three or four days to see if the venom took effect. Do we really want to wait around that long?"

"We wait," commanded the prince.

Unfortunately, a gnome spy, who was also a messenger, brought news and the news that had arrived brought the entire gnome camp into an uproar. The gnome spy, that was watching the giants guarding the mist wall, happened to overhear Analoop as she was returning from her visit to Gingoras, her giant home. She was explaining to the guard at the mist wall that the Swift Army had conquered and was now in control of Gamotz and that she was bringing her army of two hundred giants back to Gamotz in case it gets attacked.

The news swept through the gnome army like wildfire, and the gnomes were outraged. In unity they were committing mutiny. They were packing up their camp and they were starting to march, at a radically high speed, northward toward the Avol River crossing. They were going to rescue their home at all costs, and there was nothing that the prince or his puppet gnome leader Klakaly were going to be able to say to stop their departure.

The trolls had no interest in the destruction or the saving of Gamotz and they were happy to be rid of the gnomes. They decided to stay behind with the prince and continue to guard the west edge of the Amins Groves.

As the gnomes were charging toward the Avol crossing, they met a new challenge.

***

The giant forces had been organized and were on the march. Unfortunately, they were late. The giants who had marched to Amins to help protect that city, had arrived too late and the city was destroyed by the time they arrived. They had returned towards their homes in order to make camp in the fields north of Giter. Giant-giant had been commanded by the Creator to help out in this war and he wasn't going to return home until he had followed this command.

The giants had camped out for several days, uncertain about what they should do next when a giant, that was out on patrol in the area surrounding the plains, returned to camp to report to Giant-giant. "There is a camp of gnomes and trolls on the west edge of the Amins Groves. I think they are preparing another attack on Amins, hoping to wipe out the leprechauns."

Giant-giant jumped up and yelled at his troops, "We have a Kabul Army invading the Southern Plains and we need to rescue our friends. Get ready! We march in an hour."

***

Unfortunately for the gnomes who were in a hurry to return to Gamotz, as they were heading toward the Avol River crossing, they were met by Giant-giant's army. Sadly, the clubs and swords of the giants made quick work of the gnomes even though their numbers were large. Ironically, the gnomes, who had set out to rid Small World of the elf and leprechaun species, were themselves nearly eliminated.

The battle wasn't over. The prince, in his eagle form, witnessed the slaughter of the gnomes and he sent the remaining trolls to help out. Unfortunately, the trolls, although much larger and stronger than the gnomes, were still no match for the giants. The trolls were able to kill several giants, but in the end the trolls and the gnomes were completely wiped out. The Kabul Army of Prince Kakakrul which was invading the Southern Plains, was no more.

The eagle flew away toward the north. It was no use trying to identify the wizard, or to attack the Amins healer on his own. He was too weak and even if he had the strength, he would need more than just himself to accomplish his goal. He felt dejected. He didn't want to face his father Lord Krakus. It was all too much. He decided to hide out in the Kabul somewhere, maybe in the deserted city of Morgos, and try to calm down after his miserable defeat.

CHAPTER TWENTY-FOUR
THE ATTACK ON TRAGIS

The wizard found himself an excellent place to camp out, with a perfect view of Tragis, the troll city which was host to both the Kabul Lord and the Prince. He was buckling down for the night when he noticed, walking up the trail he had just come down, a dark, black figure. It walked on its arms rather than on its legs. The wizard did his best to remain concealed and quiet. However, the strange creature walked directly up to him and said, "Hello Wizard of Havinis. Do you remember us? We are the Worlepreeks. I am Ordo, assistant to Oply the council lord. We helped you escape the gnomes when you were traveling down the Albo Pass."

"Of course," replied the wizard, now that he was reminded about them. "I thought you never came out of your caves?"

"We rarely do, but we were commanded by the Creator to come and talk to you and help you."

"Excellent," responded the wizard. "But what can you do to help me?"

"I will take you down into the caves. We have a connection with the series of caves that are ruled by the evil Kwdad the Destroyer who dominates over the Lord of the Kabul. That way you don't have to go through Tragis to get to the caves. However, you needed to get this far so we could bring you into our caves. The Creator wants to leave you with the choice of how you want to accomplish your mission, but we think our route would be easier."

"Of course," responded the wizard. "You have no idea how thankful I am that you came here to help me. I was sure I was going to have a rough time of getting to that master of evil."

"Your challenges aren't finished," replied Ordo. "Once you enter Kwdad's world, there are many more challenges that you will need to conquer. And I can't help you with those. All I can do is make it easier for you to get there."

"I appreciate any help you can give me," responded the wizard.

"Please come with me," suggested Ordo. "I will get you to a safe place where you can sleep. Then tomorrow, I will show you the way."

The wizard grabbed his gear and the two were off. They soon found themselves inside a hidden cave that took them deep into the hillside. The wizard didn't like being in so many caves, but he knew that this was what was expected of him, so he pushed on.

The wizard had a comfortable night's rest. The following morning Ordo arrived, hoping to lead the wizard to the evil caves, but the wizard insisted, "Please allow me to spend another day here, studying the Tako scrolls."

"Of course," responded the worlepreek. "Perhaps you'd also like to review our Book of Psalms. That talks about the evil. Maybe you can get some clues from that."

"That would be great," responded the wizard. "Please bring it to me."

Ordo left the wizard and a short time later returned with the Book of Psalms. Then he departed with, "I'll come and check on you in the morning and see how you're doing and if you're ready to enter the evil caves."

"Thanks," was all the wizard said, and Ordo departed.

***

Analoop arrived at the gates of Gamotz with a band of about one hundred giants who were invited into the city by a cheer that echoed throughout the city. All the giants were eagerly welcomed even though many of them had never seen and were completely unfamiliar with any of the other species. The newly added strength to the Swift Army was a welcome sight.

Earlier that day, Goglbarj had transformed herself into her owl form. She wanted to survey Morgos and Tragis to see what these cities looked like. She wanted to make sure that there were no more magotites, and she wanted to see if there were any more trolls marching on Gamotz. She also wanted to check to see if there were any gnomes marching back to Gamotz. She returned and transformed herself just in time for the celebrated return of Analoop.

Goglbarj had discovered nothing. Morgos was still a stink hole with no new inhabitants. Tragis seemed barren but there were still trolls about. And there were no gnomes on a march toward Gamotz. In fact there were no gnomes anywhere but in Gamotz. The entire Kabul seemed eerily quiet.

The celebrations for Analoop's return hadn't completely ended when a hawk landed in Gamotz and transformed itself into Egisix. Goglbarj approached him and asked, "What are you doing here? Do you have some news for us?"

"I was hoping you could give me some news," responded Efisix, feeling rather strange as he noticed that he was the only male in the entire city.

Goglbarj explained the story of the female army and the destruction of the magotite army. She went on to explain the capture of Gamotz. She told Egisix that they were going to remain in Gamotz until the gnome army returned so they could wipe that out as well.

Egisix responded, "You ladies are absolute heroes! You have accomplished a lot more than we men have."

Goglbarj took pride in that statement. She took pride in being recognized as a successful leader of an army that made a significant difference.

Then Egisix continued to give an update of what he knew had happened. He explained how Amins had been destroyed but that the leprechauns were all safe. He explained how Gije and all her warriors were destroyed but that the majority of the population was hidden and was safe. He explained how the troll army was ransacking Hilebin and Hilebon right now and although a large number of trolls had been killed, there were still a lot left. They had just started their march back to Tragis.

Princess Ejijone noticed Egisix and ran up to him, giving him a big hug. Egisix was extremely uncomfortable. He had never so much as held the hand of the princess, let alone hugged her. Then she said, "It's wonderful to see a fellow dwarf." Then, seeing his embarrassment she added, "Don't be uncomfortable. War times change everything. We are all warriors together and you are my brother in battle."

Regaining his composure, Egisix said, "Don't get me wrong. I am thrilled by your hug. I just don't want to be disrespectful to someone I hold in such high esteem. I can't believe what you and your fellow warriors have been able to accomplish. The entire dwarf citizenship should be astoundingly proud of you."

After a pause Egisix commented, "We are definitely all warriors together. Please stay safe."

Then the princess said, "I'll do my best. I won't ask you how you managed to get here. I assume it's the same way as Goglbarj."

"Right you are," responded Egisix.

After giving each other updates, Egisix, Ejijone, and Goglbarj said their goodbyes and Egisix transformed himself back into a hawk, and flew off to excitedly update the north and the south on the incredibly successful efforts of the Swift Army.

After he left, Goglbarj called the leaders of the various species together in order to give them and update and to talk about next steps for the Swift Army. That included Goglbarj of the amazonionites, Jesves of the leprechauns, Queen Gushe of the elves, Princess Ejijone of the dwarfs, and Giantess Annala of the giants. Goglbarj started with the bad news, that Amins, Gije, Hilebin, and Hilebon had all been destroyed. Then she shared the good news that none of the leprechauns were killed, most of the elves were still alive and also most of the dwarfs had survived. There was a shriek of agony all around. Everyone seemed to have been directly affected except the giants and the amazonionites. But even they felt the pain of the others who had suffered extensive losses.

After about an hour, when the pain had finally sunk in, Goglbarj suggested a proposal, "Since the troll army is still up in the Hile Groves, it would be an excellent time for us to take over Tragis. With the new recruits from the giants, I think we would have an excellent chance of taking over that city, just like we did here in Gamotz."

Queen Gushe asked,

"You're proposing,
    That we move out of Gamotz,
That we conquer Tragis,
    That we do it immediately?"

"Exactly," answered Goglbarj.

In anger over her homeland being destroyed Ejijone barked, "Let's take those trolls out and that stinking Lord Krakus with them."

After her outburst, no one else wanted to say anything. Eventually Goglbarj asked, "Then it's unanimous. We're going to Tragis?"

"Absolutely," replied Jesves. The leaders of the various Swift species started organizing their warriors, letting them know the plan to go to Tragis. They would leave first thing in the morning.

The gnomes that were still living in Gamotz, even though it was under siege, had mixed emotions. They were happy about the idea that the Swift Army was leaving, but they wondered if they should warn the trolls of the pending attack. In the end they decided to send a couple messengers to Tragis to let them know what was happening.

The Swift guards that were posted on the walls noticed the gnomes trying to sneak out of Gamotz in the middle of the night. They quickly asked Goglbarj what they should do. Goglbarj, realizing the intent of the gnomes departure, sent one of the giants after them, realizing that the giants moved the fastest and could easily catch up with them. The giant chased and captured the gnomes, but since they fought back they ended up getting killed by the giant. The giant returned to the camp sharing the news to the happiness of the Swift Army, but to the disappointment of the remaining gnomes.

In the morning, everyone was ready and the march northward began. It would take them all day to get to Tragis and then they would have to make camp for the night, careful that hopefully they are not noticed by the enemy.

The leaders got together to discuss a plan of attack. Goglbarj started asking, "Should we do something similar to what we did in Morgos, and draw them out before we go after them with a full-blown attack?"

Jesves quickly jumped in and said, "Yes. Let's have the giants go to the north side because they can get there the quickest. Elves on one side and dwarfs on the other. And we leprechauns will try to draw them out as before. The amazonionites will stay with us and help us with the attack from the south."

Everyone was in agreement with the plan. "That sounds like a good plan. Why not go with a strategy that has worked so well in the past?" questioned Ejijone.

The plan was made and would be set in motion early the following day. The night's campout was successfully uneventful and early the following morning the Swift Army was on its way.

When the giants, dwarfs, and elves were in place, a small army of leprechauns approached the south walls of Tragis and started shooting flaming arrows over the walls. They were surprised that there were initially only a couple of troll guards on the walls, but the number increased dramatically and quickly as fires started burning inside the city.

The trick didn't work. There were no trolls storming out of the city gates. The gates stayed closed and the trolls on the walls continued to throw spears at the leprechauns, occasionally hitting one.

After an hour of futile effort to draw the trolls out, the giants decided to sneak in on the north side of the city. The trolls had mistakenly thought that the only attack was coming from the south side and had completely ignored the north side. A small group of giants snuck in close to the north wall of the city. Then, staying against the wall so they wouldn't be noticed, they worked their way around to the west side of the city where the gates of the city were located. After arriving at the gates, four of the strongest and biggest of the giants pushed against the gates with full force.

At first the gates resisted the attempts of the giants, not giving in very much. Then the giants backed off of the gates, and six of them, with shields on their shoulders, rushed against the gates and crashed into them, splintering and breaking the beams that held the gate secure. The gates didn't break away completely so it took a second charge to finish the job.

By now the trolls were aware of the attempt to break through the gates and trolls had rushed to the wall above the gates. More trolls ran to the inside of the gates, throwing spears at the giant intruders.

With the gates opened, the charge was on. Giants from the north and the dwarfs that were waiting on the west side of the city, came charging toward the city gates, hoping to burst through. The trolls weren't going to give in easily and they fought with all their ability, but they weren't the warrior trolls. The troll warriors were still in the Hile Groves doing battle with the dwarfs there. The trolls that were in Tragis were the women, the children, and the elderly. In spite of the fact that they put up a good fight, they were soon conquered by the dwarfs with their axes, and the stronger and more powerful giants with their clubs.

After about one hour of battle, the only trolls that were left were the ones hiding out in their homes. The Swift Army had no interest in invading every home. They weren't interested in wiping out the troll race. They were interested in preventing the Kabul takeover of Small World.

The Swift Army quickly barricaded the remaining trolls into their homes by barring their doors. They felt they needed to do this in order prevent any random attacks. Then they went about securing the city by closing and securing the front gates, and by posting guards on the tops of the walls.

Goglbarj went directly to the chambers of Lord Krakus, but he was nowhere to be found. He had completely disappeared. She knew he was hiding somewhere, but where? She had hoped to capture him as a type of trophy because she knew that his capture and surrender could mean that the Swift Army had won the war.

The army set about taking care of their dead and wounded. They were careful to make sure all parts of the city were secure and that there would be no more threats from the remaining trolls in the city.

Then it was time to celebrate. The Swift female army had accomplished what all the leaders from all the other cities of Small World had declared was impossible. They had conquered the three cities of the Kabul. They celebrated their success, but they also knew that the trolls from the north would eventually be coming home. They knew that their struggles weren't over yet.

***

Lord Krakus was beside himself. Where was this army coming from which was attacking Tragis. He couldn't believe the nerve of these foolish Small World citizens. These ridiculous leprechauns were attacking the stronghold of the entire Kabul. Did they really think they had a chance against trolls? Could this really be the army composed of the women of Small World? Was his army truly so weak that it was going to be destroyed by these women?

The Lord let out a call for his son, Prince Kakakrul. But the prince did not respond. Krakus was unsure what that meant since his son had always been responsive before.

The Lord exited his chambers to see what kind of threat these leprechaun invaders posed. He was walking towards the front gate when a loud crash occurred against the gate and he saw the beam splintering which normally was placed horizontally across both gates in order to prevent anyone gaining access.

The Lord asked the troll standing close to him, "What's happening? Leprechauns aren't strong enough to break through that gate?"

The troll answered, "There is an army of giants out there and they are the ones trying to break through the gates."

Krakus was astonished by the news. Giants here in the Kabul? How is that possible? Giants are shy and don't like to have contact with any other species. Why would they be working with leprechauns? Why would they be here in the Kabul?

The Lord rushed back into his chambers where he quickly locked the door. Then he went behind his desk and walked over to a bookcase on the wall that was behind the chair. He pulled two books halfway out and pushed two other specific books partially in, causing the bookcase to swing open like a door. He rushed through the door and pushed a button inside the opening causing a light to come on and causing the bookcase-door to close behind him. He felt safe here in Destroyer Kwdad's Caves of Dread. He assumed no one would ever be able to access these tunnels. The only problem he had was that he would never know when it would be safe to once again come out of these tunnels.

The Lord travelled down the twisted spiral staircase which was lit up by the bright red light that was generated from the power of Kwdad. The Lord was sure he would be able to find a safe place to hide out here while the battle above raged on. But what would he do if the trolls lost the battle? Would he be stuck down here forever?

***

Prince Kakakrul was discouraged and depressed as he flew northward over the Kabul. He was sure that he would be the next ruler of the Kabul, but he had hoped that by the time he became ruler that his father would have dominated all of Small World. Then Kakakrul would be the ruler of all of Small World. But now, with the failure of the Kabul Army in the Southern Plains he was no longer confident that he would be able to rule Small World. In fact his father might be so mad and discourage that he would disown Kakakrul as his son. The prince started to feel like he had lost everything.

The prince heard the call of his father, wanting him to come, but he didn't want to answer that call. He feared that his father was just going to be angry with his failures and he didn't need that level of rejection right now because he already felt frustrated and disappointed. He didn't need his father to add fuel to the fire.

The prince flew for Morgos as planned. He found the smell horrendous, but he felt like he didn't have a choice. He wanted to hide out somewhere where no one was likely to find him, and he knew that no one would want to come to Morgos with all the rotting dead body parts and the smell they made.

He cleared out a place for himself in the chambers of the previous magotite Prince Murqack. This would have to be his home for a while. This would be his place of mourning and suffering. This place would become a testament of his failure.

Chapter Twenty-Five

The Revenge of the Trolls

Egisix was flying over the Kabul on one of his message and communication missions when he noticed that the Swift Army had deserted Gamotz. He wondered where they could have gone and then it came to him; they must have attacked Tragis while the troll army was in the Hile Groves. He flew up to Tragis and discovered that it was true. The Swift Army had not only attacked Tragis, but they had conquered the city and were now in possession of it.

The discovery threw Egisix into a panic. He celebrated the bravery, strength and success of the Swift Army, but he also knew that they would probably be wiped out by the thousands of trolls that were returning from the battle with the dwarfs. In his mind, the ladies had made their mark and they had been significantly more successful than the men, but to allow this slaughter would be crazy.

Egisix decided to take it upon himself to ask for help. But who should he ask? The only thing that made sense, since the warriors from the dwarfs and the elves had been wiped out was the giants. He had to go directly to Giant-giant and announce the situation to him. They were not only the strongest, but they were the only species that could move fast enough to get to Tragis in time to help out and to save the Swift Army. Then he would go to Bydola and ask him to go to Tragis to cure the injured in the Swift Army.

Egisix flew directly to the giant army that was camped out in the plains above Giter. He informed Giant-giant, "The women of the Small World species have formed their own army and ventured into the Kabul. They include elves, dwarfs, leprechauns, amazonionites, and giants."

"Giants," barked Giant-giant. "Our women wouldn't be stupid enough to join in a crazy venture like that. Are you telling me that giant women are part of the army?"

Egisix responded, "There are over one hundred and twenty-five giants in this female army and the leader is Giantess Annala, your wife."

Giant-giant had always considered himself too strong to be shocked, but he was now stunned so badly that it could only be interpreted as shock. He just stood there with his mouth draped open in unbelief.

After a pause of several minutes Egisix continued, "The female army, which has been called the Swift Army, has been extremely successful. First they captured Morgos and successfully wiped out the magotite species. Next they attacked and conquered Gamotz, the gnome city, because the gnome warriors were gone and attacking Amins and Gije. They stayed there long enough to rebuild their weapons supply and to recruit another one hundred giants."

Egisix continued, "They learned that the trolls were in the Hile Groves, and so they decided to attack Tragis, assuming that all the warriors would be gone from that city. That turned out to be true and

they successfully conquered and invaded that city. That is where they are hold up now."

Then the dwarf added, "The reason I have come here to you is because thousands of trolls are returning from the Hile Groves and they will be arriving in Tragis, and I don't think the Swift Army will be strong enough to hold them off, even though they are inside the city walls."

Then Giant-giant said, "Then we must rush up there to help them out."

"My thoughts exactly," responded Egisix. "I didn't think you would want to sacrifice over one hundred of your women even though they have proven themselves braver than any of us. I think they need and deserve your help."

"We will leave immediately," responded Giant-giant.

Then Egisix requested, "Can one of your giants come with me to Amins. I'm hoping I can get Bydola to also go to Tragis and heal the injured there, but he would need someone to carry him. He can't move as fast as you giants can."

"Absolutely," responded Giant-giant. Someone was assigned to go with Egisix and carry him to Amins. The two left immediately for Amins while Giant-giant rounded up his troops and told them they were going to help the lady giants. Everyone was extremely surprised by the story of the Swift Army's success but no one hesitated. They all knew some giant that was probably a part of the Swift Army, and they were eager and anxious to help. They also left immediately for the Avol River crossing, and then up to the Kabul.

Upon arriving in Amins, Egisix retold the entire story that he had relayed earlier to Giant-giant. The reaction of the leprechauns was similar to the reaction of the giants. They were in shock.

Elasti said, "I knew Jesves and the rest of those women were up to something, but this is incredible. They have been heroes while we have been here hiding out in the Amins Groves, hoping the trees would protect us. I feel like a coward compared to them. What can we do to help?"

Egisix explained, "We need Bydola to come with us to Tragis. There are many injured and they desperately need healing. And there will most likely be more need for healings once the trolls get back to Tragis."

"Of course," responded Bydola. "Let's leave right now."

Egisix continued his explanation, "This giant will carry you so you can move quickly."

"Excellent," responded Bydola. "We will cut through the Amins Groves and try to catch up with the rest of the giants at the Avol River crossing. Then we will proceed with them to Tragis."

The support mission was arranged and the giants, along with Bydola, were off for the Kabul.

***

The Swift female army had accomplished what all the leaders from all the other cities of Small World had considered to be too ridiculous to even consider and declared as impossible. The Swift Army celebrated their success all the time realizing that their biggest battle was still ahead of them. The trolls from the north would eventually be coming home.

The Swift Army spent the next couple days building up defenses and preparing weapons, for example making arrows. They were nervous and scared, not knowing what was coming at them. But they were determined to win this last battle just the same way as they had won the previous two, or they would go down trying.

The first few days seemed peaceful, but then it happened. The yell came out from the centuries along the walls surrounding Tragis, "We see the troll army coming in the distance."

Yelling would turn out to be a mistake because the remaining trolls that were in the city became empowered and energized. They started trying to break free from their captivity so they could help the returning trolls. In the end, the Swift Army fought a battle inside and outside the walls surrounding Tragis.

The returning trolls were walking along as if they didn't have a care in the world. They thought they were victors and that they were returning home to a celebration of the defeat of the dwarfs. They wondered why the gates hadn't been thrown wide open and tr0lls hadn't come rushing out to celebrate and to welcome them home. Unfortunately, as they started getting close to the gates, a shower of spears and arrows greeted them, killing many of the first row of trolls immediately.

It was then that they finally realized that this city was no longer under troll control. The fell back and regrouped, trying to decide what to do about this new challenge. Their city had been conquered and probably many of their women and children slaughtered. This was not something that the troll warriors were willing to tolerate.

Although the troll leaders attempted to control their warriors, it was unsuccessful. The trolls madly rushed at the gates of the city, trying to crash through. Other trolls would climb on the shoulders of their companions, which allowed them to reach over the walls of the city since the walls of Tragis were designed to keep out all the smaller species. They never counted on the giants.

Hordes of arrows flew from the walls of the city. Hundreds of trolls fell, but there were thousands more coming behind them. The Swift Army elves, leprechauns, and amazonionites had badly underestimated the size of the troll army and, even though they had created thousands of arrows in Gamotz, the arrows were soon running in short supply.

Dwarfs had gone outside the walls of the city, crawling through a hole on the back side. They used their ax throwing techniques and cut the legs off many of the trolls. Unfortunately, even though a large number of trolls lost their legs, the dwarfs were also over-whelmed by the never-ending number of trolls, and soon fell victim to troll swords and clubs.

At one point in the battle the gates were opened, and a swarm of giants charged out of the city. They battled the trolls, and each giant killed a dozen or more trolls before they lost their own lives. The entire war seemed futile.

The battle raged on for hours. The flow of trolls seemed endless and they were wildly aggressive because it was their home that they were defending. The Swift Army was becoming decimated, but everyone knew that if they quit, they would all be wiped out. There was no other option but to continue the fight.

The trolls had found a log and using it as a battering ram they pounded against the gate. Again and again they banged hard, hoping to break through while above them the Swift warriors dropped rocks, threw spears, and shot arrows, killing off trolls as they tried repeatedly to get into Tragis. Eventually the trolls were able to break the gate. They couldn't break the beam but they splintered up one of the doors. They created a hole that was big enough for the trolls to crawl through, and with that opening the trolls started flooding into the city.

It became the task of the giants to fight off the trolls that were coming into the city. At first it was an easy battle for them because there weren't very many trolls, but as the number of the enemy in-creased it became more difficult to keep the trolls away. Trolls ganged up on individual giants and were successful in occasionally killing one. The ratio was ten to twenty trolls to every giant killed, but there were so many trolls that even this ratio seemed insigni-ficant.

The battle was becoming overwhelming for the Swift Army and they were starting to become battle weary and discouraged. They were realizing that this may be the end for all of them.

Suddenly and unexpectedly the trolls stopped their attack. The trolls that had entered the city, ran back outside. The Swift Army ran to the top of the walls to see what was happening. What they saw astounded them and gave them an enormous amount of relief.

What they saw was Giant-giant and his army of giants charging down on the troll army. And the troll army had turned to fight them. The giants were screaming and yelling, trying to draw the full attention of the trolls away from attacking Tragis and refocus it on them. When the two forces met, it was a horrendous slaughter. The giants hammered the trolls so badly that many of them started running. The fierceness of the giants, and the fact that the ratio was such that the trolls were no longer dominant in their numbers, brought fear into the hearts of the trolls. They ran off by the hundreds.

The giants didn't pursue them. Giant-giant felt they had accomplished their purpose. The Kabul forces had been defeated. Now his attention turned to the Swift Army. He walked up to the gate and asked, "You are the heroes of Small World. You have done the impossible. I never realized your incredible capabilities and I am truly astonished. I bow to Giantess Annala and hope that she is still safe. Will you now allow a vicious group of male giants to enter into your all-female domain?"

Annala responded, "What took you so long? We were ready to give up. And how did you find out about us anyway?"

"Egisix informed us about your dilemma and how badly you were outnumbered. We came running as soon as we found out. Up to now we had no idea how successful you had been in your battles here in the Kabul. We didn't even know your army existed. Your entire army is truly our heroes and we bow in respect of what you have accomplished. You almost singlehandedly saved Small World. Can we enter? We have brought a special surprise with just for you."

"Please come in," responded Annala. Then, after he had walked through the city gates, she asked, "What is this surprise?"

"We have Bydola with us and if you haven't heard of him before, he is the leprechaun healer," answered Giant-giant.

"Hurrah," yelled Jesves. "I have seen him perform numerous healings. We need him badly. We have many seriously injured warriors."

Bydola climbed off the back of the giant that has been carrying him and he asked, "Is there a fountain of water somewhere?"

"The only thing we have is a trough for drinking," answered Goglbarj. "Will that work?"

"Yes," responded Bydola. "Start bringing me your injured, starting with the most seriously injured first."

As Bydola started performing the healings there was a bittersweet reunion between Giant-giant and Giantess Annala. Giant-giant said, "Today you are my hero. I don't know what I would have done if I lost you." These same sentiments were felt by several of the giant couples who were reunited.

A special pond had to be created by digging up dirt walls and filling the pond with water. The trough was too small for healing the giants.

It took several hours, but eventually the healings were all successfully performed. Even many of the Swift warriors that had injuries from some of the previous battles at Morgos or Gamotz were now able to be healed.

During the healings, the dead were also taken care of using the rituals appropriate to their species. Some required burials, some burnings, and others were placed on rooftops for the birds to eat. The trolls that were left in the city were forced to come out of their homes and take care of their own dead. These trolls were non-warriors and they were now outnumbered so they hesitated to fight back against the Swift and Giant Armies. They went ahead taking care of their dead by building a huge pile of bodies and then burning them.

There was a lot of morning and sadness on all sides which lasted for several hours. Then, after the healings and the funerary rituals were completed, it came time to celebrate. But everyone was too exhausted to celebrate.

It was now the middle of the night, and everyone seemed to collapse wherever they ended up. Guards were assigned to watch over the city, primarily because they didn't want any of the trolls living in the city to attack anyone in revenge, and they didn't want the trolls who had run away to come back and try to recapture the city.

The following morning was a time for celebration. Although they were still war weary, everyone from the Swift Army and the Giant Army joined together in a celebration of the defeat of the Kabul. All three cities had been conquered, and the Kabul Lord and his prince were nowhere to be found.

The Giant Army hailed the Swift Army as the heroes of Small World. They had demonstrated extreme bravery and courage. There was no distinction or segregation by species. They had all become united in the type of friendship and fellowship that comes from having suffered and worked together.

Suddenly and dramatically, as if to make a statement of its own, the Kabul Volcano, which was just a short distance to the east of Tragis, exploded in excitement. The eruption was so loud that it caused everyone's ears to ring. Red hot rocks could be seen blasting out of its top and red hot lava could be seen flowing down it's sides. Red boulders could be seen flying as far as Tragis and landing in the city, casing numerous fires.

Goglbarj quickly called all the leaders together and suggested, "The war is over. Now is the time for us to get out of here before the volcano lava reaches the city and reaches us."

Queen Gushe added,

> "We need to go home,
> > And rebuild our lives,
> The worst is over,
> > Now the healing survives."

Jesves added, "There's something missing if we each go home and forget what we have accomplished here together. There is a story to be told and we need to share it with all of Small World. We should establish an annual time of celebration where all species get together and share with each other. We are no longer separated but we are all of Small World and we are united as one."

Ejijone suggested, "We need to form a delegation which will go around and tell everyone what has happened, and then invite everyone to reunite in one year from today here in Tragis."

"Agreed," added Jesves. "I will be one of those delegates since my role in leading the leprechauns has ended now that the Kabul is defeated."

"My usefulness has also ended so I will join you," responded Goglbarj.

Then Queen Gushe added,

> "And I will join you,
> > We will be a threesome.
> You can always use a queen,
> > To make us fearsome."

The three organized themselves together and departed Tragis as a group. They were fearsome indeed. They were the perfect picture of unity and strength as they marched away from Tragis with the volcano erupting and spuing its terror in the background.

The remainder of the Swift army organized themselves into two separate groups with the southerners, including the elves, leprechauns, and giants, heading south and the northerners, including the amazonionites and the dwarfs, heading north.

As far as they knew, the war had been won. The Lord and the prince were gone, and the three Kabul armies have been defeated. And, even more importantly, the species of Small World have been united in a partnership that they swore they would always maintain.

Little did they know that there was still one more battle that needed to be fought. And this was the most important battle of all. It was the battle of good vs. evil which would define the future of Small World for many years to come.

Chapter Twenty-Six

The Wizard's Showdown

The wizard spent the day studying the scrolls followed by a comfortable night's rest. The following morning Ordo again arrived, hoping to lead the wizard to the evil caves, but the wizard once again insisted, "Please allow me to spend another day here, studying the Tako scrolls. I have learned a lot but I feel like there is still more for me to learn before I am ready to take on the evil."

"Of course," responded the worlepreek. "I'll come and check on you in the morning and see how you're doing and find out if you're ready to enter the evil caves."

"Thanks," was all the wizard said, and Ordo departed.

It was a quiet and peaceful day for the wizard, and he would have gladly spent many more days like this, reading and studying. He didn't look forward to confronting the evil that existed. He wanted to find out if the Protee power would give him other strengths that he could use to fight evil. He wasn't sure why the power to make light was so important. He searched for other spells that may help him accomplish the task he had been assigned.

His continued study helped him to better understand the evil he would be confronting. He realized and understood why it had to be him and him alone who would make this connection. He also learned the role the Lamos would play in the final defeat of Kwdad the Destroyer.

The day was spent in intensive study. But in the end, the wizard was still not clear on exactly what he should be doing. He wasn't sure what it would take to defeat Kwdad.

He spent a restless night wondering and worrying about the events of the next day. However, he felt as ready as he could possibly be.

When Ordo arrived in the morning the wizard was up and ready. He was nervous but by this time he just wanted to get it over with. He felt like he had overthought all the possibilities of how this encounter would play out, and he couldn't think of any more scenarios. He had arrived at the point where he just wanted it done.

Ordo led him through a series of tunnels until they arrived at a door which was heavily sealed off with multiple locks and cross-beams. There were several guards at the door, waiting in anticipation of the wizard's arrival. The door was carefully opened, and the wizard was allowed to enter into a dark, low tunnel. He would be forced to crawl, but before anything else, he would have to make a light to help him see.

The wizard grabbed a stone that he saw lying on the ground and holding it in his hands he said the words, "By the power of the Protee, I Raviump turn this stone into light." Immediately the stone started to glow with a bright orange light. With that light the wizard could see a long distance down the tunnel. It seemed to have no end. It seemed to go on forever.

The worlepreeks closed the door behind the wizard and he could hear the lock clicked shut. This was a one-way journey for him. If he didn't find another way out, he would be locked in these caves and tunnels forever. And that didn't sound very appealing to him. Either way, he was committed to making this effort successful for the sake of all of Small World.

He started his long journey down the tunnel, hoping there would be no surprises. He watched for boobytraps which might come at him from any direction. From previous expeditions into caves he had heard stories about traps like the retants which were roots that came out of the walls of the cave and captured its victims, sucking their blood out of them. He also heard about the Erates which were floating tiles with large cracks between them that dropped away into the Lamos. He knew he had to be careful.

He travelled on, carefully making sure he wouldn't get captured by any of these traps that the previous expeditions had encountered.

After several hours, he started to wonder if this tunnel would ever end.

The tunnel took a turn and he could see the slight glimmer of a red light far off in the distance. He welcomed the end to his having to crawl in these tunnels, but he also wondered what would happen next.

It was a couple hours later when he finally arrived at a large cavern which was lit by a red light. He put his orange glowing rock in his pocket, temporarily muting it from giving off any light.

The cavern had tunnels leading off in several different directions so the wizard would have to make a decision. He decided to follow the tallest of the tunnels for no other reason than that it would allow him to walk upright for a little while.

All the tunnels were now lit with the same red light and he followed the taller one for a short while until it opened up into another cavern. He once again had to choose and he followed another tunnel that was taller. The walk was again a short one and as he started to come close to a rather large cavern he could hear someone conversing. He became cautious and approached the end of the tunnel hoping that no one would notice his presence. Eventually he arrived at a large circular cavern. The entrance to the cavern was as if he were entering the side of a ball. He could see nothing inside, but it glowed red. After arriving at the doorway, he did his best to spy into the inside of the cavern, without revealing his presence.

The conversation he was listening to was between Lord Krakus and Kwdad. Krakus said, "I'm here Master Kwdad. I came down to talk to you about my mission. Tragis is being invaded and I wanted to get your insight as to what I should be doing?" Kwdad was sitting on his throne at one end of the room and Krakus was standing in front of him with his head bowed down.

Kwdad responded, "Who would be foolish enough to invade into the Kabul? That's simply not rational. Don't they know they'll get destroyed?"

"I don't know how to answer that," replied the Lord. "They are indeed being very foolish."

"Who is this individual that you brought with you?" asked Kwdad.

"What individual?" asked Krakus.

"The one hiding at the end of the cave," replied Kwdad. Then he commanded the wizard, "Come out here you fool. Come out to where we can see you. I always wanted to meet the Wizard of Havinis."

It was obvious to the wizard that somehow Kwdad had identified his presence, so he stepped out into the cell. "What can I do for you?" asked the wizard, not really knowing what else to say."

The wizard noticed that now that he was in the Kwdad's cavern, the floor seemed to move. Looking down he noticed that he was standing on the Erates. He realized that he had to be careful to not step into the cracks which led down to the Lamos.

"How did you get here?" challenged Krakus.

"I had friends help me get into these caves," responded the wizard.

Kwdad was turning red with fury, "You asked what you can do for me. The answer is that you can die." Kwdad flashed a bolt of red light directly at the wizard, assuming that the lightning bolt would instantly destroy him. However, when the red bolt struck the wizard, it seemed to have no effect. Instantly an orange shield formed around the wizard, protecting him from Kwdad's bolt.

Kwdad screamed, "The wizard has the Protee powers. Krakus, push him into the cracks of the Erates so that he will fall into the Lamos."

The wizard received a message into his head from the Creator which said, "Throw your rock at Krakus."

Krakus charged madly at the wizard, knocking him to the ground, but he did not fall into the Erates. Instead he jumped back up again, threw his orange rock in the direction of Krakus, and it flashed its own bolt of lightning. This time the bolt was orange and it struck Krakus hard, knocking him to the ground.

But Krakus wasn't to be stopped. He jumped up and charged at the wizard a second time, this time hanging on to him as they both went down. Krakus was stubborn and would not be defeated easily. They both got up and the Lord jumped up charging towards the wizard. This time the wizard was ready. He jumped out of the way of his attacker and then stuck his staff out causing Krakus to trip, stumble a few steps, and then fall.

Kwdad was angry, both at Krakus and at the wizard. He saw them both as fools. He shot another bolt of red light at the wizard and instead of hitting the wizard an orange light again surrounded him and deflected the red energy bolt off of himself. The bolt hit Krakus instead as he was trying to get up and knocked him back to the ground. This time Krakus was a lot slower at getting up. He struggled and as the Erates tile moved he slipped again.

"You better stay down there before you fall in the crack," commented Kwdad. Then, addressing the wizard he said, "What am I supposed to do with you? I can't just allow you to invade my world."

"You can jump in the Lamos along with your friend here," chided the wizard.

Kwdad fired another red lightning bolt at the wizard. This time it was a lot more powerful than the previous bolts and it ended up knocking the wizard to the ground, causing him to slide on the Erates tile. He slipped and started falling into the crack between the tiles. He was left hanging over the edge of one of the tiles.

Krakus jumped up and ran toward the wizard, hoping to push him over, but the wizard was too quick. The wizard received a spurt of energy and jumped up just in time to save himself.

The wizard had read about how the light had more power than just offering the ability to see. He could see how Kwdad used the light as a weapon against him and he wondered if he could also use the orange light that he had been given by the Creator in any other way as a weapon against Krakus and Kwdad.

The wizard had seen how Kwdad had used his light and he decided to give it a try. In his mind he said, "By the power of the Protee, I Raviump use the light to shoot a lightning bolt." He pointed his staff at Kwdad and, to the shock and surprise of the wizard, Kwdad, and Krakus, a lightning bolt shrieked out of the end of his staff and struck Kwdad, knocking him slightly backward.

"I see that you learned something new," chided Kwdad. "Let's see which one of us is better at this new game."

Kwdad started sending a series of bolts, one right after another, at the wizard, causing him to stumble backward. Additionally, Krakus charged him attempting to push him into the Lamos.

The wizard quickly repeated the process of point his staff, this time aiming at Krakus and knocking him down and causing him to slide over several tiles, but he was unsuccessful in knocking him into the Lamos. The wizard tried a second time, this time even stronger, and pushed Krakus so far that he hit his head against a wall and wasn't able to recover for quite some time. Krakus just lay there along the wall while the wizard continued exchanging lightning bolts with Kwdad.

The wizard hoped he had seen the last of Krakus, but it was not to be. Krakus returned to consciousness and tried to get up. Unfortunately, he was still dazed from his hit on the head as he raced toward the wizard, again hoping to knock him into the Lamos.

The wizard was quick and stepped aside as Krakus came charging toward him. Then, as Krakus stumbled past the wizard, the wizard gave him a hard push and Krakus tripped, stumbled, and slid into one of the larger Erates cracks. He held onto the edge with one hand for several seconds, but in the end his effort to save himself was futile and he slipped away into the Lamos, never to be seen in Small World again.

Then a strange thing occurred. The Erates started to emit a strange, eerie, shrieking, high pitched sound that was deafening. It even made the wizard slightly dizzy. It was as if they were thanking him for sending Krakus down into the Lamos as a kind of treat.

The battle of lightning bolts continued to rage on between the wizard and Kwdad. Neither seemed to be getting the upper edge. The wizard's bolts seemed to be more effective, since Kwdad didn't have the same effective shielding, but Kwdad was better at shooting the bolts and would often deflect the wizard's bolts by shooting directly at and hitting the wizard's bolts.

The battle seemed fruitless. It seemed as if neither side had any chance of winning. Both seemed evenly matched using their secret light weapon. But then the wizard remembered something he had read in the scrolls. It didn't seem important at the time he read it, but now it made sense. The scripture in the scroll said, "The light can push and pull."

This revelation was followed by a message from the Creator which said, "Use your power to pull Kwdad off his throne."

The wizard thought he'd see what would happen if he pulled. He said the words, "By the power of the Protee, I Raviump use the light to pull."

What came out of his pointing staff this time was not a lightning bolt, but something that looked like a whip. The whip wrapped itself around Kwdad, holding his arms to his side, and yanked him up off his throne and pulled him towards the wizard. He came so close that the wizard was able to punch him in the nose. Then he said, "By the power of the Protee, I Raviump use the light to push." This time Kwdad was pushed backwards violently and slammed against the side wall.

The push replaced the magic rope with a lightning bolt and allowed Kwdad to have his hands free and, as he was being pushed backwards he also shot the wizard with another lightning bolt. This time the wizard was slightly startled and started to fall backwards. The bolt had penetrated through the wizard's shield and had given him a jerk, causing him to trip and slip and nearly fall into a Erates crack.

The battle of the lightning bolts resumed with neither of the combatants gaining the upper hand. The wizard felt he must try something different. He tried to remember anything from the scrolls that might help. He remembered a scripture which said, "The light of the Creator overpowers all light." He wondered what that meant. The orange lightning bolt didn't seem to be any stronger than the red bolt, so in what way was the orange light stronger?

Again the Creator came through with a message, "Turn off the light!"

In desperation the wizard thought he would try something. He said, "By the power of the Protee, I Raviump use the orange light to turn the red light of evil into orange."

Nothing happened. The battle of the lightning bolts continued with red and orange shooting wildly at each other.

Still in desperation the wizard thought he would try something else. He said, "By the power of the Protee, I Raviump use the Creator's light to stop the red light of evil."

This time it worked. Maybe the reference to the Creator's light made the difference. He wasn't sure what the difference was, but suddenly the red light was gone and only the orange light remained.

Kwdad, seeing that his red power was gone, was no longer able to shoot his lightning bolts. He charged headfirst toward the wizard, wrapped his arms around him, and crashed him to the ground. The charge pushed them along the ground for several feet and both the wizard and Kwdad drifted over the edge of an Erates crack.

The wizard tried to push Kwdad off, but that was also unsuccessful and they both continued to slip. Neither wanted to fall into the crack so they ended up holding on to each other in the hope they wouldn't fall, but in the end their struggling caused them both to slip over the edge. They started to fall, deeper and deeper down into the Lamos. The orange light of the Creator lit up the pit that they were falling into, but they could see no bottom.

They let go of each other. Both the wizard and Kwdad were flapping their arms as if they wished they could fly, but there was nothing; nothing to hold on to, noting to catch them, just nothing.

Chapter Twenty-Seven

The End

The Tragis volcano became more and more violent. The remaining troll residents of Tragis had to run for their lives as the lava from the volcano came closer and closer to the city. Eventually the entire town was burned and the Lord's entrance to Kwdad's cave was sealed. The source of evil had been closed.

The mist wall that surrounded the Kabul also disappeared. It was held up by the evil and when evil was destroyed, so was the wall. The entirety of the Kabul changed. It started to transform itself from brown to green. It would take many years of transformation, but eventually the Kabul would look like all the other parts of Small World.

The three Swift Army leaders who were going to share the message of the war, Queen Gushe the elf, Goglbarj the amazonionite, and Jesves the leprechaun, marched off toward the north. They decided they would visit the dwarfs first, sharing their story of the defeat of the Kabul. When they approached Hilebin they were horrified by the extend of the destruction.

The threesome told their story, to the horror and excitement of the entire community. They were all filled with excitement when they learned how much the Swift Army had accomplished.

Princess Ejijone, the dwarf, also arrived a couple days later with the remainder of her dwarf army. The dwarf community, having heard the story of the Swift Army, gave a cheer and shout for joy when they arrived. The entire community was extremely proud of their female army and even the King Egione bowed his head in reverence as they walked down the main thoroughfare of the city.

The city was destroyed but not the hearts of the people, they lived on and everyone knew that the town could be rebuilt. Saving the lives of its citizens was more critical. They couldn't be restored if they were lost.

The day of celebration was followed by a day of mourning for all those dwarfs, both male and female, who had lost their lives, in the struggle to save Small World. Following the two days, the three companions were about to leave when they were approached by Garbona, the lepelf, and Obydon, the leprechaun who was the carrier of the Southern Sword, both of which had stayed behind in Hilebin when the rest of their party headed south. Obydon spoke to the threesome first, "I would like to travel with you back to the south so I can rejoin my citizens in Amins."

"Of course," responded Jesves, who was a participant in the expedition that had brought the sword to the north for the crossing of the swords.

Then Garbona spoke up, "I've heard Giter has been destroyed and there are very few if any lepelves left but I would also like to travel with you back to my home and see for myself what has happened."

Again, Jesves answered, "Of course. There were only a few lepelves who survived because they were outside the city when it was attacked. They have moved to Amins. I am sure they will be delighted to have you join with them."

The fivesome departed from Hilebin and headed south. The journey would take several days and would require a trip through the Kabul, rather than taking the Albo or Kilo Pass. Obydon and Garbona were anxious to see the destruction of the Kabul on their way south.

***

The wizard fell further and further into the Lamos. There seemed to be no end. He clung to a second orange rock that had given him light, hoping to see something, anything that would help. All he could see was Kwdad falling away in the nothingness below him. In his mind the wizard decided to go crazy in his desperation to save himself and said, "By the power of the Protee, I Raviump give myself the power to fly."

A flash of light occurred and suddenly he was transformed into a vulture. He could fly. But now what? Since all the red light had been extinguished up above him he could no longer see where he came from. He couldn't find his way back. Everything was a dark nothingness. He fluttered upward, still carrying the orange glowing rock in his claw. Then he circled around, looking for anything, but there was nothing. He started flying in an ever-increasing circle, becoming more and more tired by the minute. He wasn't sure if his fate at becoming a vulture was any better than falling into the Lamos.

All he could do was to continue to fly until he eventually would get worn out, give up, and drop. And then the shrieking sound of the Lamos began to deafen the wizard and make him dizzy.

***

The prince Kakakrul flew to Morgos and transformed himself into an prince. Because the horrendous smell made him gag he wasn't be able to stay there. Then he flew into the woods to the southwest of Morgos and decided to stay there. He was hiding out from his father. He was hiding out from the world. He had been a complete failure and he no longer wanted to talk to or hear from anyone.

He had camped out for a couple days when a large group of trolls came rushing towards him. When they saw the prince they slowed down and the prince asked them, "Why are you here? Why aren't you defending Tragis?"

"Tragis has been conquered," was the response. "Almost all the trolls have been destroyed. We are all that was left of our species. We had to save ourselves."

The prince's first reaction was to call them all cowards but he also realized that the magotites were gone and the gnomes were almost also completely gone. These trolls were all that was left of his kingdom. "What of my father?" asked the prince.

"He just disappeared," was the response. "We don't know what happened to him."

"Where are you planning to go?" asked Kakakrul. "Morgos isn't accessible because of all the stink. Gamotz is possible because the majority of the gnomes are wiped out, but last time I checked it still had invaders in there as well. And their homes are far too small for trolls."

"We follow you my prince," was the troll's response.

"Then we camp here for now," said the prince. "I'll let you know what our plan is as soon as I decide."

"Thank you," answered the troll. "We will camp with you." The trolls proceeded to make camp.

A couple of days later more trolls appeared and this time they were even more in a panic. "What's going on in Tragis?" asked the prince.

"The volcano erupted and Tragis is now completely destroyed by lava," was the response of this new group.

"What about the invaders?" asked the prince.

"They left as soon as the volcano erupted."

"What about my father?" the prince repeated his earlier question.

"No idea. If he was in Tragis, he is lost. The lava has completely consumed the city."

The prince knew that their efforts to gain control of Small World had been a complete disaster. The only good news was that he was no longer responsible to report to his father. The prince was now the leader of what was left of the Kabul, which wasn't very much.

***

The three heroes, Goglbarj, Jesves, and Gushe, along with their two add-ons, Obydon and Garbona, made their march toward the south over the next couple days. They decided to go to Amins first because three of their party wanted to go there.

The travelled through the Kabul. At the bottom end of the Kabul they went down the Kilo Pass and onto the South Road. From there they travelled east over the Avol River and continued on to Giter. In Giter they stopped temporarily to view the destruction.

Garbona was visibly shaken. "My home, the palace, my father's tavern, all is gone. The entire city is a waste land." Tears welled up in his eyes.

The travelers spent a night in the plains above the city and then continued on the next day using the South Road. Eventually they ended up in Amins, where they encountered the leprechauns working hard to rebuild their city. As they walked into the city, citizens came out from all directions to greet them. They had already learned a lot about the capture of the Kabul from the Swift

troops that had returned and from Bydola who had returned with them, but they were anxious to learn more.

Mostly they wanted to celebrate Jesves' return. She was the hero of the hour and everyone hailed her with praise. But Jesves only had one interest and that was the safety of all her previous traveling companions. She found Elasti with Jizeel and they seemed to be happily reunited. They were soon to be married.

Gido the elf had also remained in Amins and had his arm wrapped around Goglhick the amazonionite. The two of them seemed to be making plans that would keep them in Amins, rather than return to their own homes.

In the meantime Goglbarj addressed the crowd and repeated the stories that she had told in Hilebin, focusing on the need to unite the species and work together as one. She gave a strong message about unifying and saving their cultures, and about the elimination of evil which she felt had been symbolized by the disappearance of the mist wall.

Garbona was overwhelmed by the reception that he received from the remaining lepelves. There were only ten of them, but they hailed him as their hero. One of the lepelves yelled out, "Garbona is our new king. Hail to king Garbona."

Garbona was shocked. He never expected this type of reception and his response was, "I can't be a king. I don't know anything about being a king."

The remaining lepelves responded, "We know even less. You are now our hero and king, whether you like it or not."

Garbona, resigning himself to be the king, said, "Since you insist that I am your king, then this is my wish and desire. We will rebuild our city, one small building at a time. And we will always be in debt to all the species of Small World. They will all be our friends and we will continue to help each other just as we did during this war. There will no longer be animosity between us and the other species. That ends now!"

The lepelves let out a cheer yelling, "We have truly selected the right man to be our king."

During this time Goglbarj continued telling her stories to anyone that would listen. When she finished her stories, Amaz asked, "What about the wizard, the Kabul Lord, and the prince?"

Goglbarj responded, "They have all just disappeared. We think the Lord was hiding somewhere in Tragis but that he was killed when the lava from the volcano swept over the city. But the prince and the wizard may still be around. We just don't know. Maybe the wizard has gone back to sleep until the next time the swords are crossed, but we know nothing for sure."

The three hero leaders of the Swift Army stayed in Amins for a couple days, celebrating the end of the war with them. Then they journeyed on to Gije, following the South Road the entire way. Queen Gushe was especially anxious to return to her home. After seeing the destruction in Hilebin and Amins she feared what she might find in Gije.

The journey took a couple days, but they eventually arrived to find the city in ruins. Queen Gushe was overcome and tears welled up in her eyes. There were a several elves walking around and working on cleaning up the mess. It was mostly the elf contingent of the Swift Army that was doing all the work. They were working on cleaning up the destructive mess that the Kabul Army had left behind.

Queen Gushe asked one of them,
  "Tell me what,
    Has happened here?
  Where are our warriors?
    I have great fear."
The elf answered,
  "Our warriors are gone,
    Buried they are,
  Our elders and youth,
    In caves hide out."
The queen asked,"
  "What of the king?
    How did he fare?
  Is he in caves?
    Did he beware?"
The elf answered,
  "He is a hero,
    He fought hard and brave,
  He fought with our warriors,
    But we could not save!"
The queen commanded,
  "Bring them out,
    To celebrate our victory,
  We will share,
    To tell our stories."

It wasn't long before the town center was filled with elves anxious to hear the stories that were to be shared. The queen walked out in front of the crowd and raised her hand for silence, but instead of silence, what she heard was,

"Hail Queen Gushe,
        She is our hero,
    She will lead us,
            She has been proven!"
When the chants calmed down the queen said,
    "Our amazonionite hero,
            Our story will tell,
        She will give all,
                The message from hell!"
Goglbarj then took the stage and repeated, for a third time, the story of the fall of the Kabul. The elves were enthralled. They loved hearing the stories. When she was finished the queen took over and said,

    "Tomorrow will be,
            Celebration all day,
    The next day will be,
            Morning all day,
    The third day and after,
            We will rebuild,
    The Gije of before,
            When we were thrilled."
The elves let out a cheer and applause. There would be much mourning, but that would wait for a day. First, they needed celebrate the end of the evil that was known as the Kabul.

Or was it the end?

When the celebration was over, Goglbarj transformed herself into an owl and flew toward the Central Ranges. She was exhausted. She was drained from the fighting, from the traveling, and from the story telling. She now longed to once again be safely at home.

THUS ENDS THE THIRD BOOK
IN THE SERIES

THE HISTORY OF THE
SMALL WORLD

About the Author

Gerhard Plenert

Professor Plenert has completed numerous fiction series titles thus far in his literary career. Both fantasy fiction and police procedural / woman sleuth / mystery – whodunit series are his newest passions. The professor features over 20 years of academia where he has published over 150 articles and 25 books referencing Lean methods including supply chain strategy and operations management and planning. He has also written MBA and operations planning text-books for the United Nations. His ideas and publications have been endorsed by Steven Covey and at companies such as AT&T, Black & Decker, FedEx, Motorola, etc.

As former Director of Executive Education at Utah State University Shingo Institute, Dr. Plenert features 25 plus years of professional organizational transformation reach back where he has continuously aided companies and government agencies with Shingo Model enterprise excellence. An internationally recognized expert, Professor Plenert supplies IT; leading-edge planning and scheduling methodologies; Lean Six Sigma; quality and productivity tool assurance; and supply chain management having "written the book" on innovative management concepts, such as advanced planning and scheduling, finite capacity scheduling, and world-class management.

Dr. Plenert has engaged significant initiatives with Aerojet Rocketdyne, Aramco, Cisco, Genentech, Johnson & Johnson, Microsoft, NCR Corporation, Ritz-Carlton, Seagate, Shell, Sony, US Air Force and numerous Department of Defense services and agencies. He has also consulted for major manufacturing and distribution companies such as Applied Magnetics, AT&T, Black

& Decker, Hewlett-Packard, IBM, Kraft Foods, Motorola, Raytheon, and Toyota.

Gerhard has served as a tenured full professor at California State University, Chico; a professor at BYU, BYU–Hawaii; University of Malaysia; University of San Diego; and has served as a visiting professor at numerous universities around the globe.

With degrees in math, physics, and German; he holds an MBA, MA in international studies and PhD in resource economics (oil and gas) and operations management.

Today, Dr. Gerhard Plenert continues as a Shingo examiner and Adjunct Faculty member for several universities while creating his stories, which are his greatest delectation in the current hour after his wife and family where he celebrates both and their ongoing successes first and foremost.

Dr. Gerhard is available to interview as a novelist and as a professional with expertise in his multiple disciplines.

VISIT THE AUTHOR

SOCIAL AND OTHER MEDIA

IMPRINT:

Thunderforge Pubs

PUBLISHER:

DonnaInk Publications L.L.C.
www.donnaink.com | www.donnainkpublications.com

SOCIAL MEDIA:

Facebook:
https://www.facebook.com/authorgerhardplenert

LinkedIn:
www.linkedin.com/pub/gerhard-plenert/1/b0/75b

Twitter:
https://twitter.com/GPlenert

WORDPRESS BLOG:

http://gerhard338.wordpress.com

WEBSITE:

www.gerhardplenert.com

MERCHANDISE

SAVING THE SMALL WORLD

GLOSSARY

Abogidyide - the secret name of Bydola

Agot - Leprechaun from Amins - brave, young friend of Elasti chosen for the first expedition

Algo - Leprechaun from Amins - the old "Wise Elder" of the council

Amaz - Leprechaun from Amins - Head of the Council of Amins and a "Wise Elder"

Amazonionites – Amazonian women warriors living in the Central Ranges

Amber - Southern Sword's light

Amins - the Southern Plains city of the leprechauns where the Small World saga begins

Analoop – giant warrior in Swift Army

Annala – giantess

Avre - Leprechaun from Amins - a wise member of the

Balbot - Leprechaun from Amins - outspoken, aggressive council member

Balkwood - a favorite climbing tree

Bananot - Leprechaun from Amins - the old wise foreseer

Bearess – child bearer in an Amazonionite tribe

Broch - Leprechaun from Amins - brave, young friend of Elasti chosen for the first expedition

Bydola – Leprechaun from Amins - the strong rock-mine worker – received the Protee power from the Creator

Carer – child caretaker in an Amazonionite tribe

Creator -builder of all things

Destroyer – evil name for Kwdad

Dwarfs – small but strong and heavily built inhabitants of Small World, dwelling in the North Groves

Ejijone - dwarf Princess of the Northland

Ejijtwenty – attendant to Ejijone and dwarf spy for the Kabul

Elasti - Leprechaun from Amins - the fearful son of a carpenter who was forced on the first expedition and then volunteered for the second

Egglac – assistant to Giant-giant – messenger between giants and leprechauns

Egififty-one – One of Egitsix's warriors

Egififty-seven - One of Egitwelve's warriors

Egiforty – One of Egisix's warriors

Egiforty-five – One of Egitwelve's warriors

Egiforty-four – One of Egisix's warriors

Egiforty-nine – One of Egitwelve's warriors

Egininety-nine - One of Egisix's warriors

Egininety-one – One of Egisix's warriors

Egione - King of the dwarfs

Egisix – Dwarf military leader

Egitime the fourteenth – A reference on the ceiling of the crypt at the bottom of Hile Lake

Egitwelve – Dwarf healed by Bydola

Elderess – leader of an Amazonionite tribe

Elfin Book of Learning - elfin scriptures

Elf – the pretty inhabitants of Small World living in the south-west corner of the Southern Plains

Erates - tiles with cracks that fall to the Lamos

Erock – Elf from Gije - doctor

Gabotz – The magic word that transforms Egisix in and out of his hawk shape

Gabrona – Lepelf from Giter - innkeeper's son who joined the expedition

Gagl - tribe of Amazonionites

Gamotz - the Central Ranges city of the gnomes

Gath – Elf from Gije - last to travel on the Back Road before this expedition

Geday – Elf from Gije - farmer

Geld - money, coinage

Giant-giant – ruler of the Giants

Gibbon - small cat-like creature

Gido – Elf from Gije - council member and representative on the expedition

Gigl – tribe of Amazonionites

Gije - the city of the elves, the "pretty" residents of Small World's Southern Plains

Gijivure –Elf from Gije - warrior and bowman representing Gije on the expedition

Gilbon – Lepelf military leader from Giter - Yanon's military friend

Gillgal – Elasti's secret name

Gimans – Elf from Gije - the Lord of Gije

Gingoras – the Sheere Cliffs city of the shy giants

Gione – Elf from Gije - farmer

Giter - the Southern Plains city of the lazy and apathetic lepelves

Giterod – Lepelf from Giter - representative on the expedition and king's assistant

Giterquake - earthquakes centered around Giter

Gnomes – deformed and mutant creatures created by the holocaust that occurred in Upper world

God of the Rainbow – Leprechauns' God

Gogl - tribe of Amazonionites

Goglaby - one of the younger Amazonionite warriors

Goglbarj - lead Amazonionite warrior

Goglchin – Amazonionite warrior joining Goglbarj on the expedition to the south

Goglhick – Amazonionite warrior joining Goglbarj on the expedition to the south

Gorbot – Lepelf from Giter – King

Gushe – elf queen

Hasko - Leprechaun from Amins - the scout

Hastle - nickname for Hiztin

Hector – assistant to Giant-giant

Hilebin - the North Groves royal city of the dwarfs

Hilebon - the North Groves commercial city of the dwarfs

Hile Lake – lake in the Hile Groves that once contained a great city in its depths. No rivers flow into or out of the lake.

Hiztin - Leprechaun from Amins - the bowman

Hopls - One-legged noisy birds

Jesves - Leprechaun from Amins - the fearless girl that never gets lost but keeps getting into trouble

Jizeel - Leprechaun from Amins - the daughter of Amaz, engaged to Elasti

Kabul - The Central Ranges land ruled by Krakus

Kakakrul – Prince of the Kabul and son of Lord Krakus

Kaklu – Duke and leader of the Gnomes

Karkat - tree with extremely hard wood and living roots

Kirda – Marmalide

Klakaly – Kaklu's second in command

Krakus - mutant Wizard and Emperor / Lord of the Kabul

Kwdad – the Destroyer and source of evil

Lepelves - Residents of Giter that are the result of a union of elves and leprechauns

Leprechauns – the smallest inhabitants of Small World living the furthest south in the Southern Plains

Lifefight Wars - the original invasion Small World by the gnomes from Upper world who afterward made their home in the Kabul

Magotites – Magotites were maggot-eaten dead animals brought back to life by the Kabul Lord so that he could use them for his evil designs. They lived in the northern part of the Kabul.

Mar Lake – Lake in the Central Ranges where the Mermaids live

Marmale – Male Mermaid used for reproduction

Marmalides – Advanced Mermaids living in Mar Lake who have a leadership role amongst the Mermaids

Marmaroplis – Underwater city of the mermaids

Mihorse - small, domesticated horse used in farming

Mirror Pond -a large pond west of Giter which contains a water quist and was sometimes used to get to the Creator.

Morgos - the Central Ranges city of the magotites

Mudwumps - mud caretakers of the Creator that are deaf

Murqack – Prince and leader of the Magotites

Northern Sword - magical sword given to the dwarfs after the Lifefight Wars

Obydon - Leprechaun from Amins - the son of Amaz, sword carrier on the expedition

Oply – Worlepreek from Second Tunnel - Council Lord

Opopp - Worlepreek from Second Tunnel - Doctor

Orange - Creator's light

Ordil - Worlepreek from the tunnel under the Albo Pass

Ordo - Worlepreek from Second Tunnel - Oply's assistant

Pollo Weed -narcotic weed

Protee - an organization of power against evil directed by the Creator. The organization uses a staff and a secret name to invoke its power, the presence of which was expressed by an orange light. They also have their own language for communication.

Pull boat - a boat used to cross the Avol River that has a rope tied at each shore

Purple - Raker's color

Quali Swamp Rats - rats controlling the Quali Swamps

Rakadam – King and leader of the Trolls

Raker – mysterious swamp creature

Raviump – the Wizard's secret name

Retants - living roots from the Karkat tree

Riposters - mutant bird-fish from the Kabul

Shadow Warriors – Ghosts and protectors of the Tako Temple

Shawlee – Mamalide involved in the quest

Southern Sword - magical sword given to the leprechauns after the Lifefight Wars

Staff of Protee - staff given to Bydola by the Creator

Temple at Tako - pyramid temple structure built and ruled over by the Protee in the demolished city of Tako

Tragis - the Central Ranges city of the trolls

Treeclap – leader of the Hile Groves trees

Trolls – monstrous, slow moving and slightly backwards forest dwellers

Small World - a world within the world

Swift Army – the all-female army that saved Small World

Upperworld - the outside world of Small World

Werewolves - humans turned into wolves

Water Quist - creature living in Mirror Pond

Wizard of Havinis - the helpful "Great Wizard" who was a human but was transferred into Small World during the Lifefight Wars by the power of the crossed swords

Worlepreeks - leprechauns without legs that live in the northern-most tunnels of the Kilo Pass

Worlepreeks Book of Psalms - Worlepreeks scriptures

Yanon - Leprechaun from Amins - the military leader who becomes expedition leader

Yellow - Southern Sword's light